T5-CWL-545

TALES
OF TRAIL AND TOWN

TALES
OF TRAIL AND TOWN

BY

BRET HARTE

Short Story Index Reprint Series

BOOKS FOR LIBRARIES PRESS
FREEPORT, NEW YORK

First Published 1898
Reprinted 1970

STANDARD BOOK NUMBER:
8369-3519-5

LIBRARY OF CONGRESS CATALOG CARD NUMBER:
70-121562

PRINTED IN THE UNITED STATES OF AMERICA

CONTENTS

	PAGE
THE ANCESTORS OF PETER ATHERLY	1
TWO AMERICANS	122
THE JUDGMENT OF BOLINAS PLAIN	181
THE STRANGE EXPERIENCE OF ALKALI DICK .	222
A NIGHT ON THE DIVIDE	262
THE YOUNGEST PROSPECTOR IN CALAVERAS . .	295
A TALE OF THREE TRUANTS	327

TALES OF TRAIL AND TOWN

THE ANCESTORS OF PETER ATHERLY

CHAPTER I

IT must be admitted that the civilizing processes of Rough and Ready were not marked by any of the ameliorating conditions of other improved camps. After the discovery of the famous " Eureka " lead, there was the usual influx of gamblers and saloon-keepers ; but that was accepted as a matter of course. But it was thought hard that, after a church was built and a new school erected, it should suddenly be found necessary to have doors that locked, instead of standing shamelessly open to the criticism and temptation of wayfarers, or that portable property could no longer be left out at night in the old fond reliance on universal brotherhood. The habit of borrowing was stopped with the introduction of more money into the camp, and the establishment of rates of interest; the poorer people either took what they wanted, or as indiscreetly bought on credit.   There were better clothes to be seen in its one long straggling street, but those who wore them generally lacked the grim virtue of the old pioneers, and the fairer faces that were to be seen were generally rouged.   There was a year or two of this kind of mutation, in which the youthful barbarism of Rough and Ready might have been said to struggle with adult civilized wickedness, and then the name itself disappeared.   By an Act ⌐f the Legislature the growing town was called " Atherly," after the owner of the Eureka mine, — Peter Atherly, — who had given largess to the town in its " Waterworks " and a " Gin Mill," as the new Atherly Hotel and its gilded bar-rooms were now called.   Even at the last moment, however, the new title of " Atherly " hung in the balance.   The romantic daughter of the pastor had said that Mr. Atherly should be called " Atherly of Atherly," an aristocratic title so strongly suggestive of an innovation upon democratic principles that it

was not until it was discreetly suggested that
everybody was still free to call him " Atherly, late of Rough and Ready," that opposition ceased.

Possibly this incident may have first awakened him to the value of his name, and some
anxiety as to its origin.   Roughly speaking,
Atherly's father was only a bucolic emigrant
from " Mizzouri," and his mother had done
the washing for the camp on her first arrival.
The Atherlys had suffered on their overland
journey from drought and famine, with the
addition of being captured by Indians, who
had held them captive for ten months.   Indeed, Mr. Atherly, senior, never recovered
from the effects of his captivity, and died
shortly after Mrs. Atherly had given birth
to twins, Peter and Jenny Atherly.   This
was scant knowledge for Peter in the glori-
fication of his name through his immediate
progenitors ; but " Atherly of Atherly " still
sounded pleasantly, and, as the young lady
had said, smacked of old feudal days and
honors.   It was believed beyond doubt, even
in their simple family records, — the fly
leaf of a Bible, — that Peter Atherly's great-
grandfather was an Englishman who brought

over to his Majesty's Virginian possessions
his only son, then a boy. It was not established, however, to what class of deportation
he belonged: whether he was suffering exile
from religious or judicial conviction, or if he
were only one of the articled "apprentices"
who largely made up the American immigra-
tion of those days. Howbeit, "Atherly" was
undoubtedly an English name, even suggest-
ing respectable and landed ancestry, and
Peter Atherly was proud of it. He looked
somewhat askance upon his Irish and German fellow citizens, and talked a good deal
about " race." Two things, however, con-
cerned him: he was not in looks certainly
like any type of modern Englishman as seen
either on the stage in San Francisco, or as
an actual tourist in the mining regions, and
his accent was undoubtedly Southwestern.
He was tall and dark, with deep-set eyes in
a singularly immobile countenance; he had
an erect but lithe and sinewy figure even for
his thirty odd years, and might easily have
been taken for any other American except for
the single exception that his nose was distinctly Roman, and gave him a distinguished
air. There was a suggestion of Abraham

Lincoln (and even of Don Quixote) in his tall, melancholy figure and length of limb, but nothing whatever that suggested an Englishman.

It was shortly after the christening of Atherly town that an incident occurred which at first shook, and then the more firmly established, his mild monomania. His widowed mother had been for the last two years an inmate of a private asylum for inebriates, through certain habits contracted while washing for the camp in the first year of her widowhood. This had always been a matter of open sympathy to Rough and Ready; but it was a secret reproach hinted at in Atherly, although it was known that the rich Peter Atherly kept his mother liberally supplied, and that both he and his sister " Jinny " or Jenny Atherly visited her frequently. One day he was telegraphed for, and on going to the asylum found Mrs. Atherly delirious and raving. Through her son's liberality she had bribed an attendant, and was fast succumbing to a private debauch. In the intervals of her delirium she called Peter by name, talked frenziedly and mysteriously of his " high connections " —

alluded to himself and his sister as being of the " true breed " — and with a certain vigor of epithet, picked up in the familiarity of the camp during the days when she was known as " Old Ma'am Atherly " or " Aunt Sally," declared that they were " no corn-cracking Hoosiers," " hayseed pikes," nor " northern Yankee scum," and that she should yet live to see them " holding their own lands again and the lands of their fore-fathers." Quieted at last by opiates, she fell into a more lucid but scarcely less distressing attitude. Recognizing her son again, as well as her own fast failing condition, she sarcastically thanked him for coming to "see her off," congratulated him that he would soon be spared the lie and expense of keeping her here on account of his pride, under the thin pretext of trying to "cure " her. She knew that Sally Atherly of Rough and Ready was n't considered fit company for " Atherly of Atherly " by his fine new friends. This and much more in a voice mingling maudlin sentiment with bitter resentment, and with an ominous glitter in her bloodshot and glairy eyes. Peter winced with a consciousness of the half-truth of her

reproaches, but the curiosity and excitement
awakened by the revelations of her frenzy
were greater than his remorse. He said
quickly : —

"You were speaking of father ! — of his
family — his lands and possessions. Tell
me again ! "

"Wot are ye givin' us ?" she ejaculated
in husky suspicion, opening upon him her
beady eyes, in which the film of death was
already gathering.

"Tell me of father, — my father and
his family ! his great-grandfather ! — the
Atherlys, my relations — what you were
saying. What do you know about them ?"

"*That*'s all ye wanter know — is it ?
That's what ye 'r' comin' to the old washer-
woman for — is it ?" she burst out with the
desperation of disgust. "Well — give it
up ! Ask me another ! "

"But, mother — the old records, you
know ! The family Bible — what you once
told us — me and Jinny ! "

Something gurgled in her throat like a
chuckle. With the energy of malevolence,
she stammered : "There was n't no records
— there was n't no family Bible ! it's all a

lie — you hear me! Your Atherly that
you're so proud of was just a British bum-
mer who was kicked outer his family in England and sent to buzz round in Americky.
He honey-fogled me — Sally Magregor —
out of a better family than his'n, in Kansas,
and skyugled me away, but it was a straight
out marriage, and I kin prove it. It was in
the St. Louis papers, and I've got it stored
away safe enough in my trunk! You hear
me! I'm shoutin'! But he wasn't no old
settler in Mizzouri — he wasn't descended
from any settler, either! He was a new
man outer England — fresh caught — and
talked down his throat. And he fooled *me*
— the darter of an old family that was settled on the right bank of the Mizzouri afore
Dan'l Boone came to Kentucky — with his
new philanderings. Then he broke up, and
went all to pieces when we struck Californy,
and left *me* — Sally Magregor, whose father had niggers of his own — to wash for
Rough and Ready! *That*'s your Atherly!
Take him! I don't want him — I've done
with him! I was done with him long afore
— afore" — a cough checked her utterance,
— "afore" — She gasped again, but the

words seemed to strangle in her throat. In-
tent only on her words and scarcely heeding
her sufferings, Peter was bending over her
eagerly, when the doctor rudely pulled him
away and lifted her to a sitting posture.
But she never spoke again. The strongest
restoratives quickly administered only left
her in a state of scarcely breathing uncon-
sciousness.

"Is she dying? Can't you bring her to,"
said the anxious Peter, "if only for a moment, doctor?"

"I'm thinkin'," said the visiting doctor, an
old Scotch army surgeon, looking at the rich
Mr. Atherly with cool, professional contempt,
"that your mother willna do any more washing for me as in the old time, nor give up
her life again to support her bairns. And it
isna my eentention to bring her back to pain
for the purposes of geeneral conversation!"

Nor, indeed, did she ever come back to
any purpose, but passed away with her unfinished sentence. And her limbs were
scarcely decently composed by the attend-
ants before Peter was rummaging the trunk
in her room for the paper she had spoken of.
It was in an old work-box — a now faded

yellow clipping from a newspaper, lying amidst spoils of cotton thread, buttons, and beeswax, which he even then remembered to have seen upon his mother's lap when she superadded the sewing on of buttons to her washing of the miners' shirts. And his dark and hollow cheek glowed with gratified sentiment as he read the clipping.

"We hear with regret of the death of Philip Atherly, Esq., of Rough and Ready, California. Mr. Atherly will be remembered by some of our readers as the hero of the romantic elopement of Miss Sallie Magregor, daughter of Colonel 'Bob' Magregor, which created such a stir in well-to-do circles some thirty years ago. It was known vaguely that the young couple had 'gone West,' — a then unknown region, — but it seems that after severe trials and tribulations on the frontier with savages, they emigrated early to Oregon, and then, on the outbreak of the gold fever, to California. But it will be a surprise to many to know that it has just transpired that Mr. Atherly was the second son of Sir Ashley Atherly, an English baronet, and by the death of his brother might have succeeded to the property and title."

He remained for some moments looking fixedly at the paper, until the commonplace paragraph imprinted itself upon his brain as no line of sage or poet had ever done, and then he folded it up and put it in his pocket. In his exaltation he felt that even the mother he had never loved was promoted to a certain respect as his father's wife, although he was equally conscious of a new resentment against her for her contemptuous allusions to *his* father, and her evident hopeless inability to comprehend his position. His mother, he feared, was indeed low! — but *he* was his father's son! Nevertheless, he gave her a funeral at Atherly, long remembered for its barbaric opulence and display. Thirty carriages, procured from Sacramento at great expense, were freely offered to his friends to join in the astounding pageant. A wonderful casket of iron and silver, brought from San Francisco, held the remains of the ex-washerwoman of Rough and Ready. But a more remarkable innovation was the addition of a royal crown to the other ornamentation of the casket. Peter Atherly's ideas of heraldry were very vague, — Sacramento at that time offered him no opportunity of knowing what were the arms of the Atherlys, — and the introduction of the royal crown seemed to satisfy Peter's mind as to what a crest *might* be, while to the ordinary democratic mind it simply suggested that the corpse was English! Political criticism being thus happily averted, Mrs. Atherly's body was laid in the little cemetery, not far away from certain rude wooden crosses which marked the burial-place of wanderers whose very names were unknown, and in due time a marble shaft was erected over it. But when, the next day, the county paper contained, in addition to the column-and-a-half description of the funeral, the more formal announcement of the death of " Mrs. Sallie Atherly, wife of the late Philip Atherly, second son of Sir Ashley Atherly, of England," criticism and comment broke out. The old pioneers of Rough and Ready felt that they had been imposed upon, and that in some vague way the unfortunate woman had made them the victims of a huge practical joke during all these years. That she had grimly enjoyed their ignorance of her position they did not doubt. " Why, I remember onct when I

was sorter bullyraggin' her about mixin' up
my duds with Doc Simmons's, and sendin'
me Whiskey Dick's old rags, she turned
round sudden with a kind of screech, and
ran out into the brush. I reckoned, at the
time, that it was either ' drink ' or feelin's,
and could hev kicked myself for being sassy
to the old woman, but I know now that all
this time that air critter — that barrow-
net's daughter-in-law — was just laughin'
herself into fits in the brush! No, sir, she
played this yer camp for all it was worth,
year in and out, and we just gave ourselves
away like speckled idiots! and now she's
lyin' out thar in the bone yard, and keeps
on p'intin' the joke, and a-roarin' at us in
marble."

Even the later citizens in Atherly felt an
equal resentment against her, but from different motives. That her drinking habits
and her powerful vocabulary were all the
effect of her aristocratic alliance they never
doubted. And, although it brought the virtues of their own superior republican sobriety
into greater contrast. they felt a scandal at
having been tricked into attending this gilded
funeral of dissipated rank. Peter Atherly

found himself unpopular in his own town. The sober who drank from his free " Waterworks," and the giddy ones who imbibed at his " Gin Mill," equally criticised him. He could not understand it ; his peculiar predilections had been accepted before, when they were mere presumptions ; why should they not *now*, when they were admitted facts ? He was conscious of no change in himself since the funeral ! Yet the criticism went on. Presently it took the milder but more contagious form of ridicule. In his own hotel, built with his own money, and in his own presence, he had heard a reckless frequenter of the bar-room decline some proffered refreshment on the ground that " he only drank with his titled relatives." A local humorist, amidst the applause of an admiring crowd at the post-office window, had openly accused the postmaster of withholding letters to him from his only surviving brother, " the Dook of Doncherknow." " The ole dooky never onct missed the mail to let me know wot 's goin' on in me childhood's home," remarked the humorist plaintively ; " and yer 's this dod-blasted gov'ment mule of a postmaster keepin' me letters back ! " Letters with pretentious and gilded coats of arms, taken from the decorated inner lining of cigar-boxes, were posted to prominent citizens. The neighboring and unregenerated settlement of Red Dog was more outrageous in its contribution. The Red Dog "Sentinel," in commenting on the death of "Haulbowline Tom," a drunken English man-o'-war's man, said : "It may not be generally known that our regretted fellow citizen, while serving on H. M. S. Boxer, was secretly married to Queen Kikalu of the Friendly Group ; but, unlike some of our prosperous neighbors, he never boasted of his royal alliance, and resisted with steady British pluck any invitation to share the throne. Indeed, any allusion to the subject affected him deeply. There are those among us who will remember the beautiful portrait of his royal bride tattooed upon his left arm with the royal crest and the crossed flags of the two nations." Only Peter Atherly and his sister understood the sting inflicted either by accident or design in the latter sentence. Both he and his sister had some singular hieroglyphic branded on their arms, — probably a reminiscence of their life on the plains in

their infant Indian captivity. But there was
no mistaking the general sentiment. The
criticisms of a small town may become ine-
vasible. Atherly determined to take the
first opportunity to leave Rough and Ready.
He was rich ; his property was secure ; there
was no reason why he should stay where his
family pretensions were a drawback. And
a further circumstance determined his resolution.

He was awaiting his sister in his new house
on a little crest above the town. She had
been at the time of her mother's death, and
since, a private boarder in the Sacred Heart
Convent at Santa Clara, whence she had
been summoned to the funeral, but had returned the next day. Few people had noticed in her brother's carriage the veiled
figure which might have belonged to one of
the religious orders ; still less did they remember the dark, lank, heavy-browed girl
who had sometimes been seen about Rough
and Ready. For she had her brother's melancholy, and greater reticence, and had continued of her own free will, long after her
girlish pupilage at the convent, to live secluded under its maternal roof without tak-

ing orders. A general suspicion that she
was either a religious " crank," or considered
herself too good to live in a mountain mining
town, had not contributed to her brother's
popularity. In her abstraction from worldly
ambitions she had, naturally, taken no part
in her brother's family pretensions. He had
given her an independent allowance, and she
was supposed to be equally a sharer in his
good fortune. Yet she had suddenly declared
her intention of returning to Atherly, to con-
sult him on affairs of importance. Peter
was both surprised and eager ; there was but
little affection between them, but, preoccupied
with his one idea, he was satisfied that she
wanted to talk about the family.

But he was amazed, disappointed, and dis-
concerted. For Jenny Atherly, the sober
recluse of Santa Clara, hidden in her sombre draperies at the funeral, was no longer
to be recognized in the fashionable, smartly
but somewhat over-dressed woman he saw
before him. In spite of her large features
and the distinguishing Roman nose, like his
own, she looked even pretty in her excitement. She had left the convent, she was
tired of the life there, she was satisfied that

a religious vocation would not suit her. In brief, she intended to enjoy herself like other women. If he really felt a pride in the family he ought to take her out, like other brothers, and "give her a show." He could do it there if he liked, and she would keep house for him. If he did n't want to, she must have enough money to keep her fashionably in San Francisco. But she wanted excitement, and that she *would have !* She wanted to go to balls, theatres, and entertainments, and she intended to ! Her voice grew quite high, and her dark cheek glowed with some new-found emotion.

Astounded as he was, Peter succumbed. It was better that she should indulge her astounding caprice under his roof than elsewhere. It would not do for the sister of an Atherly to provoke scandal. He gave entertainments, picnics, and parties, and "Jinny" Atherly plunged into these mild festivities with the enthusiasm of a schoolgirl. She not only could dance with feverish energy all night, but next day could mount a horse — she was a fearless rider — and lead the most accomplished horsemen. She was a good shot, she walked with the untiring foot of a coyote, she threaded the woods with the instinct of a pioneer. Peter regarded her with a singular mingling of astonishment and fear. Surely she had not learned this at school! These were not the teachings nor the sports of the good sisters! He once dared to interrogate her regarding this change in her habits. " I always *felt* like it," she answered quickly, " but I kept it down. I used sometimes to feel that I could n't stand it any longer, but must rush out and do something," she said passionately : · but," she went on with furtive eyes, and a sudden wild timidity like that of a fawn, " I was afraid! I was afraid *it was like mother!* It seemed to me to be *her* blood that was rising in me, and I kept it down, — I did n't want to be like her, — and I prayed and struggled against it. Did you," she said, suddenly grasping his hand, " ever feel like that ? "

But Peter never had. His melancholy faith in his father's race had left no thought of his mother's blood mingling with it. " But," he said gravely, " believing this, why did you change ? "

" Because I could hold out no longer. I

should have gone crazy. Times I wanted to take some of those meek nuns, some of those white-faced pupils with their blue eyes and wavy flaxen hair, and strangle them. I could n't strive and pray and struggle any longer *there*, and so I came here to let myself out! I suppose when I get married — and I ought to, with my money — it may change me! You don't suppose," she said, with a return of her wild-animal-like timidity, " it is anything that was in *father*, in those *Atherlys*, — do you?"

But Peter had no idea of anything but virtue in the Atherly blood ; he had heard that the upper class of Europeans were fond of field sports and of hunting ; it was odd that his sister should inherit this propensity and not he. He regarded her more kindly for this evidence of race. " You think of getting married ? " he said more gently, yet with a certain brotherly doubt that any man could like her enough, even with her money. " Is there any one here would — suit you ? " he added diplomatically.

" No — I hate them all ! " she burst out. " There is n't one I don't despise for his sickening, foppish, womanish airs."

Nevertheless, it was quite evident that some of the men were attracted by her singular originality and a certain good comradeship in her ways. And it was on one of their riding excursions that Peter noticed that she was singled out by a good-looking, blond-haired young lawyer of the town for his especial attentions. As the cavalcade straggled in climbing the mountain, the young fellow rode close to her saddle-bow, and as the distance lengthened between the other stragglers, they at last were quite alone. When the trail became more densely wooded, Peter quite lost sight of them. But when, a few moments later, having lost the trail himself, they again appeared in the distance before him, he was so amazed that he unconsciously halted. For the two horses were walking side by side, and the stranger's arm was round his sister's waist.

Had Peter any sense of humor he might have smiled at this weakness in his Amazonian sister, but he saw only the serious, practical side of the situation, with, of course, its inevitable relation to his one controlling idea. The young man was in good practice, and would have made an eligible husband to any one else. But was he fit to mate with an Atherly? What would those as yet unknown and powerful relatives say to it? At the same time he could not help knowing that "Jinny," in the eccentricities of her virgin spinsterhood, might be equally objectionable to them, as she certainly was a severe trial to him here. If she were off his hands he might be able to prosecute his search for his relatives with more freedom. After all, there were *mésalliances* in all families, and being a woman she was not in the direct line. Instead, therefore, of spurring forward to join them, he lingered a little until they passed out of sight, and until he was joined by a companion from behind. Him, too, he purposely delayed. They were walking slowly, breathing their mustangs, when his companion suddenly uttered a cry of alarm, and sprang from his horse. For on the trail before them lay the young lawyer quite unconscious, with his riderless steed nipping the young leaves of the underbrush. He was evidently stunned by a fall, although across his face was a livid welt which might have been caused by collision with the small elastic limb of a sapling, or a blow from a

riding-whip; happily the last idea was only
in Peter's mind. As they lifted him up he
came slowly to consciousness. He was bewildered and dazed at first, but as he began
to speak the color came back freshly to his
face. He could not conceive, he stammered,
what had happened. He was riding with
Miss Atherly, and he supposed his horse had
slipped upon some withered pine needles and
thrown him! A spasm of pain crossed his
face suddenly, and he lifted his hand to the
top of his head. Was he hurt *there?* No,
but perhaps his hair, which was flowing and
curly, had caught in the branches — like
Absalom's! He tried to smile, and even
begged them to assist him to his horse that
he might follow his fair companion, who
would be wondering where he was; but
Peter, satisfied that he had received no serious injury, hurriedly enjoined him to stay,
while he himself would follow his sister.
Putting spurs to his horse, he succeeded, in
spite of the slippery trail, in overtaking her
near the summit. At the sound of his
horse's hoofs she wheeled quickly, came
dashing furiously towards him, and only
pulled up at the sound of his voice. But

she had not time to change her first attitude
and expression, which was something which
perplexed and alarmed him.   Her long lithe
figure was half crouching, half clinging to
the horse's back, her loosened hair flying
over her shoulders, her dark eyes gleaming
with an odd nymph-like mischief.   Her white
teeth flashed as she recognized him, but her
laugh was still mocking and uncanny.   He
took refuge in indignation.

" What has happened ? " he said sharply.

" The fool tried to kiss me! " she said
simply.   " And I — I — let out at him —
like mother! "

Nevertheless, she gave him one of those
shy, timid glances he had noticed before, and
began coiling something around her fingers,
with a suggestion of coy embarrassment, in-
describably inconsistent with her previous
masculine independence.

" You might have killed him," said Peter
angrily.

" Perhaps I might!   *Ought* I have killed
him, Peter ? " she said anxiously, yet with
the same winning, timid smile.   If she had
not been his sister, he would have thought
her quite handsome.

" As it is," he said impetuously, " you
have made a frightful scandal here."

" *He* won't say anything about it — will
he?" she inquired shyly, still twisting the
something around her finger.

Peter did not reply; perhaps the young
lawyer really loved her and would keep her
secret! But he was vexed, and there was
something maniacal in her twisting fingers.
" What have you got there?" he said
sharply.

She shook the object in the air before her
with a laugh. " Only a lock of his hair,"
she said gayly ; " but I did n't *cut* it off!'"

" Throw it away, and come here!" he said
angrily.

But she only tucked the little blond curl
into her waist belt and shook her head. He
urged his horse forward, but she turned and
fled, laughing as he pursued her. Being the
better rider she could easily evade him whenever he got too near, and in this way they
eventually reached the town and their house
long before their companions. But she was
far enough ahead of her brother to be able
to dismount and hide her trophy with childish glee before he arrived.

She was right in believing that her unfortunate cavalier would make no revelation of her conduct, and his catastrophe passed as an accident. But Peter could not disguise the fact that much of his unpopularity was shared by his sister. The matrons of Atherly believed that she was " fast," and remembered more distinctly than ever the evil habits of her mother. That she would, in the due course of time, " take to drink," they never doubted. Her dancing was considered outrageous in its unfettered freedom, and her extraordinary powers of endurance were looked upon as " masculine" by the weaker girls whose partners she took from them. She reciprocally looked down upon them, and made no secret of her contempt for their small refinements and fancies. She affected only the society of men, and even treated them with a familiarity that was both fearless and scornful. Peter saw that it was useless to face the opposition ; Miss Atherly did not seem to encourage the renewal of the young lawyer's attentions, although it was evident that he was still attracted by her, nor did she seem to invite

advances from others. He must go away —
and he would have to take her with him.
It seemed ridiculous that a woman of thirty,
of masculine character, should require a
chaperon in a brother of equal age; but
Peter knew the singular blending of childlike ignorance with this Amazonian quality.
He had made his arrangements for an absence from Atherly of three or four years,
and they departed together. The young fair-
haired lawyer came to the stage-coach office
to see them off. Peter could detect no sentiment in his sister's familiar farewell of
her unfortunate suitor. At New York, however, it was arranged that " Jinny " should
stay with some friends whom they had made
en route, and that, if she wished, she could
come to Europe later, and join him in London.

Thus relieved of one, Peter Atherly of
Atherly started on his cherished quest of his
other and more remote relations.

CHAPTER II

PETER ATHERLY had been four months in England, but knew little of the country until one summer afternoon when his carriage rolled along the well - ordered road between Nonningsby Station and Ashley Grange.

In that four months he had consulted authorities, examined records, visited the Heralds' College, written letters, and made a few friends. A rich American, tracing his genealogical tree, was not a new thing — even in that day — in London; but there was something original and simple in his methods, and so much that was grave, reserved, and un-American in his personality that it awakened interest. A recognition that he was a foreigner, but a puzzled doubt, however, of his exact nationality, which he found everywhere, at first pained him, but he became reconciled to it at about the same time that his English acquaintances abandoned their own reserve and caution before the greater reticence of this melancholy American, and actually became the questioners! In this way his quest became known only as a disclosure of his own courtesy, and offers of assistance were pressed eagerly upon him. That was why Sir Edward Atherly found himself gravely puzzled, as he sat with his family solicitor one morning in the library of Ashley Grange.

"Humph!" said Sir Edward. "And you say he has absolutely no other purpose in making these inquiries?"

"Positively none," returned the solicitor. "He is even willing to sign a renunciation of any claim which might arise out of this information. It is rather a singular case, but he seems to be a rich man and quite able to indulge his harmless caprices."

"And you are quite sure he is Philip's son?"

"Quite, from the papers he brings me. Of course I informed him that even if he should be able to establish a legal marriage he could expect nothing as next of kin, as you had children of your own. He seemed to know that already, and avowed that his only wish was to satisfy his own mind."

"I suppose he wants to claim kinship and all that sort of thing for society's sake?"

"I do not think so," said the solicitor dryly. "I suggested an interview with you, but he seemed to think it quite unnecessary, if *I* could give him the information he required."

"Ha!" said Sir Edward promptly, "we'll invite him here. Lady Atherly can bring in some people to see him. Is he — ahem — What is he like? The usual American, I suppose?"

"Not at all. Quite foreign-looking — dark, and rather like an Italian. There is no resemblance to Mr. Philip," he said, glancing at the painting of a flaxen-haired child fondling a greyhound under the elms of Ashley Park.

"Ah! Yes, yes! Perhaps the mother was one of those Southern creoles, or mulattoes," said Sir Edward with an Englishman's tolerant regard for the vagaries of people who were clearly not English; "they're rather attractive women, I hear."

"I think you do quite well to be civil to him," said the solicitor. "He seems to take an interest in the family, and being rich, and apparently only anxious to enhance the family prestige, you ought to know him.

Now, in reference to those mortgages on Appleby Farm, if you could get " —

"Yes, yes!" said Sir Edward quickly; "we'll have him down here; and, I say! *you*'ll come too?"

The solicitor bowed. "And, by the way," continued Sir Edward, "there was a girl too, — wasn't there? He has a sister, I believe?"

"Yes, but he has left her in America."

"Ah, yes! — very good — yes! — of course. We'll have Lord Greyshott and Sir Roger and old Lady Everton, — she knows all about Sir Ashley and the family. And — er — is he young or old?"

"About thirty, I should say, Sir Edward."

"Ah, well! We'll have Lady Elfrida over from the Towers."

Had Peter known of these preparations he might have turned back to Nonningsby without even visiting the old church in Ashley Park, which he had been told held the ashes of his ancestors. For during these four months the conviction that he was a foreigner and that he had little or nothing in common with things here had been clearly forced upon him. He could recognize some kinship in the manners and customs of the people to those he had known in the West and on the Atlantic coast, but not to his own individuality, and he seemed even more a stranger here — where he had expected to feel the thrill of consanguinity — than in the West. He had accepted the invitation of the living Atherly for the sake of the Atherlys long dead and forgotten. As the great quadrangle of stone and ivy lifted itself out of the park, he looked longingly towards the little square tower which peeped from between the yews nearer the road. As the carriage drove up to the carved archway whence so many Atherlys had issued into the world, he could not believe that any of his blood had gone forth from it, or, except himself, had ever entered it before. Once in the great house he felt like a prisoner as he wandered through the long corridors to his room ; even the noble trees beyond his mullioned windows seemed of another growth than those he had known.

There was no doubt that he created a sensation at Ashley Grange, not only from his singular kinship, but from his striking

individuality. The Atherlys and their guests
were fascinated and freely admiring. His
very originality, which prevented them from
comparing him with any English or American standard of excellence, gave them a
comfortable assurance of safety in their admiration. His reserve, his seriousness, his
simplicity, very unlike their own, and yet
near enough to suggest a delicate flattery,
was in his favor. So was his naïve frankness in regard to his status in the family,
shown in the few words of greeting with
Sir Ashley, and in his later simple yet free
admissions regarding his obscure youth, his
former poverty, and his present wealth. He
boasted of neither; he was disturbed by
neither. Standing alone, a stranger, for the
first time in an assemblage of distinguished
and titled men and women, he betrayed no
consciousness; surrounded for the first time
by objects which he knew his wealth could
not buy, he showed the most unmistakable
indifference, — the indifference of temperament. The ladies vied with each other to
attack this unimpressible nature, — this profound isolation from external attraction.
They followed him about, they looked into

his dark, melancholy eyes ; it was impossible, they thought, that he could continue this superb acting forever. A glance, a smile, a burst of ingenuous confidence, a covert appeal to his chivalry would yet catch him tripping. But the melancholy eyes that had gazed at the treasures of Ashley Grange and the opulent ease of its guests without kindling, opened to their first emotion, — wonder! At which Lady Elfrida, who had ingenuously admired him, hated him a little, as the first step towards a kindlier feeling.

The next day, having declared his intention of visiting Ashley Church, and, as frankly, his intention of going there alone, he slipped out in the afternoon and made his way quietly through the park to the square ivied tower he had first seen. In this tranquil level length of the wood there was the one spot, the churchyard, where, oddly enough, the green earth heaved into little billows as if to show the turbulence of that life which those who lay below them had lately quitted. It was a relief to the somewhat studied and formal monotony of the well-ordered woodland, — every rood of which had been paced by visitors, keepers, or poachers, — to find those decrepit and bending tombstones, lurching at every angle, or deeply sinking into the green sea of forgetfulness around them. All this, and the trodden paths of the villagers towards that common place of meeting, struck him as being more human than anything he had left behind him at the Grange.

He entered the ivy-grown porch and stared for a moment at the half-legal official parochial notices posted on the oaken door, — his first obtrusive intimation of the combination of church and state, — and hesitated. He was not prepared to find that this last resting - place of his people had something to do with taxes and tithes, and that a certain material respectability and security attended his votive sigh. God and the reigning sovereign of the realm preserved a decorous alliance in the royal arms that appeared above the official notices. Presently he pushed open the door gently and entered the nave. For a moment it seemed to him as if the arched gloom of the woods he had left behind was repeated in the dim aisle and vaulted roof; there was an earthy odor, as if the church itself, springing from the fertilizing dust below, had taken root in the soil ; the chequers of light from the faded stained-glass windows fell like the flicker of leaves on the pavement. He paused before the cold altar, and started, for beside him lay the recumbent figure of a warrior pillowed on his helmet with the paraphernalia of his trade around him. A sudden childish memory of the great Western plains, and the biers of the Indian " braves " raised on upright poles against the staring sky and above the sun-baked prairie, rushed upon him. There, too, had lain the weapons of the departed chieftain ; there, too, lay the Indian's " faithful hound," here simulated by the cross-legged crusader's canine effigy. And now, strangest of all, he found that this unlooked-for recollection and remembrance thrilled him more at that moment than the dead before him. Here they rested, — the Atherlys of centuries ; recumbent in armor or priestly robes, upright in busts that were periwigged or hidden in long curls, above the marble record of their deeds and virtues. Some of these records were in Latin, — an unknown tongue to Peter, — some in a quaint English almost as unintelligible ; but none as foreign to him as the dead themselves. Their banners waved above his head ; their voices filled the silent church, but fell upon his vacant eye and duller ear. He was none of them.

Presently he was conscious of a footstep, so faint, so subtle, that it might have come from a peregrinating ghost. He turned quickly and saw Lady Elfrida, half bold, yet half frightened, halting beside a pillar of the chancel. But there was nothing of the dead about her : she was radiating and pulsating with the uncompromising and material freshness of English girlhood. The wild rose in the hedgerow was not more tangible than her cheek, nor the summer sky more clearly cool and blue than her eyes. The vigor of health and unfettered freedom of limb was in her figure from her buckled walking-shoe to her brown hair topped by a sailor hat. The assurance and contentment of a well-ordered life, of secured position and freedom from vain anxieties or expectations, were visible in every line of her refined, delicate, and evenly quiescent features. And yet Lady Elfrida, for the first time in her girlhood, felt a little nervous.

Yet she was frank, too, with the frankness of those who have no thought of being misunderstood. She said she had come there out of curiosity to see how he would " get on " with his ancestors. She had been watching him from the chancel ever since he came, — and she was disappointed. As far as emotion went she thought he had the advantage of the stoniest and longest dead of them all. Perhaps he did not like them? But he must be careful what he *said*, for some of her own people were there, — manifestly this one. (She put the toe of her buckled shoe on the crusader Peter had just looked at.) And then there was another in the corner. So she had a right to come there as well as he, — and she could act as cicerone! This one was a De Brecy, one of King John's knights, who married an Atherly. (She swung herself into a half-sitting posture on the effigy of the dead knight, composed her straight short skirt over her trim ankles, and looked up in Peter's dark face.) That would make them some kind of relations, — would n't it? He must come over to Bentley Towers and see the rest of the De Brecys in the chapel there to-morrow.

Perhaps there might be some he liked better, and who looked more like him. For there was no one here or at the Grange who resembled him in the least.

He assented to the truth of this with such grave, disarming courtesy, and yet with such undisguised wonder, — as she appeared to talk with greater freedom to a stranger than an American girl would, — that she at once popped off the crusader, and accompanied him somewhat more demurely around the church. Suddenly she stopped with a slight exclamation.

They had halted before a tablet to the memory of a later Atherly, an officer of his Majesty's 100th Foot, who was killed at Braddock's defeat. The tablet was supported on the one side by a weeping Fame, and on the other by a manacled North American Indian. She stammered and said: " You see there are other Atherlys who went to America even before your father," and then stopped with a sense of having made a slip.

A wild and inexplicable resentment against this complacent historical outrage suddenly took possession of Peter. He knew that his rage was inconsistent with his usual calm, but he could not help it! His swarthy cheek glowed, his dark eyes flashed, he almost trembled with excitement as he hurriedly pointed out to Lady Elfrida that the Indians were *victorious* in that ill-fated expedition of the British forces, and that the captive savage was an allegorical lie. So swift and convincing was his emotion that the young girl, knowing nothing of the subject and caring less, shared his indignation, followed him with anxious eyes, and their hands for an instant touched in innocent and generous sympathy. And then — he knew not how or why — a still more wild and terrible idea sprang up in his fancy. He knew it was madness, yet for a moment he could only stand and grapple with it silently and breathlessly. It was to seize this young and innocent girl, this witness of his disappointment, this complacent and beautiful type of all they valued here, and bear her away — a prisoner, a hostage — he knew not why — on a galloping horse in the dust of the prairie — far beyond the seas! It was only when he saw her cheek flush and pale, when he saw her staring at him with helpless,

frightened, but fascinated eyes, — the eyes
of the fluttering bird under the spell of the
rattlesnake, — that he drew his breath and
turned bewildered away. "And do you
know, dear," she said with naïve simplicity
to her sister that evening, "that although
he was an American, and everybody says
that they don't care at all for those poor
Indians, he was so magnanimous in his indignation that I fancied he looked like one
of Cooper's heroes himself rather than an
Atherly. It was such a stupid thing for me
to show him that tomb of Major Atherly,
you know, who fought the Americans, —
did n't he? — or was it later? — but I quite
forgot he was an American." And with this
belief in her mind, and in the high expiation of a noble nature, she forbore her characteristic raillery, and followed him meekly,
manacled in spirit like the allegorical figure,
to the church porch, where they separated,
to meet on the morrow. But that morrow
never came.

For late in the afternoon a cable message
reached him from California asking him to
return to accept a nomination to Congress
from his own district. It determined his

resolution, which for a moment at the church porch had wavered under the bright eyes of Lady Elfrida. He telegraphed his acceptance, hurriedly took leave of his honestly lamenting kinsman, followed his dispatch to London, and in a few days was on the Atlantic.

How he was received in California, how he found his sister married to the blond lawyer, how he recovered his popularity and won his election, are details that do not belong to this chronicle of his quest. And that quest seems to have terminated forever with his appearance at Washington to take his seat as Congressman.

It was the night of a levee at the White House. The East Room was crowded with smartly dressed men and women of the capital, quaintly simple legislators from remote States in bygone fashions, officers in uniform, and the diplomatic circle blazing with orders. The invoker of this brilliant assembly stood in simple evening dress near the door, — unattended and hedged by no formality. He shook the hand of the new Congressman heartily, congratulated him by name, and turned smilingly to the next comer. Presently there was a slight stir at one of the opposite doors, the crowd fell back, and five figures stalked majestically into the centre of the room. They were the leading chiefs of an Indian reservation coming to pay their respects to their "Great Father," the President. Their costumes were a mingling of the picturesque with the grotesque; of tawdriness with magnificence; of artificial tinsel and glitter with the regal spoils of the chase; of childlike vanity with barbaric pride. Yet before these the glittering orders and ribbons of the diplomats became dull and meaningless, the uniforms of the officers mere servile livery. Their painted, immobile faces and plumed heads towered with grave dignity above the meaner crowd; their inscrutable eyes returned no response to the timid glances directed towards them. They stood by themselves, alone and impassive, — yet their presence filled the room with the sense of kings. The unostentatious, simple republican court suddenly seemed to have become royal. Even the interpreter who stood between their remote dignity and the nearer civilized world acquired the status of a court chamberlain.

When their " Great Father," apparently the less important personage, had smilingly received them, a political colleague approached Peter and took his arm. " Gray Eagle would like to speak with you. Come on ! Here 's your chance ! You may be put on the Committee on Indian Relations, and pick up a few facts. Remember we want a firm policy ; no more palaver about the ' Great Father ' and no more blankets and guns ! You know what we used to say out West, ' The only " Good Indian " is a dead one.' So wade in, and hear what the old plug hat has to say."

Peter permitted himself to be led to the group. Even at that moment he remembered the figure of the Indian on the tomb at Ashley Grange, and felt a slight flash of satisfaction over the superior height and bearing of Gray Eagle.

" How ! " said Gray Eagle. " How ! " said the other four chiefs. " How ! " repeated Peter instinctively. At a gesture from Gray Eagle the interpreter said : " Let your friend stand back ; Gray Eagle has nothing to say to him. He wishes to speak only with you."

Peter's friend reluctantly withdrew, but threw a cautioning glance towards him. " Ugh ! " said Gray Eagle. " Ugh ! " said the other chiefs. A few guttural words followed to the interpreter, who turned, and facing Peter with the monotonous impassiveness which he had caught from the chiefs, said : " He says he knew your father. He was a great chief, — with many horses and many squaws. He is dead."

" My father was an Englishman, — Philip Atherly ! " said Peter, with an odd nervousness creeping over him.

The interpreter repeated the words to Grey Eagle, who, after a guttural " Ugh ! " answered in his own tongue.

" He says," continued the interpreter with a slight shrug, yet relapsing into his former impassiveness, " that your father was a great chief, and your mother a pale face, or white woman. She was captured with an Englishman, but she became the wife of the chief while in captivity. She was only released before the birth of her children, but a year or two afterwards she brought them as infants to see their father, — the Great Chief, — and to get the mark of their tribe.

He says you and your sister are each marked on the left arm."

Then Gray Eagle opened his mouth and uttered his first English sentence. " His father, big Injin, take common white squaw ! Papoose no good, — too much white squaw mother, not enough big Injin father ! Look ! He big man, but no can bear pain ! Ugh ! "

The interpreter turned in time to catch Peter. He had fainted.

CHAPTER III

A HOT afternoon on the plains. A dusty cavalcade of United States cavalry and commissary wagons, which from a distance preserved a certain military precision of movement, but on nearer view resolved itself into straggling troopers in twos and fours interspersed between the wagons, two non-commissioned officers and a guide riding ahead, who had already fallen into the cavalry slouch, but off to the right, smartly erect and cadet-like, the young lieutenant in command. A wide road that had the appearance of being at once well traveled and yet

deserted, and that, although well defined
under foot, still seemed to disappear and lose
itself a hundred feet ahead in the monotonous level. A horizon that in that clear,
dry, hazeless atmosphere never mocked you,
yet never changed, but kept its eternal rim
of mountains at the same height and distance from hour to hour and day to day.
Dust — a parching alkaline powder that
cracked the skin — everywhere, clinging to
the hubs and spokes of the wheels, without being disturbed by movement, incrusting
the cavalryman from his high boots to the
crossed sabres of his cap ; going off in small
puffs like explosions under the plunging
hoofs of the horses, but too heavy to rise
and follow them. A reeking smell of horse
sweat and boot leather that lingered in the
road long after the train had passed. An
external silence broken only by the cough
of a jaded horse in the suffocating dust, or
the cracking of harness leather. Within
one of the wagons that seemed a miracle of
military neatness and methodical stowage,
a lazy conversation carried on by a grizzled
driver and sunbrowned farrier.

" ' Who be you ? ' sezee. ' I 'm Philip

Atherly, a member of Congress,' sez the long, dark-complected man, sezee, ' and I 'm on a commission for looking into this yer Injin grievance,' sezee. ' You may be God Almighty,' sez Nebraska Bill, sezee, ' but you look a d——d sight more like a hoss-stealin' Apache, and we don't want any of your psalm-singing, big-talkin' peacemakers interferin' with our ways of treatin' pizen, — you hear me? I 'm shoutin',' sezee. With that the dark-complected man's eyes began to glisten, and he sorter squirmed all over to get at Bill, and Bill outs with his battery. — Whoa, will ye; what 's up with *you* now? " The latter remark was directed to the young spirited near horse he was driving, who was beginning to be strangely excited.

" What happened then ? " said the farrier lazily.

" Well," continued the driver, having momentarily quieted his horse, " I reckoned it was about time for me to wheel into line, for fellers of the Bill stripe, out on the plains, would ez leave plug a man in citizen's clothes, even if he was the President him-self, as they would drop on an Injin or a

nigger. 'Look here, Bill,' sez I, 'I'm es-
cortin' this stranger under gov'ment orders,
and I'm responsible for him. I ain't allowed to waste gov'ment powder and shot
on *your* kind onless I've orders, but if
you'll wait till I strip off this shell[1] I'll
lam the stuffin' outer ye, afore the stranger.' With that Bill just danced with rage,
but dassent fire, for *he* knew, and *I* knew,
that if he'd plugged me he'd been a dead
frontiersman afore the next mornin'.'"

"But you'd have had to give him up to
the authorities, and a jury of his own kind
would have set him free."

"Not much! If you hadn't just joined,
you'd know that ain't the way o' 30th Cavalry," returned the driver. "The kernel
would have issued his orders to bring in
Bill dead or alive, and the 30th would have
managed to bring him in *dead!* Then your
jury might have sat on him! Tell you what,
chaps of the Bill stripe don't care overmuch
to tackle the yaller braid."[2]

"But what's this yer Congressman interferin' for, anyway?"

[1] Cavalry jacket.
[2] Characteristic trimming of cavalry jacket.

" He 's a rich Californian. Thinks he 's got a ' call,' I reckon, to look arter Injins, just as them Abolitionists looked arter slaves. And get hated just as they was by the folks here, — and as *we* are, too, for the matter of that."

" Well, I dunno," rejoined the farrier, " it don't seem nateral for white men to quarrel with each other about the way to treat an Injin, and that Injin lyin' in ambush to shoot 'em both. And ef gov'ment would only make up its mind how to treat 'em, instead of one day pretendin' to be their ' Great Father' and treatin' them like babies, and the next makin' treaties with 'em like as they wos forriners, and the next sendin' out a handful of us to lick ten thousand of them— Wot 's the use of *one* regiment — even two — agin a nation — on their own ground ? "

" A nation, — and on their own ground, — that 's just whar you 've hit it, Softy. That 's the argument of that Congressman Atherly, as I 've heard him talk with the kernel."

" And what did the kernel say ? "

" The kernel reckoned it was his business

to obey orders, — and so should you. So
shut your head ! If ye wanted to talk about
gov'ment ye might say suthin' about its usin'
us to convoy picnics and excursion parties
around, who come out here to have a day's
shootin', under some big-wig of a political
boss or a railroad president, with a letter to
the general. And *we* 're told off to look
arter their precious skins, and keep the Injins off 'em, — and they shootin' or skeerin'
off the Injins' nat'ral game, and our proven-
der ! Darn my skin ef there 'll be much to
scout for ef this goes on. And b'gosh ! —
ef they are n't now ringin' in a lot of titled
forriners to hunt ' big game,' as they call
it, — Lord This-and-That and Count So-
and-So, — all of 'em with letters to the general from the Washington cabinet to show
' hospitality,' or from millionaires who 've
bin hobnobbin' with 'em in the old country. And darn my skin ef some of 'em
ain't bringin' their wives and sisters along
too. There was a lord and lady passed
through here under escort last week, and
we 're goin' to pick up some more of 'em at
Fort Biggs to-morrow, — and I reckon some
of us will be told off to act as ladies' maids

or milliners. Nothin' short of a good Injin scare, I reckon, would send them and us about our reg'lar business. Whoa, then, will ye? At it again, are ye? What's gone of the d——d critter?"

Here the fractious near horse was again beginning to show signs of disturbance and active terror. His quivering nostrils were turned towards the wind, and he almost leaped the centre pole in his frantic effort to avoid it. The eyes of the two men were turned instinctively in that direction. Nothing was to be seen, — the illimitable plain and the sinking sun were all that met the eye. But the horse continued to struggle, and the wagon stopped. Then it was discovered that the horse of an adjacent trooper was also laboring under the same mysterious excitement, and at the same moment wagon No. 3 halted. The infection of some inexplicable terror was spreading among them. Then two non-commissioned officers came riding down the line at a sharp canter, and were joined quickly by the young lieutenant, who gave an order. The trumpeter instinctively raised his instrument to his lips, but was stopped by another order.

And then, as seen by a distant observer, a singular spectacle was unfolded. The straggling train suddenly seemed to resolve itself into a large widening circle of horsemen, revolving round and partly hiding the few heavy wagons that were being rapidly freed from their struggling teams. These, too, joined the circle, and were driven before the whirling troopers. Gradually the circle seemed to grow smaller under the "winding-up" of those evolutions, until the horseless wagons reappeared again, motionless, fronting the four points of the compass, thus making the radii of a smaller inner circle, into which the teams of the wagons as well as the troopers' horses were closely " wound up " and densely packed together in an immovable mass. As the circle became smaller the troopers leaped from their horses, — which, however, continued to blindly follow each other in the narrower circle, — and ran to the wagons, carbines in hand. In five minutes from the time of giving the order the straggling train was a fortified camp, the horses corralled in the centre, the dismounted troopers securely posted with their repeating carbines in the angles of the rude bastions formed by the deserted wagons, and ready for an attack. The stampede, if such it was, was stopped.

And yet no cause for it was to be seen! Nothing in earth or sky suggested a reason for this extraordinary panic, or the marvelous evolution that suppressed it. The guide, with three men in open order, rode out and radiated across the empty plain, returning as empty of result. In an hour the horses were sufficiently calmed and fed, the camp slowly unwound itself, the teams were set to and were led out of the circle, and as the rays of the setting sun began to expand fanlike across the plain the cavalcade moved on. But between them and the sinking sun, and visible through its last rays, was a faint line of haze parallel with their track. Yet even this, too, quickly faded away.

Had the guide, however, penetrated half a mile further to the west he would have come upon the cause of the panic, and a spectacle more marvelous than that he had just witnessed. For the illimitable plain with its monotonous prospect was far from being level; a hundred yards further on he would have slowly and imperceptibly de-

scended into a depression nearly a mile in
width. Here he not only would have completely lost sight of his own cavalcade, but
have come upon another thrice its length.
For here was a trailing line of jog-trotting
dusky shapes, some crouching on dwarf
ponies half their size, some trailing lances,
lodge-poles, rifles, women and children after
them, all moving with a monotonous rhyth-
mic motion as marked as the military precision of the other cavalcade, and always
on a parallel line with it. They had done
so all day, keeping touch and distance
by stealthy videttes that crept and crawled
along the imperceptible slope towards the
unconscious white men. It was, no doubt,
the near proximity of one of those watchers
that had touched the keen scent of the troopers' horses.

The moon came up; the two cavalcades,
scarcely a mile apart, moved on in unison
together. Then suddenly the dusky caravan
seemed to arise, stretch itself out, and swept
away like a morning mist towards the west.
The bugles of Fort Biggs had just rung out.

.   .   .   .

Peter Atherly was up early the next morn-

ing pacing the veranda of the commandant's house at Fort Biggs. It had been
his intention to visit the new Indian Reservation that day, but he had just received a
letter announcing an unexpected visit from
his sister, who wished to join him. He had
never told her the secret of their Indian
paternity, as it had been revealed to him
from the scornful lips of Gray Eagle a year
ago ; he knew her strangely excitable nature ; besides, she was a wife now, and the
secret would have to be shared with her
husband. When he himself had recovered
from the shock of the revelation, two things
had impressed themselves upon his reserved
and gloomy nature : a horror of his previous claim upon the Atherlys, and an infinite pity and sense of duty towards his own
race. He had devoted himself and his increasing wealth to this one object; it seemed
to him at times almost providential that his
position as a legislator, which he had accepted as a whim or fancy, should have given
him this singular opportunity.

Yet it was not an easy task or an enviable
position. He was obliged to divorce himself
from his political party as well as keep clear

of the wild schemes of impractical enthusi-
asts, too practical " contractors," and the still
more helpless bigotry of Christian civilizers,
who would have regenerated the Indian
with a text which he did not understand
and they were unable to illustrate by example. He had expected the opposition of
lawless frontiersmen and ignorant settlers —
as roughly indicated in the conversation
already recorded; indeed he had felt it difficult to argue his humane theories under the
smoking roof of a raided settler's cabin,
whose owner, however, had forgotten his
own repeated provocations, or the trespass
of which he was proud. But Atherly's unaffected and unobtrusive zeal, his fixity of
purpose, his undoubted courage, his self-
abnegation, and above all the gentle melancholy and half-philosophical wisdom of this
new missionary, won him the respect and
assistance of even the most callous or the
most skeptical of officials. The Secretary
of the Interior had given him carte blanche;
the President trusted him, and it was said
had granted him extraordinary powers.
Oddly enough it was only his own Californian constituency, who had once laughed

at what they deemed his early aristocratic pretensions, who now found fault with his democratic philanthropy. That a man who had been so well received in England — the news of his visit to Ashley Grange had been duly recorded — should sink so low as " to take up with the Injins " of his own country galled their republican pride. A few of his personal friends regretted that he had not brought back from England more conservative and fashionable graces, and had not improved his opportunities. Unfortunately there was no essentially English policy of trusting aborigines that they knew of.

In his gloomy self-scrutiny he had often wondered if he ought not to openly proclaim his kinship with the despised race, but he was always deterred by the thought of his sister and her husband, as well as by the persistent doubt whether his advocacy of Indian rights with his fellow countrymen would be as well served by such a course. And here again he was perplexed by a singular incident of his early missionary efforts which he had at first treated with cold surprise, but to which later reflection had given a new significance. After Gray Eagle's revelation

he had made a pilgrimage to the Indian
country to verify the statements regarding
his dead father, — the Indian chief Silver
Cloud. Despite the confusion of tribal dia-
lects he was amazed to find that the Indian
tongue came back to him almost as a forgotten boyish memory, so that he was soon able
to do without an interpreter ; but not until
that functionary, who knew his secret, appeared one day as a more significant ambas-
sador. " Gray Eagle says if you want truly
to be a brother to his people you must take
a wife among them. He loves you — take
one of his ! " Peter, through whose veins —
albeit of mixed blood — ran that Puritan ice
so often found throughout the Great West,
was frigidly amazed. In vain did the interpreter assure him that the wife in question,
Little Daybreak, was a wife only in name,
a prudent reserve kept by Gray Eagle in
the orphan daughter of a brother brave.
But Peter was adamant. Whatever answer
the interpreter returned to Gray Eagle he
never knew. But to his alarm he presently
found that the Indian maiden Little Daybreak had been aware of Gray Eagle's offer,
and had with pathetic simplicity already

considered herself Peter's spouse. During his stay at the encampment he found her sitting before his lodge every morning. A girl of sixteen in years, a child of six in intellect, she flashed her little white teeth upon him when he lifted his tent flap, content to receive his grave, melancholy bow, or patiently trotted at his side carrying things he did not want, which she had taken from the lodge. When he sat down to work, she remained seated at a distance, looking at him with glistening beady eyes like blackberries set in milk, and softly scratching the little bare brown ankle of one foot with the turned-in toes of the other, after an infantine fashion. Yet after he had left — a still single man, solely through his interpreter's diplomacy, as he always believed — he was very worried as to the wisdom of his course. Why should he not in this way ally himself to his unfortunate race irrevocably? Perhaps there was an answer somewhere in his consciousness which he dared not voice to himself. Since his visit to the English Atherlys, he had put resolutely aside everything that related to that episode, which he now considered was an unhappy imposture. But

there were times when a vision of Lady Elfrida, gazing at him with wondering, fascinated eyes, passed across his fancy; even the
contact with his own race and his thoughts
of their wrongs recalled to him the tomb of
the soldier Atherly and the carven captive
savage supporter. He could not pass the
upright supported bier of an Indian brave —
slowly desiccating in the desert air — without seeing in the dead warrior's paraphernal-
lia of arms and trophies some resemblance
to the cross-legged crusader on whose marble effigy *she* had girlishly perched herself
as she told the story of her ancestors. Yet
only the peaceful gloom and repose of the
old church touched him now; even she,
too, with all her glory of English girlhood,
seemed to belong to that remote past. She
was part of the restful quiet of the church;
the yews in the quaint old churchyard might
have waved over her as well.

Still, he was eager to see his sister, and
if he should conclude to impart to her his
secret, she might advise him. At all events,
he decided to delay his departure until her
arrival, a decision with which the commanding officer concurred, as a foraging party

had that morning discovered traces of Indians in the vicinity of the fort, and the lately arrived commissary train had reported the unaccountable but promptly prevented stampede.

Unfortunately, his sister Jenny appeared accompanied by her husband, who seized an early opportunity to take Peter aside and confide to him his anxiety about her health, and the strange fits of excitement under which she occasionally labored. Remembering the episode of the Californian woods three years ago, Peter stared at this good-natured, good-looking man, whose life he had always believed she once imperiled, and wondered more than ever at their strange union.

" Do you ever quarrel ? " asked Peter bluntly.

" No," said the good-hearted fellow warmly, " never ! We have never had a harsh word ; she 's the dearest girl, — the best wife in the world to me, but " — he hesitated, " you know there are times when I think she confounds me with somebody else, and is strange ! Sometimes when we are in company she stands alone and stares at everybody, without saying a word, as if she did n't understand them. Or else she gets painfully excited and dances all night until she is exhausted. I thought, perhaps," he added timidly, " that you might know, and would tell me if she had any singular experience as a child, — any illness, or," he went on still more gently, " if perhaps her mother or father " —

" No," interrupted Peter almost brusquely, with the sudden conviction that this was no time for revelation of his secret, " no, nothing."

" The doctor says," continued Lascelles with that hesitating, almost mystic delicacy with which most gentlemen approach a subject upon which their wives talk openly, " that it may be owing to Jenny's peculiar state of health just now, you know, and that if — all went well, you know, and there should be — don't you see — a little child " —

Peter interrupted him with a start. A child! Jenny's child! Silver Cloud's grandchild! This was a complication he had not thought of. No! It was too late to tell his secret now. He only nodded his head abstractedly and said coldly, " I dare say he is right."

Nevertheless, Jenny was looking remarkably well. Perhaps it was the excitement of travel and new surroundings; but her tall, lithe figure, nearly half a head taller than her husband's, was a striking one among the officers' wives in the commandant's sitting-room. Her olive cheek glowed with a faint illuminating color; there was something even patrician in her slightly curved nose and high cheek bones, and her smile, rare even in her most excited moments, was, like her brother's, singularly fascinating. The officers evidently thought so too, and when the young lieutenant of the commissary escort, fresh from West Point and Flirtation Walk, gallantly attached himself to her, the ladies were slightly scandalized at the naïve air of camaraderie with which Mrs. Lascelles received his attentions. Even Peter was a little disturbed. Only Lascelles, delighted with his wife's animation, and pleased at her success, gazed at her with unqualified admiration. Indeed, he was so satisfied with her improvement, and so sanguine of her ultimate recovery, that he felt justified in leaving her with her brother and returning to Omaha by the regular mail wagon next day.

There was no danger to be apprehended in her accompanying Peter; they would have a full escort; the reservation lay in a direction unfrequented by marauding tribes; the road was the principal one used by the government to connect the fort with the settlements, and well traveled; the officers' wives had often journeyed thither.

The childish curiosity and high spirits which Jenny showed on the journey to the reservation was increased when she reached it and drew up before the house of the Indian agent. Peter was relieved; he had been anxious and nervous as to any instinctive effect which might be produced on her excitable nature by a first view of her own kinsfolk, although she was still ignorant of her relationship. Her interest and curiosity, however, had nothing abnormal in it. But he was not prepared for the effect produced upon *them* at her first appearance. A few of the braves gathered eagerly around her, and one even addressed her in his own guttural tongue, at which she betrayed a slight feeling of alarm; and Peter saw with satisfaction that she drew close to him. Knowing that his old interpreter and Gray Eagle were of a different and hostile tribe a hundred miles away, and that his secret was safe with them, he simply introduced her as his sister. But he presently found that the braves had added to their curiosity a certain suspiciousness and sullen demeanor, and he was glad to resign his sister into the hands of the agent's wife, while he prosecuted his business of examination and inspection. Later, on his return to the cabin, he was met by the agent, who seemed to be with difficulty suppressing a laugh.

" Your sister is exciting quite a sensation here," he said. " Do you know that some of these idiotic braves and the Medicine Man insist upon it that she 's *a squaw*, and that you 're keeping her in captivity against your plighted faith to them! You 'll excuse me," he went on with an attempt to recover his gravity, " troubling you with their d——d fool talk, and you won't say anything to *her* about it, but I thought you ought to know it on account of your position among 'em. You don't want to lose their confidence, and you know how easily their skeery faculties are stampeded with an idea ! "

"Where is she now?" demanded Peter, with a darkening face.

"Somewhere with the squaws, I reckon. I thought she might be a little skeered of the braves, and I've kept them away. *She*'s all right, you know; only if you intend to stay here long I'd" —

But Peter was already striding away in the direction of a thicket of cottonwood where he heard the ripple of women's and children's voices. When he had penetrated it, he found his sister sitting on a stump, surrounded by a laughing, gesticulating crowd of young girls and old women, with a tightly swaddled papoose in her lap. Some of them had already half mischievously, half curiously possessed themselves of her dust cloak, hat, parasol, and gloves, and were parading before her in their grotesque finery, apparently as much to her childish excited amusement as their own. She was even answering their gesticulations with equivalent gestures in her attempt to understand them, and trying amidst shouts of laughter to respond to the monotonous chant of the old women who were zigzagging a dance before her. With the gayly striped blankets lying on the

ground, the strings of beads, wampum, and
highly colored feathers hanging from the
trees, and the flickering lights and shadows,
it was an innocent and even idyllic picture,
but the more experienced Peter saw in the
performances only the uncertain temper and
want of consecutive idea of playing animals,
and the stolid unwinking papoose in his sister's lap gave his sentiment a momentary
shock.

Seeing him approach she ran to meet him,
the squaws and children slinking away from
his grave face.   " I have had such a funny
time, Peter !   Only to think of it, I believe
they 've never seen men or women with decent clothes before, — of course the settlers'
wives don't dress much, — and I believe
they 'd have had everything I possess if
you had n't come.   But they 're *too* funny
for anything.   It was killing to see them
put on my hat wrong side before, and try to
make one out of my parasol.   But I like
them a great deal better than those gloomy
chiefs, and I think I understand them almost.   And do you know, Peter, somehow I
seem to have known them all before.   And
those dear little papooses, are n't they ridicu-

lously lovely. I only wish " — she stopped,
for Peter had somewhat hurriedly taken the
Indian boy from her arms and restored it
to the frightened mother. A singular change
came over her face, and she glanced at him
quickly. But she resumed, with a heightened color, " I like it ever so much better
here than down at the fort. And ever so
much better than New York. I don't wonder that you like them so much, Peter, and
are so devoted to them. Don't be angry,
dear, because I let them have my things ;
I 'm sure I never cared particularly for them,
and I think it would be such fun to dress
as they do." Peter remembered keenly his
sudden shock at her precipitate change to
bright colors after leaving her novitiate at
the Sacred Heart. " I do hope," she went
on eagerly, " that we are going to stay a long
time here."

" We are leaving to-morrow," he said
curtly. " I find I have urgent business at
the fort."

And they did leave. None too soon,
thought Peter and the Indian agent, as they
glanced at the faces of the dusky chiefs
who had gathered around the cabin. Luckily

the presence of their cavalry escort rendered any outbreak impossible, and the stoical taciturnity of the race kept Peter from any verbal insult. But Mrs. Lascelles noticed their lowering dissatisfaction, and her eyes flashed. " I wonder you don't punish them," she said simply.

For a few days after their return she did not allude to her visit, and Peter was beginning to think that her late impressions were as volatile as they were childlike. He devoted himself to his government report, and while he kept up his communications with the reservation and the agent, for the present domiciled himself at the fort.

Colonel Bryce, the commandant, though doubtful of civilians, was not slow to appreciate the difference of playing host to a man of Atherly's wealth and position, and even found in Peter's reserve and melancholy an agreeable relief to the somewhat boisterous and material recreations of garrison life, and a gentle check upon the younger officers. For, while Peter did not gamble or drink, there was yet an unobtrusive and gentle dignity in his abstention that relieved him from the attitude of a prig or an " ex-

ample." Mrs. Lascelles was popular with
the officers, and accepted more tolerantly by
the wives, since they recognized her harm-
lessness. Once or twice she was found apparently interested in the gesticulations of
a few "friendlies" who had penetrated the
parade ground of the fort to barter beads
and wampum. The colonel was obliged at
last to caution her against this, as it was
found that in her inexperience she had given
them certain articles that were contraband
of the rules, and finally to stop them from
an intrusion which was becoming more frequent and annoying. Left thus to herself,
she relieved her isolation by walks beyond
the precincts of the garrison, where she frequently met those "friendly" wanderers,
chiefly squaws and children. Here she was
again cautioned by the commander, —

"Don't put too much faith in those creatures, Mrs. Lascelles."

Jenny elevated her black brows and threw
up her arched nose like a charger. "I 'm
not afraid of old women and children," she
said loftily.

"But *I* am," said the colonel gravely.
"It 's a horrible thing to think of, but these

feeble old women and innocent children are always selected to torture the prisoners taken by the braves, and, by Jove, they seem to like it."

Thus restricted, Mrs. Lascelles fell back upon the attentions of Lieutenant Forsyth, whose gallantry was always as fresh as his smart cadet-like tunics, and they took some rides together. Whether it was military caution or the feminine discretion of the colonel's wife, — to the quiet amusement of the other officers, — a trooper was added to the riding party by the order of the colonel, and thereafter it consisted of three. One night, however, the riders did not appear at dinner, and there was considerable uneasiness mingled with some gossip throughout the garrison. It was already midnight before they arrived, and then with horses blown and trembling with exhaustion, and the whole party bearing every sign of fatigue and disturbance. The colonel said a few sharp, decisive words to the subaltern, who, pale and reticent, plucked at his little moustache, but took the whole blame upon himself. *He* and Mrs. Lascelles had, he said, outridden the trooper and got lost; it was late when Cassidy (the trooper) found them, but it was no fault of *his*, and they had to ride at the top of their speed to cover the ground between them and the fort. It was noticed that Mrs. Lascelles scarcely spoke to Forsyth, and turned abruptly away from the colonel's interrogations and went to her room.

Peter, absorbed in his report, scarcely noticed the incident, nor the singular restraint that seemed to fall upon the little military household for a day or two afterwards. He had accepted the lieutenant's story without comment or question; he knew his own sister too well to believe that she had lent herself to a flirtation with Forsyth; indeed, he had rather pitied the young officer when he remembered Lascelles' experience in his early courtship. But he was somewhat astonished one afternoon to find the trooper Cassidy alone in his office.

"Oi thought Oi 'd make bould to have a word wid ye, sorr," he said, recovering from a stiff salute with his fingers nipping the cord of his trousers. "It 's not for meeself, sorr, although the ould man was harrd on me, nor for the leddy, your sister, but for the sake of the leftenant, sorr, who the ould man was harrdest on of all. Oi was of the parrty that rode with your sister."

"Yes, yes, I remember, I heard the story," said Peter. "She and Mr. Forsyth got lost."

"Axin' your pardin, sorr, she didn't. Mr. Forsyth loid. Loid like an officer and a jintleman — as he is, God bless him — to save a leddy, more betoken your sister, sorr. They never got lost, sorr. We was all three together from the toime we shtarted till we got back, and it's the love av God that we ever got back at all. And it's breaking me hearrt, sorr, to see *him* goin' round with the black looks of everybody upon him, and he a-twirlin' his moustache and purtending not to mind."

"What do you mean?" said Peter, uneasily.

"Oi mane to be tellin' you what happened, sorr," said Cassidy stoutly. "When we shtarted out Oi fell three files to the rear, as became me, so as not to be in the way o' their colloguing, but sorra a bit o' stragglin' was there, and Oi kept them afore me all the toime. When we got to Post Oak Bottom

the leddy p'ints her whip off to the roight,
and sez she : ' It 's a fine bit of turf there,
Misther Forsyth,' invitin' like, and with that
she gallops away to the right. The leftenant follys her, and Oi closed up the rear. So
we rides away innoshent like amongst the
trees, me thinkin' only it wor a mighty queer
place for manoovrin', until we seed, just beyond us in the hollow, the smoke of an Injin
camp and a lot of women and childer. And
Mrs. Lascelles gets off and goes to discours-
in' and blarneying wid 'em : and Oi sees
Mr. Forsyth glancin' round and lookin' on-
easy. Then he goes up and sez something
to your sister, and she won't give him a
hearin'. And then he tells her she must
mount and be off. And she turns upon him,
bedad, like a tayger, and bids him be off
himself. Then he comes to me and sez he,
' Oi don't like the look o' this, Cassidy,' sez
he ; ' the woods behind is full of braves,'
sez he. ' Thrue for you, leftenant,' sez Oi,
' it 's into a trap that the leddy hez led us,
God save her ! ' ' Whisht,' he sez, ' take my
horse, it 's the strongest. Go beside her,
and when Oi say the word lift her up into
the saddle before ye, and gallop like blazes.

Oi 'll bring up the rear and the other horse.'
Wid that we changed horses and cantered
up to where she was standing, and he gives
the word when she is n't lookin', and Oi
grabs her up — she sthrugglin' like mad but
not utterin' a cry — and Oi lights out for
the trail agin. And sure enough the braves
made as if they would folly, but the leftenant throws the reins of her horse over the
horn of his saddle, and whips out his revolver
and houlds 'em back till I 've got well away
to the trail again. And then they let fly
their arrows, and begorra the next thing a
bullet whizzes by him. And then he knows
they have arrms wid 'em and are 'hostiles,'
and he rowls the nearest one over, wheelin'
and fightin' and coverin' our retreat till we
gets to the road agin. And they dare n't
folly us out of cover. Then the lady gets
more sinsible, and the leftenant pershuades
her to mount her horse agin. But before
we comes to the fort, he sez to me : 'Cassidy,' sez he, 'not a word o' this on account
of the leddy.' And I was mum, sorr, while
he was shootin' off his mouth about him
bein' lost and all that, and him bein' bully-
ragged by the kernel, and me knowin' that

but for him your sister would n't be between these walls here, and Oi would n't be talkin' to ye. And shure, sorr, ye might be tellin's the kernel as how the leddy was took by the hysterics, and was that loony that she did n't know whatever she was sayin', and so get the leftenant in favor again."

"I will speak with the colonel to-night," said Peter gloomily.

"Lord save yer honor," returned the trooper gratefully, "and if ye could be sayin' that the *leddy* tould you, — it would only be the merest taste of a loi ye 'd be tellin', — and you 'd save me from breakin' me word to the leftenant."

"I shall of course speak to my sister first," returned Peter, with a guilty consciousness that he had accepted the trooper's story mainly from his previous knowledge of his sister's character. Nevertheless, in spite of this foregone conclusion, he *did* speak to her. To his surprise she did not deny it. Lieutenant Forsyth, — a vain and conceited fool, — whose silly attentions she had accepted solely that she might get recreation beyond the fort, — had presumed to tell her what *she* must do! As if *she* was one of

those stupid officers' wives or sisters! And
it never would have happened if he — Peter
— had let her remain at the reservation with
the Indian agent's wife, or if "Charley"
(the gentle Lascelles) were here! *He*
would have let her go, or taken her there.
Besides all the while she was among friends;
his, Peter's own friends, — the people whose
cause he was championing! In vain did
Peter try to point out to her that these "people" were still children in mind and impulse,
and capable of vacillation or even treachery.
He remembered he was talking to a child
in mind and impulse, who had shown the
same qualities, and in trying to convince her
of her danger he felt he was only voicing
the common arguments of his opponents.

He spoke also to the colonel, excusing
her through her ignorance, her trust in his
influence with the savages, and the general
derangement of her health. The colonel,
relieved of his suspicions of a promising
young officer, was gentle and sympathetic,
but firm as to Peter's future course. In a
moment of caprice and willfulness she might
imperil the garrison as she had her escort,
and, more than that, she was imperiling

Peter's influence with the Indians. Absurd stories had come to his ears regarding the attitude of the reservation towards him. He thought she ought to return home as quickly as possible. Fortunately an opportunity offered. The general commanding had advised him of the visit to the fort of a party of English tourists who had been shooting in the vicinity, and who were making the fort the farthest point of their western excursion. There were three or four ladies in the party, and as they would be returning to the line of railroad under escort, she could easily accompany them. This, added Colonel Carter, was also Mrs. Carter's opinion, — she was a woman of experience, and had a married daughter of her own. In the mean time Peter had better not broach the subject to his sister, but trust to the arrival of the strangers, who would remain for a week, and who would undoubtedly divert Mrs. Lascelles' impressible mind, and eventually make the proposition more natural and attractive.

In the interval Peter revisited the reservation, and endeavored to pacify the irritation that had sprung from his previous in-

spection. The outrage at Post Oak Bottom
he was assured had no relation to the incident at the reservation, but was committed
by some stragglers from other tribes who
had not yet accepted the government bounty,
yet had not been thus far classified as " hostile." There had been no " Ghost Dancing " nor other indication of disturbance.
The colonel had not deemed it necessary to
send out an exemplary force, or make a
counter demonstration. The incident was allowed to drop. At the reservation Peter had
ignored the previous conduct of the chiefs
towards him ; had with quiet courage exposed
himself fully — unarmed and unattended —
amongst them, and had as fully let it be
known that this previous incident was the
reason that his sister had not accompanied
him on his second visit. He left them at
the close of the second day more satisfied in
his mind, and perhaps in a more enthusiastic
attitude towards his report.

As he came within sound of the sunset
bugles, he struck a narrower trail which
led to the fort, through an oasis of oaks
and cottonwoods and a small stream or
" branch," which afterwards lost itself in

the dusty plain. He had already passed
a few settler's cabins, a sutler's shop, and
other buildings that had sprung up around
this armed nucleus of civilization — which,
in due season, was to become a frontier
town. But as yet the brief wood was wild
and secluded; frequented only by the women and children of the fort, within whose
protecting bounds it stood, and to whose
formal "parade," and trim white and green
cottage "quarters," it afforded an agreeable relief. As he rode abstractedly forward
under the low cottonwood vault he felt a
strange influence stealing over him, an influence that was not only a present experience
but at the same time a far-off memory. The
concave vault above deepened; the sunset
light from the level horizon beyond streamed
through the leaves as through the chequers
of stained glass windows; through the two
shafts before him stretched the pillared aisles
of Ashley Church! He was riding as in a
dream, and when a figure suddenly slipped
across his pathway from a column-like tree
trunk, he woke with the disturbance and
sense of unreality of a dream. For he saw
Lady Elfrida standing before him!

It was not a mere memory conjured up by association, for although the figure, face, and attitude were the same, there were certain changes of costume which the eye of recollection noticed. In place of the smart narrow-brimmed sailor hat he remembered, she was wearing a slouched cavalry hat with a gold cord around its crown, that, with all its becomingness and picturesque audacity, seemed to become characteristic and respectable, as a crest to her refined head, and as historic as a Lely canvas. She wore a flannel shirt, belted in at her slight waist with a band of yellow leather, defining her small hips, and short straight pleatless skirts that fell to her trim ankles and buckled leather shoes. She was fresh and cool, wholesome and clean, free and unfettered; indeed, her beauty seemed only an afterthought or accident. So much so that when Peter saw her afterwards, amidst the billowy, gauzy, and challenging graces of the officer's wives, who were dressed in their best and prettiest frocks to welcome her, the eye turned naturally from that suggestion of enhancement to the girl who seemed to defy it. She was clearly not an idealized memory, a spirit or a

ghost, but naturalistic and rosy; he thought
a trifle rosier, as she laughingly addressed
him : —

"I suppose it is n't quite fair to surprise
you like that," she said, with an honest girlish hand-shake, "for you see I know all
about you now, and what you are doing here,
and even when you were expected; and I
dare say you thought we were still in England, if you remembered us at all. And
we have n't met since that day at Ashley
Church when I put my foot in it, — or rather
on your pet protégé's, the Indian's: you
remember Major Atherly's tomb? And to
think that all the while we did n't know
that you were a public man and a great
political reformer, and had a fad like this.
Why, we 'd have got up meetings for you,
and my father would have presided, — he 's
always fond of doing these things, — and
we 'd have passed resolutions, and given you
subscriptions, and Bibles, and flannel shirts,
and revolvers — but I believe you draw the
line at that. My brother was saying only
the other day that you were n't half praised
enough for going in for this sort of thing
when you were so rich, and need n't care.

And so that's why you rushed away from Ashley Grange, — just to come here and work out your mission ? "

His whole life, his first wild Californian dream, his English visit, the revelation of Gray Eagle, the final collapse of his old beliefs, were whirling through his brain to the music of this clear young voice. And by some cruel irony of circumstance it seemed now to even mock his later dreams of expiation as it also called back his unhappy experience of the last week.

" Have you — have you " — he stammered with a faint smile, " seen my sister ? "

" Not yet," said Lady Elfrida. " I believe she is not well and is confined to her room ; you will introduce me, won't you ? " she added eagerly. " Of course, when we heard that there was an Atherly here we inquired about you ; and I told them you were a relation of ours," she went on with a half-mischievous shyness, — " you remember the de Bracys, — and they seemed surprised and rather curious. I suppose one does not talk so much about these things over here, and I dare say you have so much to occupy your mind you don't talk of us

in England." With the quickness of a refined perception she saw a slight shade in
his face, and changed the subject. "And
we have had such a jolly time; we have met
so many pleasant people; and they've all
been so awfully good to us, from the officials
and officers down to the plainest working-
man. And all so naturally too — so different from us. I sometimes think we have to
work ourselves up to be civil to strangers."
"No," she went on gayly, in answer to his
protesting gesture, and his stammered reminder of his own reception. "No. You
came as a sort of kinsman, and Sir Edward
knew all about you before he asked you
down to the Grange — or even sent over for
me from the Towers. No! you Americans
take people on their 'face value,' as my
brother Reggy says, and we always want to
know what are the 'securities.' And then
American men are more gallant, though,"
she declared mischievously, "I think you
are an exception in that way. Indeed," she
went on, "the more I see of your countrymen the less you seem like them. You are
more like us, — more like an Englishman
— indeed, more like an Englishman than

most Englishmen, — I mean in the matter
of reserve and all that sort of thing, you
know. It 's odd, — is n't it ? Is your sister
like you ? "

" You shall judge for yourself," said Peter
with a gayety that was forced in proportion
as his forebodings became more gloomy.
Would his sister's peculiarities — even her
secret — be safe from the clear eyes of the
young girl ?

" I know I shall like her," said Lady
Elfrida, simply. " I mean to make friends
with her before we leave, and I hope to see
a great deal of her ; and," she said with a
naïve *non sequitur*, that, however, had its
painful significance to Peter, " I do want
you to show me some Indians — your Indians, you know — *your* friends. I 've seen
some of them, of course ; I am afraid I am
a little prejudiced, for I did not like them.
You see my taste has to be educated, I suppose ; but I thought them so foolishly vain
and presuming."

" That is their perfect childishness," said
Peter quickly. " It is not, I believe, considered a moral defect," he added bitterly.

Lady Elfrida laughed, and yet at the

same moment a look of appeal that was in itself quite as childlike shone in her blue eyes. " There, I have blundered again, I know ; but I told you I have such ridiculous prejudices ! And I really want to like them as you do. Only," she laughed again, " it seems strange that *you*, of all men, should have interested yourself in people so totally different to you. But what will be the result if your efforts are successful ? Will they remain a distinct race ? Will you make citizens, soldiers, congressmen, governors of them ? Will they intermarry with the whites ? Is that a part of your plan ? I hope not ! "

It was a part of Peter's sensitive excitement that even through the unconscious irony of this speech he was noticing the difference between the young English girl's evident interest in a political problem and the utter indifference of his own countrywomen. Here was a girl scarcely out of her teens, with no pretension to being a blue stocking, with half the *aplomb* of an American girl of her own age, gravely considering a question of political economy. Oddly enough, it added to his other irritation, and he said almost abruptly, " Why not ? "

She took the question literally and with a little youthful timidity. " But these mixed races never attain to anything, do they ? I thought that was understood. But," she added with feminine quickness, " and I suppose it 's again only a *personal* argument, *you* would n't like your sister to have married an Indian, would you ? "

The irony of the situation had reached its climax to Peter. It did n't seem to be his voice that said, " I can answer by an argument still more personal. I have even thought myself of marrying an Indian woman."

It seemed to him that what he said was irrevocable, but he was desperate. It seemed to him that in a moment more he would have told her his whole secret. But the young girl drew back from him with a slight start of surprise. There may have been something in the tone of his voice and in his manner that verged upon a seriousness she was never contemplating in her random talk ; it may have been an uneasiness of some youthful imprudence in pressing the subject

upon a man of his superiority, and that his
abrupt climax was a rebuke. But it was
only for a moment; her youthful buoyancy,
and, above all, a certain common sense that
was not incompatible to her high nature,
came to her rescue. "But that," she said
with quick mischievousness, "would be a
sacrifice taken in the interest of these people, don't you see; and being a sacrifice, it's
no argument."

Peter saw his mistake, but there was something so innocent and delightful in the youthful triumph of this red-lipped logician, that
he was forced to smile. I have said that his
smile was rare and fascinating, a concession
wrung from his dark face and calm beard-
less lips that most people found irresistible,
but it was odd, nevertheless, that Lady Elfrida now for the first time felt a sudden
and not altogether unpleasant embarrassment
over the very subject she had approached
with such innocent fearlessness. There was
a new light in her eyes, a fresher color in her
cheeks as she turned her face — she knew
not why — away from him. But it enabled
her to see a figure approaching them from
the fort. And I grieve to say that, perhaps

for the first time in her life, Lady Elfrida was guilty of an affected start.

" Oh, here 's Reggy coming to look for me.   I 'd quite forgotten, but I 'm so glad. I want you to know my brother Reggy.   He was always so sorry he missed you at the Grange."

The tall, young, good-looking brown Englishman who had sauntered up bestowed a far more critical glance upon Peter's horse than upon Peter, but nevertheless grasped his hand heartily as his sister introduced him.   Perhaps both men were equally undemonstrative, although the reserve of one was from temperament and the other from education.   Nevertheless Lord Reginald remarked, with a laugh, that it was awfully jolly to be there, and that it had been a beastly shame that he was in Scotland when Atherly was at the Grange.   That none of them had ever suspected till they came to the fort that he, Atherly, was one of those government chappies, and so awfully keen on Indian politics.   " Friddy " had been the first to find it out, but they thought she was chaffing.   At which " Friddy," who had suddenly resolved herself into the youthfulest of schoolgirls in the presence of her brother, put her parasol like an Indian club behind her back, and still rosy, beamed admiringly upon Reggy. Then the three, Peter leading his horse, moved on towards the fort, presently meeting "Georgy," the six-foot Guardsman cousin in extraordinary tweeds and flannel shirt; Lord Runnybroke, uncle of Friddy, middle-aged and flannel-shirted, a mighty hunter; Lady Runnybroke, in a brown duster, but with a stately head that suggested ostrich feathers; Moyler-Spence, M. P., with an eyeglass, and the Hon. Evelyn Kayne, closely attended by the always gallant Lieutenant Forsyth. Peter began to feel a nervous longing to be alone on the burning plain and the empty horizon beyond them, until he could readjust himself to these new conditions, and glanced halfwearily around him. But his eye met Friddy's, who seemed to have evoked this gathering with a wave of her parasol, like the fairy of a pantomime, and he walked on in silence.

A day or two of unexpected pleasure passed for Peter. In these new surroundings he found he could separate Lady Elfrida from his miserable past, and the conventional restraint of Ashley Grange. Again, the revelation of her familiar name Friddy seemed to make her more accessible and human to him than her formal title, and suited the girlish simplicity that lay at the foundation of her character, of which he had seen so little before. At least so he fancied, and so excused himself ; it was delightful to find her referring to him as an older friend ; pleasant, indeed, to see that her family tacitly recognized it, and frequently appealed to him with the introduction, " Friddy says you can tell us," or " You and Friddy had better arrange it between you." Even the dreaded introduction of his sister was an agreeable surprise, owing to Lady Elfrida's frank and sympathetic prepossession, which Jenny could not resist. In a few moments they were walking together in serious and apparently confidential conversation. For to Peter's wonder it was the " Lady Elfrida " side of the English girl's nature that seemed to have attracted Jenny, and not the playfulness of " Friddy," and he was delighted to see that the young girl had assumed a grave chaperonship of

the tall Mrs. Lascelles that would have done
credit to Mrs. Carter or Lady Runnybroke.
Had he been less serious he might have been
amused, too, at the importance of his own
position in the military outpost, through the
arrival of the strangers. That this grave
political enthusiast and civilian should be on
familiar terms with a young Englishwoman
of rank was at first inconceivable to the officers. And that he had never alluded to it
before seemed to them still more remarkable.

Nevertheless, there was much liveliness
and good fellowship at the fort. Captains
and lieutenants down to the youngest " cub,"
Forsyth, vied with each other to please the
Englishmen, supplied them with that characteristic American humor and anecdote
which it is an Englishman's privilege to
bring away with him, and were picturesquely
and chivalrously devoted in their attentions
to the ladies, who were pleased and amused
by it, though it is to be doubted if it increased their respect for the giver, although
they were more grateful for it than the average American woman. Lady Elfrida found
the officers very entertaining and gallant.
Accustomed to the English officer, and his

somewhat bored way of treating his profession and his duties, she may have been amused at the zeal, earnestness, and enthusiasm of these youthful warriors, who aspired to appear as nothing but soldiers, when she contrasted them with her Guardsmen relatives who aspired to be everything else but that; but she kept it to herself. It was a recognized, respectable, and even superior occupation for gentlemen in England; what it might be in America, — who knows? She certainly found Peter, the civilian, more attractive, for there really was nothing English to compare him with, and she had something of the same feeling in her friendship for Jenny, except the patronage which Jenny seemed to solicit, and perhaps require, as a foreigner.

One afternoon the English guests, accompanied by a few of their hosts and a small escort, were making a shooting expedition to the vicinity of Green Spring, when Peter, plunged in his report, looked up to find his sister entering his office. Her face was pale, and there was something in her expression which reawakened his old anxiety. Nevertheless he smiled, and said gently: —

" Why are you not enjoying yourself with the others ? "

" I have a headache," she said, languidly, " but," lifting her eyes suddenly to his, " why are *you* not? You are their good friend, you know, — even their relation."

" No more than you are," he returned, with affected gayety. " But look at the report — it is only half finished! I have already been shirking it for them."

" You must n't let your devotion to the Indians keep you from your older friends," said Mrs. Lascelles, with an odd laugh. " But you never told me about these people before, Peter ; tell me now. They were very kind to you, were n't they, on account of your relationship ? "

" Entirely on account of that," said Peter, with a sudden bitterness he could not repress. " But they are very pleasant," he added quickly, " and very simple and unaffected, in spite of their rank ; perhaps I ought to say, *because* of it."

" You mean they are kind to us because they feel themselves superior, — just as you are kind to the Indians, Peter."

" I am afraid they have no such sense of

political equality towards us, Jenny, as impels me to be just to the Indian," he said with affected lightness. " But Lady Elfrida sympathizes with the Indians — very much."

" She ! " The emphasis which his sister put upon the personal pronoun was unmistakable, but Peter ignored it, and so apparently did she, as she said the next moment in a different voice, " She 's very pretty, don't you think? "

" Very," said Peter coldly.

There was a long pause. Peter slightly fingered one of the sheets of his delayed report on his desk. His sister looked up. " I 'm afraid I 'm as bad as Lady Elfrida in keeping you from your Indians ; but I had something to say to you. No matter, another time will do when you 're not so busy."

" Please go on now," said Peter, with affected unconcern, yet with a feeling of uneasiness creeping over him.

" It was only this," said Jenny, seating herself with her elbow on the desk and her chin in a cup-like hollow of her hand, " did you ever think that in the interests of these poor Indians, you know, purely for the sake of your belief in them, and just to show that you were above vulgar prejudices, — did you ever think you could marry one of them?"

Two thoughts flashed quickly on Peter's mind, — first, that Lady Elfrida had repeated something of their conversation to his sister; secondly, that some one had told her of Little Daybreak. Each was equally disturbing. But he recovered himself quickly and said, "I might if I thought it was required. But even a sacrifice is not always an example."

"Then you think it would be a sacrifice?" she said, slowly raising her dark eyes to his.

"If I did something against received opinion, against precedent, and for aught I know against even the prejudices of those I wish to serve, however lofty my intention was and however great the benefit to them in the end, it would still be a sacrifice in the present." He saw his own miserable logic and affected didactics, but he went on lightly, "But why do you ask such a question? You have n't any one in your mind for me, have you?"

She had risen thoughtfully and was moving towards the door. Suddenly she turned with a quick, odd vivacity : " Perhaps I had. Oh, Peter, there was such a lovely little squaw I saw the last time I was at Oak Bottom! She was no darker than I am, but so beautiful. Even in her little cotton gown and blanket, with only a string of beads around her throat, she was as pretty as any one here. And I dare say she could be educated and appear as well as any white woman. I should so like to have you see her. I would have tried to bring her to the fort, but the braves are very jealous of their wives or daughters seeing white men, you know, and I was afraid of the colonel."

She had spoken volubly and with a strange excitement, but even at the moment her face changed again, and as she left the office, with a quick laugh and parting gesture, there were tears in her eyes.

Accustomed to her moods and caprices, Peter thought little of the intrusion, relieved as he was of his first fears. She had come to him from loneliness and curiosity, and, perhaps, he thought with a sad smile, from a little sisterly jealousy of the young girl who had evinced such an interest in him, and had known him before. He took up his pen and continued the interrupted paragraph of his report.

"I am satisfied that much of the mischievous and extravagant prejudice against the half breed and all alliances of the white and red races springs from the ignorance of the frontiersman and his hasty generalization of facts. There is no doubt that an intermixture of blood brings out purely superficial contrasts the more strongly, and that against the civilizing habits and even costumes of the half breed, certain Indian defects appear the more strongly as in the case of the color line of the quadroon and octoroon, but it must not be forgotten that these are only the contrasts of specific improvement, and the inference that the borrowed defects of a half breed exceed the original defects of the full-blooded aborigine is utterly illogical." He stopped suddenly and laid down his pen with a heightened color; the bugle had blown, the guard was turning out to receive the commandant and his returning party, among whom was Friddy.

. . . .

Through the illusions of depression and distance the "sink" of Butternut Creek seemed only an incrustation of blackish moss on the dull gray plain. It was not until one approached within half a mile of it that it resolved itself into a copse of butternut-trees sunken below the distant levels. Here once, in geological story, the waters of Butternut Creek, despairing of ever crossing the leagues of arid waste before them, had suddenly disappeared in the providential interposition of an area of looser soil, and so given up the effort and the ghost forever, their grave being marked by the butternut copse, chance-sown by bird or beast in the saturated ground. In Indian legend the " sink " commemorated the equally providential escape of a great tribe who, surrounded by enemies, appealed to the Great Spirit for protection, and was promptly conveyed by subterraneous passages to the banks of the Great River a hundred miles away. Its outer edges were already invaded by the dust of • the plain, but within them ran cool recesses, a few openings, and the ashes of some long-forgotten camp-fires. To-day its sombre shadows were relieved by bright colored dresses, the jackets of the drivers of a large sutler's wagon, whose white canvas

head marked the entrance of the copse, and
all the paraphernalia of a picnic. It was a
party gotten up by the foreign guests to the
ladies of the fort, prepared and arranged by
the active Lady Elfrida, assisted by the only
gentleman of the party, Peter Atherly, who,
from his acquaintance with the locality, was
allowed to accompany them. The other gentlemen, who with a large party of officers
and soldiers were shooting in the vicinity,
were sufficiently near for protection. They
would rejoin the ladies later.

"It does not seem in the least as if we
were miles away from any town or habitation," said Lady Runnybroke, complacently
seating herself on a stump, " and I should n't
be surprised to see a church tower through
those trees. It 's very like the hazel copse
at Longworth, you know. Not at all what
I expected."

" For the matter of that neither are the
Indians," said the Hon. Evelyn Rayne. "Did
you ever see such grotesque creatures in their
cast-off boots and trousers ? They 're no better than gypsies. I wonder what Mr. Atherly
can find in them."

" And he a rich man, too, — they say he's

got a mine in California worth a million, — to take up a craze like this," added the lively Mrs. Captain Joyce, " that's what gets me! You know," she went on confidentially, " that cranks and reformers are always poor — it's quite natural; but I don't see what he, a rich man, expects to make by his reforms, I'm sure."

" He'll get over it in time," said the Hon. Evelyn Kayne, " they all do. At least he expects to get the reforms he wants in a year, and then he's coming over to England again."

" Indeed, how very nice," responded Lady Runnybroke quickly. " Did he say so? "

" No. But Friddy says he is."

The two officers' wives glanced at each other. Lady Runnybroke put up her eyeglass in default of ostrich feathers, and said didactically, " I'm sure Mr. Atherly is very much in earnest, and sincerely devoted to his work. And in a man of his wealth and position here it's most estimable. My dear," she said, getting up and moving towards Mrs. Lascelles, " we were just saying how good and unselfish your brother was in his work for these poor people."

But Jenny Lascelles must have been in one of those abstracted moods which so troubled her husband, for she seemed to be staring straight before her into the recesses of the wood. In her there was a certain resemblance to the attitude of a listening animal.

"I wish Mr. Atherly was a little more unselfish to *us* poor people," said the Hon. Evelyn Kayne, "for he and Friddy have been nearly an hour looking for a place to spread our luncheon baskets. I wish they'd leave the future of the brown races to look after itself and look a little more after us. I'm famished."

"I fancy they find it difficult to select a clear space for so large a party as we will be when the gentlemen come in," returned Lady Runnybroke, glancing in the direction of Jenny's abstracted eyes.

"I suppose you must feel like chicken and salad, too, Lady Runnybroke," suggested Mrs. Captain Joyce.

"I don't think I quite know *how* chicken and salad feel, dear," said Lady Runnybroke with a puzzled air, "but if that's one of your husband's delightful American stories,

do tell us. I never *can* get Runnybroke
to tell me any, although he roars over them
all. And I dare say he gets them all wrong.
But look, here comes our luncheon."

Peter and Lady Elfrida were advancing
towards them. The scrutiny of a dozen pairs
of eyes — wondering, mischievous, critical,
impertinent, or resentful — would have been
a trying ordeal to any errant couple; but
there was little if any change in Peter's
grave and gentle demeanor, albeit his dark
eyes were shining with a peculiar light, and
Lady Elfrida had only the animation, color,
and slight excitability that became the responsible leader of the little party. They
neither apologized or alluded to their delay.
They had selected a spot on the other side
of the copse, and the baskets could be sent
around by the wagon; they had seen a slight
haze on the plain towards the east which
betokened the vicinity of the rest of the
party, and they were about to propose that
as the gentlemen were so near they had
better postpone the picnic until they came
up. Lady Runnybroke smiled affably; the
only thing she had noticed was that Lady
Elfrida in joining them had gone directly

to the side of the abstracted Jenny, and
placed her arm around her waist. At which
Lady Runnybroke airily joined them.

The surmises of Peter and Friddy appeared to be correct. The transfer of the
provisions and the party to the other side
was barely concluded before they could see
the gentlemen coming; they were riding a
little more rapidly than when they had set
out, and were arriving fully three hours
before their time. They burst upon the
ladies a little boisterously but gayly; they
had had a glorious time, but little sport;
they had hurried back to join the ladies so
as to be able to return with them betimes.
They were ravenously hungry; they wanted
to fall to at once. Only the officers' wives
noticed that the two files of troopers *did not
dismount*, but filed slowly before the entrance
to the woods. Lady Elfrida as hostess was
prettily distressed by it, but was told by
Captain Joyce that it was "against rules,"
and that she could "feed" them at the fort.
The officers' wives put a few questions in
whispers, and were promptly frowned down.
Nevertheless, the luncheon was a successful
festivity: the gentlemen were loud in the

praises of their gracious hostess; the deli-
cacies she had provided by express from distant stations, and much that was distinctly
English and despoiled from her own stores,
were gratefully appreciated by the officers
of a remote frontier garrison. Lady Elfrida's health was toasted by the gallant colonel
in a speech that was the soul of chivalry.
Lord Runnybroke responded, perhaps without the American abandon, but with the
steady conscientiousness of an hereditary
legislator, but the M. P. summed up a
slightly exaggerated but well meaning episode by pointing out that it was on occasions
like this that the two nations showed their
common ancestry by standing side by side.
Only one thing troubled the rosy, excited,
but still clear-headed Friddy; the plates
were whisked away like magic after each
delicacy, by the military servants, and vanished; the tables were in the same mysterious
way cleared as rapidly as they were set, and
any attempt to recall a dish was met by the
declaration that it was already packed away
in the wagon. As they at last rose from
the actually empty board, and saw even the
tables disappear, Lady Elfrida plaintively

protested that she felt as if she had been presiding over an Arabian Nights entertainment, served by genii, and she knew that they would all awaken hungry when they were well on their way back. Nevertheless, in spite of this expedition, the officers lounged about smoking until every trace of the festivity had vanished. Reggy found himself standing near Peter. " You know," he said, confidentially, " I don't think the colonel has a very high opinion of your pets, — the Indians. And, by Jove, if the ' friendlies' are as nasty towards you as they were to us this morning, I wonder what you call the ' hostile' tribes."

" Did you have any difficulty with them ? " said Peter quickly.

" No, not exactly, don't you know — we were too many, I fancy ; but, by Jove, the beggars whenever we met them, — and we met one or two gypsy bands of them, — you know, they seemed to look upon us as *trespassers*, don't you know."

" And you were, in point of fact," said Peter, smiling grimly.

" Oh, I say, come now ! " said Reggy, opening his eyes. After a moment he

laughed. "Oh, yes, I see — of course, looking at it from their point of view. By Jove,
I dare say the beggars were right, you know ;
all the same, — don't you see, — *your* people were poaching too."

"So we were," said Peter gravely.

But here, at a word from the major, the
whole party debouched from the woods.
Everything appeared to be awaiting them, —
the large covered carryall for the guests, and
the two saddle horses for Mrs. Lascelles
and Lady Elfrida, who had ridden there
together. Peter, also mounted, accompanied
the carryall with two of the officers; the
troopers and wagons brought up the rear.

It was very hot, with little or no wind.
On this part of the plain the dust seemed
lighter and finer, and rose with the wheels
of the carryall and the horses of the escort,
trailing a white cloud over the cavalcade
like the smoke of an engine over a train.
It was with difficulty the troopers could be
kept from opening out on both sides of the
highway to escape it. The whole atmosphere seemed charged with it ; it even appeared in a long bank to the right, rising
and obscuring the declining sun. But they

were already within sight of the fort and
the little copse beside it. Then trooper Cassidy trotted up to the colonel, who was riding
in a dusty cloud beside the carryall, "Captain Fleetwood's compliments, sorr, and there
are two sthragglers, — Mrs. Lascelles and
the English lady." He pointed to the rapidly flying figures of Jenny and Friddy
making towards the wood.

The colonel made a movement of impatience. "Tell Mr. Forsyth to bring them
back at once," he said.

But here a feminine chorus of excuses and
expostulations rose from the carryall. "It's
only Mrs. Lascelles going to show Friddy
where the squaws and children bathe," said
Lady Runnybroke, "it's near the fort, and
they'll be there as quick as we shall."

"One moment, colonel," said Peter, with
mortified concern. "It's another folly of
my sister's! pray let me take it upon myself to bring them back."

"Very well, but see you don't linger,
and," turning to Cassidy, as Peter galloped
away, he added, "you follow him."

Peter kept the figures of the two women
in view, but presently saw them disappear in

the wood. He had no fear for their safety, but he was indignant at this last untimely caprice of his sister. He knew the idea had originated with her, and that the officers knew it, and yet she had made Lady Elfrida bear an equal share of the blame. He reached the edge of the copse, entered the first opening, but he had scarcely plunged into its shadow and shut out the plain behind him before he felt his arms and knees quickly seized from behind. So sudden and unexpected was the attack that he first thought his horse had stumbled against a coil of wild grapevine and was entangled, but the next moment he smelled the rank characteristic odor and saw the brown limbs of the Indian who had leaped on his crupper, while another rose at his horse's head. Then a warning voice in his ear said in the native tongue : —

" If the great white medicine man calls to his fighting men, the pale-faced girl and the squaw he calls his sister die ! They are here, he understands."

But Peter had neither struggled nor uttered a cry. At that touch, and with the accents of that tongue in his ears, all his own Indian blood seemed to leap and tingle through his veins. His eyes flashed; pinioned as he was he drew himself erect and answered haughtily in his captor's own speech : —

"Good ! The great white medicine man obeys, for he and his sister have no fear. But if the pale-face girl is not sent back to her people before the sun sets, then the yellow jackets will swarm the woods, and they will follow her trail to the death. My brother is wise; let the girl go. I have spoken."

"My brother is very cunning too. He would call to his fighting men through the lips of the pale-face girl."

"He will not. The great white medicine man does not lie to his red brother. He will tell the pale-face girl to say to the chief of the yellow jackets that he and his sister are with his brothers, and all is peace. But the pale-face girl must not see the great white medicine man in these bonds, nor as a captive ! I have spoken."

The two Indians fell back. There was so much of force and dignity in the man, so much of their own stoic calmness, that they at once mechanically loosened the thongs of plaited deer hide with which they had bound him, and side by side led him into the recesses of the wood.

. . . .

There was some astonishment, although little alarm at the fort, when Lady Elfrida returned accompanied by the orderly who had followed Peter to the wood, but without Peter and his sister. The reason given was perfectly natural and conceivable. Mrs. Lascelles had preceded Lady Elfrida in entering the wood and taken another opening, so that Lady Elfrida had found herself suddenly lost, and surrounded by two or three warriors in dreadful paint. They motioned her to dismount, and said something she did not understand, but she declined, knowing that she had heard Mr. Atherly and the orderly following her, and feeling no fear. And sure enough Mr. Atherly presently came up with a couple of braves, apologized to her for their mistake, but begged her to return to the fort at once and assure the colonel that everything was right, and that he and his sister were safe. He was perfectly cool and collected and like himself ;

she blushed slightly, as she said she thought
that he wished to impress upon her, for some
reason she could not understand, that he
did not want the colonel to send any assistance. She was positive of that. She told
her story unexcitedly; it was evident that
she had not been frightened, but Lady Runnybroke noticed that there was a shade of
anxious abstraction in her face.

When the officers were alone the colonel
took hurried counsel of them. "I think,"
said Captain Fleetwood, "that Lady Elfrida's story quite explains itself. I believe
this affair is purely a local one, and has nothing whatever to do with the suspicious
appearances we noticed this afternoon, or the
presence of so large a body of Indians near
Butternut. Had this been a hostile movement they would have scarcely allowed so
valuable a capture as Lady Elfrida to escape
them."

"Unless they kept Atherly and his sister
as a hostage," said Captain Joyce.

"But Atherly is one of their friends;
indeed he is their mediator and apostle, a
non-combatant, and has their confidence,"
returned the colonel. "It is much more

reasonable to suppose that Atherly has noticed some disaffection among these 'friendlies,' and he fears that our sending a party
to his assistance might precipitate a collision.
Or he may have reason to believe that this
stopping of the two women under the very
walls of the fort is only a feint to draw
our attention from something more serious.
Did he know anything of our suspicions of
the conduct of those Indians this morning?"

"Not unless he gathered it from what
Lord Reginald foolishly told him. We said
nothing, of course," returned Captain Fleetwood, with a soldier's habitual distrust of the
wisdom of the civil arm.

"That will do, gentlemen," said the colonel, as the officers dispersed; "send Cassidy
here."

The colonel was alone on the veranda as
Cassidy came up.

"You followed Mr. Atherly to-day?"

"Yes sorr."

"And you saw him when he gave the message to the young lady?"

"Yes sorr."

"Did you form any opinion from anything

else you saw, of his object in sending that message ? "

" Only from what I saw of *him*."

" Well, what was that ? "

" I saw him look afther the young leddy as she rode away, and then wheel about and go straight back into the wood."

" And what did you think of that ? " said the colonel, with a half smile.

" I thought it was shacrifice, sorr."

" What do you mean ? " said the colonel sharply.

" I mane, sorr," said Cassidy stoutly, " that he was givin' up hisself and his sister for that young leddy."

The colonel looked at the sergeant. " Ask Mr. Forsyth to come to me privately, and return here with him."

As darkness fell, some half a dozen dismounted troopers, headed by Forsyth and Cassidy, passed quietly out of the lower gate and entered the wood. An hour later the colonel was summoned from the dinner table, and the guests heard the quick rattle of a wagon turning out of the road gate — but the colonel did not return. An indefinable uneasiness crept over the little party, which reached its climax in the summoning of the other officers, and the sudden flashing out of news. The reconnoitring party had found the dead bodies of Peter Atherly and his sister on the plains at the edge of the empty wood.

The women were gathered in the commandant's quarters, and for the moment seemed to have been forgotten. The officers' wives talked with professional sympathy and disciplined quiet; the English ladies were equally sympathetic, but collected. Lady Elfrida, rather white, but patient, asked a few questions in a voice whose contralto was rather deepened. One and all wished to " do something " — anything " to help " — and one and all rebelled that the colonel had begged them to remain within doors. There was an occasional quick step on the veranda, or the clatter of a hoof on the parade, a continued but subdued murmur from the whitewashed barracks, but everywhere a sense of keen restraint.

When they emerged on the veranda again, the whole aspect of the garrison seemed to have changed in that brief time. In the faint moonlight they could see motionless

files of troopers filling the parade, the officers in belted tunics and slouched hats, —
but apparently not the same men ; the half
lounging ease and lazy dandyism gone, a
grim tension in all their faces, a set abstraction in all their acts. Then there was
the rolling of heavy wheels in the road, and
the two horses of the ambulance appeared.
The sentries presented arms ; the colonel
took off his hat ; the officers uncovered ; the
wagon wheeled into the parade ; the surgeon
stepped out. He exchanged a single word
with the colonel, and lifted the curtain of the
ambulance.

As the colonel glanced within, a deep but
embarrassed voice fell upon his ear. He
turned quickly. It was Lord Reginald,
flushed and sympathetic.

" He was a friend, — a relation of ours,
you know," he stammered. " My sister
would like — to look at him again."

" Not now," said the colonel in a low
voice. The surgeon added something in a
voice still lower, which scarcely reached the
veranda.

Lord Reginald turned away with a white
face.

" Fall back there ! " Captain Fleetwood rode up.

" All ready, sir."

" One moment, captain," said the colonel quietly. " File your first half company before that ambulance, and bid the men look in."

The singular order was obeyed. The men filed slowly forward, each in turn halting before the motionless wagon and its immobile freight. They were men inured to frontier bloodshed and savage warfare ; some halted and hurried on ; others lingered, others turned to look again. One man burst into a short laugh, but when the others turned indignantly upon him, they saw that in his face that held them in awe. What they saw in the ambulance did not transpire ; what they felt was not known. Strangely enough, however, what they repressed themselves was mysteriously communicated to their horses, who snorted and quivered with eagerness and impatience as they rode back again. The horse of the trooper who had laughed almost leaped into the air. Only Sergeant Cassidy was communicative ; he took a larger circuit in returning to his place, and managed to lean over and whisper hoarsely in the ear of a camp follower spectator, " Tell the young leddy that the torturin' divvils could n't take the smile off him! "

The little column filed out of the gateway into the road. As Captain Fleetwood passed Colonel Carter the two men's eyes met. The colonel said quietly, " Good night, captain. Let us have a good report from you."

The captain replied only with his gauntleted hand against the brim of his slouched hat, but the next moment his voice was heard strong and clear enough in the road. The little column trotted away as evenly as on parade. But those who climbed the roof of the barracks a quarter of an hour later saw, in the moonlight, a white cloud drifting rapidly across the plain towards the west. It was a small cloud in that bare, menacing, cruel, and illimitable waste ; but in its breast was crammed a thunderbolt.

It fell thirty miles away, blasting and scattering a thousand warriors and their camp, giving and taking no quarter, vengeful, exterminating, and complete. Later there were different opinions about it and the horrible crime that had provoked it: the opposers of Peter's policy jubilant over the irony of the assassination of the Apostle of Peace, Peter's disciples as actively deploring the merciless and indiscriminating vengeance of the military; and so the problem that Peter had vainly attempted to solve was left an open question. There were those, too, who believed that Peter had never sacrificed himself and his sister for the sake of another, but had provoked and incensed the savages by the blind arrogance of a reformer. There were wild stories by scouts and interpreters how he had challenged his fate by an Indian bravado; how himself and his sister had met torture with an Indian stoicism, and how the Indian braves themselves at last in a turmoil of revulsion had dipped their arrows and lances in the heroic heart's blood of their victims, and worshiped their still palpitating flesh.

But there was one honest loyal little heart that carried back — three thousand miles — to England the man as it had known and loved him. Lady Elfrida Runnybroke never married; neither did she go into retirement, but lived her life and ful-

filled her duties in her usual clear-eyed fashion. She was particularly kind to all Americans, — barring, I fear, a few pretty-faced,
finely-frocked title-hunters, — told stories of
the Far West, and had theories of a people
of which they knew little, cared less, and
believed to be vulgar. But I think she
found a new pleasure in the old church at
Ashley Grange, and loved to linger over the
effigy of the old Crusader, — her kinsman,
the swashbuckler De Bracy, — with a vague
but pretty belief that devotion and love do
not die with brave men, but live and flourish
even in lands beyond the seas.

TWO AMERICANS

PERHAPS if there was anything important in the migration of the Maynard family to Europe it rested solely upon the singular fact that Mr. Maynard did not go there in the expectation of marrying his daughter to a nobleman. A Charleston merchant, whose house represented two honorable generations, had, thirty years ago, a certain self-respect which did not require extraneous aid and foreign support, and it is exceedingly probable that his intention of spending a few years abroad had no ulterior motive than pleasure seeking and the observation of many things — principally of the past — which his own country did not possess. His future and that of his family lay in his own land, yet with practical common sense he adjusted himself temporarily to his new surroundings. In doing so, he had much to learn of others, and others had something to learn of him ; he found that the best people had a high

simplicity equal to his own; he corrected
their impressions that a Southerner had
more or less negro blood in his veins, and
that, although a slave owner, he did not
necessarily represent an aristocracy. With
a distinguishing dialect of which he was not
ashamed, a frank familiarity of approach
joined to an invincible courtesy of manner,
which made even his republican "Sir" equal
to the ordinary address to royalty, he was
always respected and seldom misunderstood.
When he was — it was unfortunate for those
who misunderstood him. His type was as
distinctive and original as his cousin's, the
Englishman, whom it was not the fashion
then to imitate. So that, whether in the
hotel of a capital, the Kursaal of a Spa, or
the humbler pension of a Swiss village, he
was always characteristic. Less so was his
wife, who, with the chameleon quality of her
transplanted countrywomen, was already Parisian in dress; still less so his daughter,
who had by this time absorbed the peculiarities of her French, German, and Italian gov-
ernesses. Yet neither had yet learned to
evade their nationality — or apologize for it.

Mr. Maynard and his family remained for

three years in Europe, his stay having been
prolonged by political excitement in his own
State of South Carolina.   Commerce is apt
to knock the insularity out of people; distance from one's own distinctive locality gives
a wider range to the vision, and the retired
merchant foresaw ruin in his State's politics, and from the view-point of all Europe
beheld instead of the usual collection of individual States — his whole country.   But the
excitement increasing, he was finally impelled
to return in a faint hope of doing something
to allay it, taking his wife with him, but
leaving his daughter at school in Paris.   At
about this time, however, a single cannon
shot fired at the national flag on Fort Sum-
ter shook the whole country, reverberated
even in Europe, sending some earnest hearts
back to do battle for State or country, sending others less earnest into inglorious exile,
but, saddest of all! knocking over the school
bench of a girl at the Paris *pensionnat*.   For
that shot had also sunk Maynard's ships at
the Charleston wharves, scattered his piled
cotton bales awaiting shipment at the quays,
and drove him, a ruined man, into the
"Home Guard" against his better judg-

ment. Helen Maynard, like a good girl,
had implored her father to let her return and
share his risks. But the answer was " to
wait" until this nine days' madness of an
uprising was over. That madness lasted six
years, outlived Maynard, whose gray, mis-
doubting head bit the dust at Ball's Bluff;
outlived his colorless widow, and left Nelly a
penniless orphan.

Yet enough of her country was left in her
to make her courageous and independent of
her past. They say that when she got the
news she cried a little, and then laid the
letter and what was left of her last monthly
allowance in Madame Ablas' lap. Madame
was devastated. " But you, impoverished
and desolated angel, what of you?" " I
shall get some of it back," said the desolated
angel with ingenuous candor, " for I speak
better French and English than the other
girls, and I shall teach *them* until I can get
into the Conservatoire, for I have a voice.
You yourself have told papa so." From
such angelic directness there was no appeal.
Madame Ablas had a heart, — more, she
had a French manageress's discriminating
instinct. The American schoolgirl was in-

stalled in a teacher's desk; her bosom friends
and fellow students became her pupils. To
some of the richest, and they were mainly
of her own country, she sold her smartest,
latest dresses, jewels, and trinkets at a very
good figure, and put the money away against
the Conservatoire in the future. She worked
hard, she endured patiently everything but
commiseration. " I 'd have you know, Miss,"
she said to Miss de Laine, daughter of the
famous house of Musslin, de Laine & Co.,
of New York, "that whatever my position
here may be, it is not one to be patronized
by a tapeseller's daughter. My case is not
such a very ' sad one,' thank you, and I prefer not to be spoken of as having seen ' better days ' by people who have n't. There !
Don't rap your desk with your pencil when
you speak to me, or I shall call out ' Cash ! '
before the whole class." So regrettable an
exhibition of temper naturally alienated certain of her compatriots who were unduly
sensitive of their origin, and as they formed a
considerable colony who were then reveling
in the dregs of the Empire and the last or-
gies of a tottering court, eventually cost her
her place. A republican so aristocratic was

not to be tolerated by the true-born Americans who paid court to De Morny for the
phosphorescent splendors of St. Cloud and
the Tuileries, and Miss Helen lost their
favor. But she had already saved enough
money for the Conservatoire and a little attic
in a very tall house in a narrow street that
trickled into the ceaseless flow of the Rue
Lafayette. Here for four years she trotted
backwards and forwards regularly to work
with the freshness of youth and the inflexible
set purpose of maturity. Here, rain or shine,
summer or winter, in the mellow season
when the large cafés expanded under the
white sunshine into an overflow of little tables on the pavement, or when the red glow
of the *Brasserie* shone through frosty panes
on the turned-up collars of pinched Parisians
who hurried by, she was always to be seen.

Half Paris had looked into her clear, gray
eyes and passed on; a smaller and not very
youthful portion of Paris had turned and
followed her with small advantage to itself
and happily no fear to her. For even in
her young womanhood she kept her child's
loving knowledge of that great city; she
even had an innocent camaraderie with

street sweepers, kiosk keepers, and lemonade venders, and the sternness of conciergedom melted before her.   In this wholesome, practical child's experience she naturally avoided or overlooked what would not have interested a child, and so kept her freshness and a certain national shrewd simplicity invincible.   There is a story told of her girlhood that, one day playing in the Tuileries gardens, she was approached by a gentleman with a waxed mustache and a still more waxen cheek beneath his heavy-lidded eyes. There was an exchange of polite amenities.

" And your name, ma petite ? "

" Helen," responded the young girl naïvely.   " What's yours ? "

" Ah," said the kind gentleman, gallantly pulling at his mustache, " if you are Helen I am Paris."

The young girl raised her clear eyes to his and said gravely, " I reckon your majesty is *France !* "

She retained this childish fearlessness as the poor student of the Conservatoire ; went alone all over Paris with her maiden skirts untarnished by the gilded dust of the boulevards or the filth of by-ways ; knew all the best shops for her friends, and the cheapest for her own scant purchases ; discovered breakfasts for a few sous with pale sempstresses, whose sadness she understood, and reckless chorus girls, whose gayety she did n't; she knew where the earliest chestnut buds were to be found in the Bois, when the slopes of the Buttes Chaumont were green, and which was the old woman who sold the cheapest flowers before the Madeleine. Alone and independent, she earned the affection of Madame Bibelot, the concierge, and, what was more, her confidence. Her outgoings and incomings were never questioned. The little American could take care of herself. Ah, if her son Jacques were only as reasonable ! Miss Maynard might have made more friends had she cared ; she might have joined hands with the innocent and light-hearted poverty of the coterie of her own artistic compatriots, but something in her blood made her distrust Bohemianism; her poverty was something to her too sacred for jest or companionship ; her own artistic aim was too long and earnest for mere temporary enthusiasms. She might have found friends in her own profession.

Her professor opened the sacred doors of his family circle to the young American girl. She appreciated the delicacy, refinement, and cheerful equal responsibilities of that household, so widely different from the accepted Anglo-Saxon belief, but there were certain restrictions that rightly or wrongly galled her American habits of girlish freedom, and she resolutely tripped past the first étage four or five flights higher to her attic, the free sky, and independence! Here she sometimes met another kind of independence in Monsieur Alphonse, aged twenty-two, and she who ought to have been Madame Alphonse, aged seventeen, and they often exchanged greetings on the landing with great respect towards each other, and, oddly enough, no confusion or *distrait*. Later they even borrowed each other's matches without fear and without reproach, until one day Monsieur Alphonse's parents took him away, and the desolated soi-disant Madame Alphonse, in a cheerful burst of confidence, gave Helen her private opinion of monsieur, and from her seventeen years' experience warned the American infant of twenty against possible similar complications.

One day — it was near the examination for prizes, and her funds were running low — she was obliged to seek one of those humbler restaurants she knew of for her frugal breakfast. But she was not hungry, and after a few mouthfuls left her meal unfinished as a young man entered and half abstractedly took a seat at her table. She had already moved towards the comptoir to pay her few sous, when, chancing to look up in a mirror which hung above the counter, reflecting the interior of the café, she saw the stranger, after casting a hurried glance around him, remove from her plate the broken roll and even the crumbs she had left, and as hurriedly sweep them into his pocket - handkerchief. There was nothing very strange in this; she had seen something like it before in these humbler cafés, — it was a crib for the birds in the Tuileries Gardens, or the poor artist's substitute for rubber in correcting his crayon drawing ! But there was a singular flushing of his handsome face in the act that stirred her with a strange pity, made her own cheek hot with sympathy, and compelled her to look at him more attentively. The back that was turned towards her was broad-shouldered and symmetrical, and showed a frame that seemed to require stronger nourishment than the simple coffee and roll he had ordered and was devouring slowly. His clothes, well made though worn, fitted him in a smart, soldier-like way, and accentuated his decided military bearing. The singular use of his left hand in lifting his cup made her uneasy, until a slight movement revealed the fact that his right sleeve was empty and pinned to his coat. He was one-armed. She turned her compassionate eyes aside, yet lingered to make a few purchases at the counter, as he paid his bill and walked away. But she was surprised to see that he tendered the waiter the unexampled gratuity of a sou. Perhaps he was some eccentric Englishman; he certainly did not look like a Frenchman.

She had quite forgotten the incident, and in the afternoon had strolled with a few fellow pupils into the galleries of the Louvre. It was " copying-day," and as her friends loitered around the easels of the different students with the easy consciousness of being themselves " artists," she strolled on somewhat abstractedly before them. Her own

art was too serious to permit her much sympathy with another, and in the chatter of
her companions with the young painters a
certain levity disturbed her. Suddenly she
stopped. She had reached a less frequented
room ; there was a single easel at one side,
but the stool before it was empty, and its
late occupant was standing in a recess by
the window, with his back towards her.
He had drawn a silk handkerchief from his
pocket. She recognized his square shoulders, she recognized the handkerchief, and
as he unrolled it she recognized the fragments of her morning's breakfast as he began
to eat them. It was the one-armed man.

She remained so motionless and breathless
that he finished his scant meal without noticing her, and even resumed his place before
the easel without being aware of her presence. The noise of approaching feet gave
a fresh impulse to her own, and she moved
towards him. But he was evidently accustomed to these interruptions, and worked on
steadily without turning his head. As the
other footsteps passed her she was embold-
ened to take a position behind him and
glance at his work. It was an architectural

study of one of Canaletto's palaces. Even her inexperienced eyes were struck with its vigor and fidelity. But she was also conscious of a sense of disappointment. Why was he not — like the others — copying one of the masterpieces? Becoming at last aware of a motionless woman behind him, he rose, and with a slight gesture of courtesy and a half-hesitating " Vous verrez mieux là, mademoiselle," moved to one side.

" Thank you," said Miss Maynard in English, " but I did not want to disturb you."

He glanced quickly at her face for the first time. " Ah, you are English ! " he said.

" No.   I am American."

His face lightened.   " So am I."

" I thought so," she said.

" From my bad French ? "

" No.   Because you did not look up to see if the woman you were polite to was old or young."

He smiled.   " And you, mademoiselle, — you did not murmur a compliment to the copy over the artist's back."

She smiled, too, — yet with a little pang over the bread. But she was relieved to see that he evidently had not recognized her. " You are modest," she said ; " you do not attempt masterpieces."

" Oh, no ! The giants like Titian and Corregio must be served with both hands. I have only one," he said half lightly, half sadly.

" But you have been a soldier," she said with quick intuition.

" Not much. Only during our war, — until I was compelled to handle nothing larger than a palette knife. Then I came home to New York, and, as I was no use there, I came here to study."

" I am from South Carolina," she said quietly, with a rising color.

He put his palette down, and glanced at her black dress. " Yes," she went on doggedly, " my father lost all his property, and was killed in battle with the Northerners. I am an orphan, — a pupil of the Conservatoire." It was never her custom to allude to her family or her lost fortunes ; she knew not why she did it now, but something impelled her to rid her mind of it to him at once. Yet she was pained at his grave and pitying face.

" I am very sorry," he said simply. Then, after a pause, he added, with a gentle smile, " At all events you and I will not quarrel here under the wings of the French eagles that shelter us both."

" I only wanted to explain why I was alone in Paris," she said, a little less aggressively.

He replied by unhooking his palette, which was ingeniously fastened by a strap over his shoulder under the missing arm, and opened a portfolio of sketches at his side. " Perhaps they may interest you more than the copy, which I have attempted only to get at this man's method. They are sketches I have done here."

There was a buttress of Notre Dame, a black arch of the Pont Neuf, part of an old courtyard in the Faubourg St. Germain, — all very fresh and striking. Yet, with the recollection of his poverty in her mind, she could not help saying, " But if you copied one of those masterpieces, you know you could sell it. There is always a demand for that work."

" Yes," he replied, " but these help me in my line, which is architectural study.   It

is, perhaps, not very ambitious," he added
thoughtfully, " but," brightening up again,
" I sell these sketches, too. They are quite
marketable, I assure you."

Helen's heart sank again. She remembered now to have seen such sketches — she
doubted not they were his — in the cheap
shops in the Rue Poissonière, ticketed at
a few francs each. She was silent as he
patiently turned them over. Suddenly she
uttered a little cry.

He had just uncovered a little sketch of
what seemed at first sight only a confused
cluster of roof tops, dormer windows, and
chimneys, level with the sky-line. But it
was bathed in the white sunshine of Paris,
against the blue sky she knew so well.
There, too, were the gritty crystals and rust
of the tiles, the red, brown, and greenish
mosses of the gutters, and lower down the
more vivid colors of geraniums and pansies
in flower-pots under the white dimity curtains which hid the small panes of garret
windows ; yet every sordid detail touched
and transfigured with the poetry and romance of youth and genius.

" You have seen this ? " she said.

"Yes; it is a study from my window. One must go high for such effects. You would be surprised if you could see how different the air and sunshine " —

" No," she interrupted gently, " I *have* seen it."

" You ? " he repeated, gazing at her curiously.

Helen ran the point of her slim finger along the sketch until it reached a tiny dormer window in the left-hand corner, half-hidden by an irregular chimney-stack. The curtains were closely drawn. Keeping her finger upon the spot, she said, interrogatively, " And you saw *that* window ? "

" Yes, quite plainly. I remember it was always open, and the room seemed empty from early morning to evening, when the curtains were drawn."

" It is my room," she said simply.

Their eyes met with this sudden confession of their equal poverty. " And mine," he said gayly, " from which this view was taken, is in the rear and still higher up on the other street."

They both laughed as if some singular restraint had been removed ; Helen even forgot the incident of the bread in her relief. Then they compared notes of their experiences, of their different concierges, of their housekeeping, of the cheap stores and the cheaper restaurants of Paris, — except *one*. She told him her name, and learned that his was Philip, or, if she pleased, Major Ostrander. Suddenly glancing at her companions, who were ostentatiously lingering at a little distance, she became conscious for the first time that she was talking quite confidentially to a very handsome man, and for a brief moment wished, she knew not why, that he had been plainer. This momentary restraint was accented by the entrance of a lady and gentleman, rather distingué in dress and bearing, who had stopped before them, and were eying equally the artist, his work, and his companion with somewhat insolent curiosity. Helen felt herself stiffening ; her companion drew himself up with soldierly rigidity. For a moment it seemed as if, under that banal influence, they would part with ceremonious continental politeness, but suddenly their hands met in a national handshake, and with a frank smile they separated.

Helen rejoined her companions.

"So you have made a conquest of the recently acquired but unknown Greek statue?" said Mademoiselle Renée lightly. "You should take up a subscription to restore his arm, ma petite, if there is a modern sculptor who can do it. You might suggest it to the two Russian cognoscenti, who have been hovering around him as if they wanted to buy him as well as his work. Madame La Princesse is rich enough to indulge her artistic taste."

"It is a countryman of mine," said Helen simply.

"He certainly does not speak French," said mademoiselle mischievously.

"Nor think it," responded Helen with equal vivacity. Nevertheless, she wished she had seen him alone.

She thought nothing more of him that day in her finishing exercises. But the next morning as she went to open her window after dressing, she drew back with a new consciousness, and then, making a peephole in the curtain, looked over the opposite roofs. She had seen them many times before, but now they had acquired a new picturesque-

ness, which as her view was, of course. the
reverse of the poor painter's sketch. must
have been a transfigured memory of her own.
Then she glanced curiously along the line of
windows level with hers. All these, however, with their occasional revelations of the
ménage behind them, were also familiar to
her, but now she began to wonder which
was his. A singular instinct at last impelled her to lift her eyes. Higher in the
corner house, and so near the roof that it
scarcely seemed possible for a grown man
to s^t.and upright behind it, was an *œil de
bœuf* looking down upon the other roofs,
and framed in that circular opening like a
vignette was the handsome face of Major
Ostrander. His eyes seemed to be turned
towards her window. Her first impulse was
to open it and recognize him with a friendly
nod. But an odd mingling of mischief and
shyness made her turn away quickly.

Nevertheless, she met him the next morning walking slowly so near her house that
their encounter might have been scarcely
accidental on his part. She walked with
him as far as the Conservatoire. In the
light of the open street she thought he looked

pale and hollow-cheeked ; she wondered if
it was from his enforced frugality, and was
trying to conceive some elaborate plan of
obliging him to accept her hospitality at least
for a single meal, when he said : —

" I think you have brought me luck, Miss
Maynard."

Helen opened her eyes wonderingly.

" The two Russian connoisseurs who stared
at us so rudely were pleased, however, to
also stare at my work. They offered me a
fabulous sum for one or two of my sketches.
It did n't seem to me quite the square thing
to old Favel the picture-dealer, whom I had
forced to take a lot at one fifteenth the price,
so I simply referred them to him."

" No ! " said Miss Helen indignantly ;
" you were not so foolish ? "

Ostrander laughed.

" I 'm afraid what you call my folly did n't
avail, for they wanted what they saw in my
portfolio."

" Of course," said Helen. " Why, that
sketch of the housetop alone was worth a
hundred times more than what you " —
She stopped ; she did not like to reveal
what he got for his pictures, and added,

" more than what any of those usurers would give."

" I am glad you think so well of it, for I do not mean to sell it," he said simply, yet with a significance that kept her silent.

She did not see him again for several days. The preparation for her examination left her no time, and her earnest concentration in her work fully preoccupied her thoughts. She was surprised, but not disturbed, on the day of the awards to see him among the audience of anxious parents and relations. Miss Helen Maynard did not get the first prize, nor yet the second; an *accessit* was her only award. She did not know until afterwards that this had long been a foregone conclusion of her teachers on account of some intrinsic defect in her voice. She did not know until long afterwards that the handsome painter's nervousness on that occasion had attracted even the sympathy of some of those who were near him. For she herself had been calm and collected. No one else knew how crushing was the blow which shattered her hopes and made her three years of labor and privation a useless struggle. Yet though no longer a

pupil she could still teach; her master had
found her a small patronage that saved her
from destitution. That night she circled up
quite cheerfully in her usual swallow flight
to her nest under the eaves, and even twittered on the landing a little over the con-
dolences of the concierge — who knew, *mon
Dieu!* what a beast the director of the Conservatoire was and how he could be bribed;
but when at last her brown head sank on
her pillow she cried — just a little.

But what was all this to that next morning — the glorious spring morning which
bathed all the roofs of Paris with warmth
and hope, rekindling enthusiasm and ambition in the breast of youth, and gilding
even much of the sordid dirt below. It
seemed quite natural that she should meet
Major Ostrander not many yards away as
she sallied out. In that bright spring sunshine and the hopeful spring of their youth
they even laughed at the previous day's disappointment. Ah! what a claque it was,
after all! For himself, he, Ostrander, would
much rather see that satin-faced Parisian
girl who had got the prize smirking at the
critics from the boards of the Grand Opera

than his countrywoman ! The Conservatoire
settled things for Paris, but Paris wasn't the
world ! America would come to the fore
yet in art of all kinds — there was a free
academy there now — there should be a
Conservatoire of its own. Of course, Paris
schooling and Paris experience were n't to
be despised in art ; but, thank heaven ! she
had *that*, and no directors could take it from
her ! This and much more, until, comparing
notes, they suddenly found that they were
both free for that day. Why should they
not take advantage of that rare weather and
rarer opportunity to make a little suburban
excursion ? But where ? There was the
Bois, but that was still Paris. Fontaine-
bleau ? Too far ; there were always artists
sketching in the forest, and he would like
for that day to " sink the shop." Versailles ?
Ah, yes ! Versailles !

Thither they went. It was not new to
either of them. Ostrander knew it as an
artist and as an American reader of that
French historic romance — a reader who
hurried over the sham intrigues of the *Œil
de Bœuf*, the sham pastorals of the *Petit
Trianon*, and the sham heroics of a shifty

court, to get to Lafayette. Helen knew it
as a child who had dodged these lessons from
her patriotic father, but had enjoyed the
woods, the parks, the terraces, and particularly the restaurant at the park gates. That
day they took it like a boy and girl, — with
the amused, omniscient tolerance of youth
for a past so inferior to the present. Ostrander thought this gray-eyed, independent
American-French girl far superior to the
obsequious *filles d'honneur*, whose brocades
had rustled through those *quinquonces*, and
Helen vaguely realized the truth of her fellow pupil's mischievous criticism of her companion that day at the Louvre. Surely there
was no classical statue here comparable to
the one-armed soldier-painter!

All this was as yet free from either sentiment or passion, and was only the frank
pride of friendship. But, oddly enough, their
mere presence and companionship seemed to
excite in others that tenderness they had not
yet felt themselves. Family groups watched
the handsome pair in their innocent confidences, and, with French exuberant recognition of sentiment, thought them the
incarnation of Love. Something in their

manifest equality of condition kept even the
vainest and most susceptible of spectators
from attempted rivalry or cynical interruption. And when at last they dropped side by
side on a sun-warmed stone bench on the
terrace, and Helen, inclining her brown head
towards her companion, informed him of the
difficulty she had experienced in getting
gumbo soup, rice and chicken, corn cakes, or
any of her favorite home dishes in Paris, an
exhausted but gallant boulevardier rose from
a contiguous bench, and, politely lifting his
hat to the handsome couple, turned slowly
away from what he believed were tender confidences he would not permit himself to hear.

But the shadow of the trees began to
lengthen, casting broad bars across the *allé*,
and the sun sank lower to the level of their
eyes. They were quite surprised, on looking
around a few moments later, to discover that
the gardens were quite deserted, and Ostrander, on consulting his watch, found that
they had just lost a train which the other
pleasure-seekers had evidently availed themselves of. No matter; there was another
train an hour later; they could still linger
for a few moments in the brief sunset and

then dine at the local restaurant before they left. They both laughed at their forgetfulness, and then, without knowing why, suddenly lapsed into silence. A faint 'wind blew in their faces and trilled the thin leaves above their heads. Nothing else moved. The long windows of the palace in that sunset light seemed to glisten again with the incendiary fires of the Revolution, and then went out blankly and abruptly. The two companions felt that they possessed the terrace and all its memories as completely as the shadows who had lived and died there.

" I am so glad we have had this day together," said the painter, with a very conscious breaking of the silence, " for I am leaving Paris to-morrow."

Helen raised her eyes quickly to his.

" For a few days only," he continued. " My Russian customers — perhaps I ought to say my *patrons* — have given me a commission to make a study of an old chateau which the princess lately bought."

A swift recollection of her fellow pupil's raillery regarding the princess's possible attitude towards the painter came over her and gave a strange artificiality to her response.

" I suppose you will enjoy it very much,"
she said dryly.

" No," he returned with the frankness
that she had lacked.   " I 'd much rather
stay in Paris, but," he added with a faint
smile, " it 's a question of money, and that
is not to be despised.   Yet I — I — somehow feel that I am deserting you, — leaving
you here all alone in Paris."

" I 've been all alone for four years," she
said, with a bitterness she had never felt
before, " and I suppose I 'm accustomed to
it."

Nevertheless she leaned a little forward,
with her fawn-colored lashes dropped over
her eyes, which were bent upon the ground
and the point of the parasol she was holding
with her little gloved hands between her
knees.   He wondered why she did not look
up ; he did not know that it was partly because there were tears in her eyes and partly
for another reason.   As she had leaned forward his arm had quite unconsciously moved
along the back of the bench where her shoulders had rested, and she could not have
resumed her position except in his half em-
brace.

He had not thought of it. He was lost in a greater abstraction. That infinite tenderness, — far above a woman's, — the tenderness of strength and manliness towards weakness and delicacy, the tenderness that looks down and not up, was already possessing him. An instinct of protection drew him nearer this bowed but charming figure, and if he then noticed that the shoulders were pretty, and the curves of the slim waist symmetrical, it was rather with a feeling of timidity and a half-consciousness of unchivalrous thought. Yet why should he not try to keep the brave and honest girl near him always? Why should he not claim the right to protect her? Why should they not — they who were alone in a strange land — join their two lonely lives for mutual help and happiness?

A sudden perception of delicacy, the thought that he should have spoken before her failure at the Conservatoire had made her feel her helplessness, brought a slight color to his cheek. Would it not seem to her that he was taking an unfair advantage of her misfortune? Yet it would be so easy now to slip a loving arm around her waist,

while he could work for her and protect her
with the other. *The other!* His eye fell
on his empty sleeve. Ah, he had forgotten
that! He had but *one* arm!

He rose up abruptly, — so abruptly that
Helen, rising too, almost touched the arm
that was hurriedly withdrawn. Yet in that
accidental contact, which sent a vague tremor through the young girl's frame, there
was still time for him to have spoken. But
he only said : —

" Perhaps we had better dine."

She assented quickly, — she knew not
why, — with a feeling of relief. They walked
very quietly and slowly towards the restaurant. Not a word of love had been spoken ;
not even a glance of understanding had passed
between them. Yet they both knew by some
mysterious instinct that a crisis of their lives
had come and gone, and that they never
again could be to each other as they were
but a brief moment ago. They talked very
sensibly and gravely during their frugal
meal ; the previous spectator of their confidences would have now thought them only
simple friends and have been as mistaken as
before. They talked freely of their hopes

and prospects, — all save one! They even
spoke pleasantly of repeating their little expedition after his return from the country,
while in their secret hearts they had both
resolved never to see each other again. Yet
by that sign each knew that this was love,
and were proud of each other's pride which
kept it a secret.

The train was late, and it was past ten
o'clock when they at last appeared before
the concierge of Helen's home. During
their journey, and while passing through
the crowds at the station and in the streets,
Ostrander had exhibited a new and grave
guardianship over the young girl, and, on
the first landing, after a scrutinizing and an
almost fierce glance at one or two of Helen's
odd fellow lodgers, he had extended his protection so far as to accompany her up the
four flights to the landing of her apartment.
Here he took leave of her with a grave courtesy that half pained, half pleased her. She
watched his broad shoulders and dangling
sleeve as he went down the stairs, and then
quickly turned, entered her room, and locked
the door. The smile had faded from her lips.
Going to the window, she pressed her hot

forehead against the cool glass and looked
out upon the stars nearly level with the black
roofs around her. She stood there some
moments until another star appeared higher
up against the roof ridge, the star she was
looking for. But here the glass pane before
her eyes became presently dim with moisture ; she was obliged to rub it out with her
handkerchief ; yet, somehow, it soon became
clouded, at which she turned sharply away
and went to bed.

But Miss Helen did not know that when
she had looked after the retreating figure of
her protector as he descended the stairs that
night that he was really carrying away on
those broad shoulders the character she had
so laboriously gained during her four years'
solitude. For when she came down the next
morning the concierge bowed to her with an
air of easy, cynical abstraction, the result of
a long conversation with his wife the night
before. He had taken Helen's part with a
kindly cynicism. " Ah ! what would you — it
was bound to come. The affair of the Conservatoire had settled that. The poor child
could not starve ; penniless, she could not
marry. Only why consort with other swallows

under the eaves when she could have had a
gilded cage on the first *étage?* "   But girls
were so foolish — in their first affair; then
it was always *love!*   The second time they
were wiser.   And this maimed warrior and
painter was as poor as she.   A compatriot,
too; well, perhaps that saved some scandal;
one could never know what the Americans
were accustomed to do.   The first floor, which
had been inclined to be civil to the young
teacher, was more so, but less respectful; one
or two young men were tentatively familiar
until they looked in her gray eyes and remembered the broad shoulders of the painter.
Oddly enough, only Mademoiselle Fifine, of
her own landing, exhibited any sympathy
with her, and for the first time Helen was
frightened.   She did not show it, however,
only she changed her lodgings the next day.
But before she left she had a few moments'
conversation with the concierge and an exchange of a word or two with some of her
fellow lodgers.   I have already hinted that
the young lady had great precision of statement; she had a pretty turn for handling
colloquial French and an incisive knowledge
of French character.   She left No. 34, Rue

de Frivole, working itself into a white rage, but utterly undecided as to her real character.

But all this and much more was presently blown away in the hot breath that swept the boulevards at the outburst of the Franco-German War, and Miss Helen Maynard disappeared from Paris with many of her fellow countrymen. The excitement reached even a quaint old chateau in Brittany where Major Ostrander was painting. The woman who was standing by his side as he sat before his easel on the broad terrace observed that he looked disturbed.

"What matters?" she said gently. "You have progressed so well in your work that you can finish it elsewhere. I have no great desire to stay in France with a frontier garrisoned by troops while I have a villa in Switzerland where you could still be my guest. Paris can teach you nothing more, my friend; you have only to create now — and be famous."

"I must go to Paris," he said quietly. "I have friends — countrymen — there, who may want me now."

"If you mean the young singer of the Rue

de Frivole, you have compromised her already. You can do her no good."

" Madame ! "

The pretty face which he had been familiar with for the past six weeks somehow seemed to change its character. Under the mask of dazzling skin he fancied he saw the high cheek-bones and square Tartar angle; the brilliant eyes were even brighter than before, but they showed more of the white than he had ever seen in them.

Nevertheless she smiled, with an equally stony revelation of her white teeth, yet said, still gently, " Forgive me if I thought our friendship justified me in being frank, — perhaps too frank for my own good."

She stopped as if half expecting an interruption ; but as he remained looking wonderingly at her, she bit her lip, and went on: " You have a great career before you. Those who help you must do so without entangling you ; a chain of roses may be as impeding as lead. Until you are independent, you — who may in time compass everything yourself — will need to be helped. You know," she added with a smile, " you have but one arm."

" In your kindness and appreciation you have made me forget it," he stammered. Yet he had a swift vision of the little bench at Versailles where he had *not* forgotten it, and as he glanced around the empty terrace where they stood he was struck with a fateful resemblance to it.

"And I should not remind you now of it," she went on, " except to say that money can always take its place. As in the fairy story, the prince must have a new arm made of gold." She stopped, and then suddenly coming closer to him said, hurriedly and almost fiercely, " Can you not see that I am advising you against my interests, — against myself ? Go, then, to Paris, and go quickly, before I change my mind. Only if you do not find your friends there, remember you have always *one* here." Before he could reply, or even understand that white face, she was gone.

He left for Paris that afternoon. He went directly to the Rue de Frivole; his old resolution to avoid Helen was blown to the winds in the prospect of losing her utterly. But the concierge only knew that mademoiselle had left a day or two after monsieur had accompanied her home. And, point-edly, there was another gentleman who had inquired eagerly — and bountifully as far as money went — for any trace of the young lady. It was a *Russe*. The concierge smiled to himself at Ostrander's flushed cheek. It served this one-armed, conceited American poseur right. Mademoiselle was wiser in this *second* affair.

Ostrander did not finish his picture. The princess sent him a cheque, which he coldly returned. Nevertheless he had acquired through his Russian patronage a local fame which stood him well with the picture deal-ers, — in spite of the excitement of the war. But his heart was no longer in his work; a fever of unrest seized him, which at another time might have wasted itself in mere dis-sipation. Some of his fellow artists had already gone into the army. After the first great reverses he offered his one arm and his military experience to that Paris which had given him a home. The old fighting instinct returned to him with a certain de-speration he had never known before. In the sorties from Paris the one-armed Amer-ican became famous, until a few days before the capitulation, when he was struck down by a bullet through the lung, and left in a temporary hospital. Here in the whirl and terror of Commune days he was forgotten, and when Paris revived under the republic he had disappeared as completely as his compatriot Helen.

But Miss Helen Maynard had been only obscured and not extinguished. At the first outbreak of hostilities a few Americans had still kept giddy state among the ruins of the tottering empire. A day or two after she left the Rue de Frivole she was invited by one of her wealthy former schoolmates to assist with her voice and talent at one of their extravagant entertainments. "You will understand, dear," said Miss de Laine, with ingenious delicacy, as she eyed her old comrade's well-worn dress, "that Poppa expects to pay you professional prices, and it may be an opening for you among our other friends."

"I should not come otherwise, dear," said Miss Helen with equal frankness. But she played and sang very charmingly to the fashionable assembly in the Champs Elysées, — so charmingly, indeed, that Miss de Laine patronizingly expatiated upon her worth and her better days in confidence to some of the guests.

"A most deserving creature," said Miss de Laine to the dowager duchess of Soho, who was passing through Paris on her way to England; "you would hardly believe that Poppa knew her father when he was one of the richest men in South Carolina."

"Your father seems to have been very fortunate," said the duchess quietly, "and so are *you*. Introduce me."

This not being exactly the reply that Miss de Laine expected, she momentarily hesitated: but the duchess profited by it to walk over to the piano and introduce herself. When she rose to go she invited Helen to luncheon with her the next day. "Come early, my dear, and we'll have a long talk." Helen pointed out hesitatingly that she was practically a guest of the de Laines. "Ah, well, that's true, my dear; then you may bring one of them with you."

Helen went to the luncheon, but was unaccompanied. She had a long talk with the dowager. "I am not rich, my dear, like your friends, and cannot afford to pay ten

napoleons for a song. Like you I have seen
' better days.' But this is no place for you,
child, and if you can bear with an old woman's company for a while I think I can find
you something to do." That evening Helen
left for England with the duchess, a piece
of "ingratitude, indelicacy, and shameless
snobbery," which Miss de Laine was never
weary of dilating upon. "And to think *I* introduced her, though she was a professional!"

. . . .

It was three years after. Paris, reviving
under the republic, had forgotten Helen and
the American colony; and the American
colony, emigrating to more congenial courts,
had forgotten Paris.

It was a bleak day of English summer
when Helen, standing by the window of the
breakfast-room at Hamley Court, and looking over the wonderful lawn, kept peren-
nially green by humid English skies, heard
the practical, masculine voice of the duchess
in her ear at the same moment that she felt
the gentle womanly touch of her hand on
her shoulder.

"We are going to luncheon at Moreland
Hall to-day, my dear."

" Why, we were there only last week ! " said Helen.

" Undoubtedly," returned the duchess dryly, " and we may luncheon there next week and the next following. And," she added, looking into her companion's gray eyes, " it rests with *you* to stay there if you choose."

Helen stared at her protector.

" My dear," continued the duchess, slipping her arm around Helen's waist, " Sir James has honored *me* — as became my relations to *you* — with his confidences. As you have n't given me *yours* I suppose you have none, and that I am telling you news when I say that Sir James wishes to marry you."

The unmistakable astonishment in the girl's eye satisfied the duchess even before her voice.

" But he scarcely knows me or anything of me ! " said the young girl quickly.

" On the contrary, my dear, he knows *everything* about you. I have been particular in telling him all *I* know — and some things even *you* don't know and could n't tell him. For instance, that you are a very

nice person. Come, my dear, don't look so
stupefied, or I shall really think there's
something in it that I don't know. It's
not a laughing nor a crying matter yet — at
present it's only luncheon again with a civil
man who has three daughters and a place in
the county. Don't make the mistake, however, of refusing him before he offers —
whatever you do afterwards."

" But " — stammered Helen.

" But — you are going to say that you
don't love him and have never thought of
him as a husband," interrupted the duchess;
" I read it in your face, — and it's a very
proper thing to say."

" It is so unexpected," urged Helen.

" Everything is unexpected from a man
in these matters," said the duchess. " We
women are the only ones that are prepared."

" But," persisted Helen, " if I don't want
to marry at all ? "

" I should say, then, that it is a sign that
you ought; if you were eager, my dear, I
should certainly dissuade you." She paused,
and then drawing Helen closer to her, said,
with a certain masculine tenderness, " As
long as I live, dear, you know that you have

a home here. But I am an old woman living on the smallest of settlements. Death
is as inevitable to me as marriage should be
to you."

Nevertheless, they did not renew the conversation, and later received the greetings
of their host at Moreland Hall with a simplicity and frankness that were, however,
perfectly natural and unaffected in both
women. Sir James, — a tall, well-preserved
man of middle age, with the unmistakable
bearing of long years of recognized and un-
challenged position, — however, exhibited on
this occasion that slight consciousness of
weakness and susceptibility to ridicule which
is apt to indicate the invasion of the tender
passion in the heart of the average Briton.
His duty as host towards the elder woman
of superior rank, however, covered his embarrassment, and for a moment left Helen
quite undisturbed to gaze again upon the
treasures of the long drawing-room of Moreland Hall with which she was already
familiar. There were the half-dozen old
masters, whose respectability had been as
recognized through centuries as their owner's
ancestors ; there were the ancestors them-

selves, — wigged, ruffled, and white-handed,
by Vandyke, Lely, Romney, and Gainsbor-
ough; there were the uniform, expression-
less ancestresses in stiff brocade or short-
waisted, clinging draperies, but all possessing
that brilliant coloring which the gray skies
outside lacked, and which seemed to have
departed from the dresses of their descendants. The American girl had sometimes
speculated upon what might have been the
appearance of the lime-tree walk, dotted
with these gayly plumaged folk, and wondered if the tyranny of environment had at
last subdued their brilliant colors. And a
new feeling touched her. Like most of her
countrywomen, she was strongly affected by
the furniture of life; the thought that all
that she saw there *might be hers;* that
she might yet stand in succession to these
strange courtiers and stranger shepherdesses,
and, like them, look down from the canvas
upon the intruding foreigner, thrilled her
for a moment with a half-proud, half-pas-
sive sense of yielding to what seemed to be
her fate. A narrow-eyed, stiff-haired Dutch
maid of honor before whom she was standing gazed at her with staring vacancy.

Suddenly she started. Before the portrait upon a fanciful easel stood a small elaborately framed sketch in oils. It was evidently some recently imported treasure. She had not seen it before. As she moved quickly forward, she recognized at a glance that it was Ostrander's sketch from the Paris grenier.

The wall, the room, the park beyond, even the gray sky, seemed to fade away before her. She was standing once more at her attic window looking across the roofs and chimney stacks upward to the blue sky of Paris. Through a gap in the roofs she could see the chestnut-trees trilling in the little square; she could hear the swallows twittering in the leaden troughs of the gutter before her; the call of the chocolate vender or the cry of a gamin floated up to her from the street below, or the latest song of the café chantant was whistled by the blue-bloused workman on the scaffolding hard by. The breath of Paris, of youth, of blended work and play, of ambition, of joyous freedom, again filled her and mingled with the scent of the mignonette that used to stand on the old window-ledge.

" I am glad you like it. I have only just put it up."

It was the voice of Sir James — a voice that had regained a little of its naturalness — a calm, even lazy English voice — confident from the experience of years of respectful listeners. Yet it somehow jarred upon her nerves with its complacency and its utter incongruousness to her feelings. Nevertheless, the impulse to know more about the sketch was the stronger.

" Do you mean you have just bought it ? " asked Helen. " It 's not English ? "

" No," said Sir James, gratified with his companion's interest. " I bought it in Paris just after the Commune."

" From the artist ? " continued Helen, in a slightly constrained voice.

" No," said Sir James, " although I knew the poor chap well enough. You can easily see that he was once a painter of great promise. I rather think it was stolen from him while he was in hospital by those incendiary wretches. I recognized it, however, and bought for a few francs from them what I would have paid *him* a thousand for."

" In hospital ? " repeated Helen dazedly.

" Yes," said Sir James. " The fact is it was the ending of the usual Bohemian artist's life. Though in this case the man was a real artist, — and I believe, by the way, was a countryman of yours."

" In hospital ? " again repeated Helen. " Then he was poor ? "

" Reckless, I should rather say; he threw himself into the fighting before Paris and was badly wounded. But it was all the result of the usual love affair — the girl, they say, ran off with the usual richer man. At all events, it ruined him for painting; he never did anything worth having afterwards."

" And now ? " said Helen in the same unmoved voice.

Sir James shrugged his shoulders. " He disappeared. Probably he 'll turn up some day on the London pavement — with chalks. That sketch, by the way, was one that had always attracted me to his studio — though he never would part with it. I rather fancy, don't you know, that the girl had something to do with it. It 's a wonderfully realistic sketch, don't you see ; and I should n't wonder if it was the girl herself who lived behind one of those queer little windows in the roof there."

" She did live there," said Helen in a low voice.

Sir James uttered a vague laugh.

Helen looked around her. The duchess had quietly and unostentatiously passed into the library, and in full view, though out of hearing, was examining, with her glass to her eye, some books upon the shelves.

" I mean," said Helen, in a perfectly clear voice, " that the young girl did *not* run away from the painter, and that he had neither the right nor the cause to believe her faithless or attribute his misfortunes to her." She hesitated, not from any sense of her indiscretion, but to recover from a momentary doubt if the girl were really her own self — but only for a moment.

" Then you knew the painter, as I did ? " he said in astonishment.

" Not as *you* did," responded Helen. She drew nearer the picture, and, pointing a slim finger to the canvas, said : —

" Do you see that small window with the mignonette ? "

" Perfectly."

" That was *my* room.   His was opposite.
He told me so when I first saw the sketch.
I am the girl you speak of, for he knew no
other, and I believe him to have been a
truthful, honorable man."

" But what were you doing there ?   Surely
you are joking ? " said Sir James, with a
forced smile.

" I was a poor pupil at the Conservatoire,
and lived where I could afford to live."

" Alone ? "

" Alone."

" And the man was " —

" Major Ostrander was my friend.   I even
think I have a better right to call him that
than you had."

Sir James coughed slightly and grasped
the lapel of his coat.   " Of course ; I dare
say ; I had no idea of this, don't you know,
when I spoke."   He looked around him as
if to evade a scene.   " Ah ! suppose we ask
the duchess to look at the sketch ; I don't
think she 's seen it."   He began to move in
the direction of the library.

" She had better wait," said Helen quietly.

" For what ? "

" Until " — hesitated Helen smilingly.

"Until? I am afraid I don't understand," said Sir James stiffly, coloring with
a slight suspicion.

"Until you have *apologized*."

"Of course," said Sir James, with a half-
hysteric laugh. "I do. You understand I
only repeated a story that was told me, and
had no idea of connecting *you* with it. I
beg your pardon, I'm sure. I er — er —
in fact," he added suddenly, the embarrassed
smile fading from his face as he looked at
her fixedly, "I remember now it must have
been the concierge of the house, or the opposite one, who told me. He said it was
a Russian who carried off that young girl.
Of course it was some made-up story."

"I left Paris with the duchess," said Helen
quietly, "before the war."

"Of course. And she knows all about
your friendship with this man."

"I don't think she does. I have n't told
her. Why should I?" returned Helen, raising her clear eyes to his.

"Really, I don't know," stammered Sir
James. "But here she is. Of course if
you prefer it, I won't say anything of this
to her."

Helen gave him her first glance of genuine emotion; it happened, however, to be scorn.

" How odd ! " she said, as the duchess leisurely approached them, her glass still in her eye. " Sir James, quite unconsciously, has just been showing me a sketch of my dear old mansarde in Paris. Look! That little window was my room. And, only think of it, Sir James bought it of an old friend of mine, who painted it from the opposite attic, where he lived. And quite unconsciously, too."

" How very singular ! " said the duchess ; " indeed, quite romantic ! "

" Very ! " said Sir James.

" Very ! " said Helen.

The tone of their voices was so different that the duchess looked from one to the other.

" But that is n't all," said Helen with a smile, " Sir James actually fancied " —

" Will you excuse me for a moment ? " said Sir James, interrupting, and turning hastily to the duchess with a forced smile and a somewhat heightened color. " I had forgotten that I had promised Lady Harriet to drive you over to Deep Hill after luncheon to meet that South American who has taken such a fancy to your place, and I must send to the stables."

As Sir James disappeared, the duchess turned to Helen. " I see what has happened, dear ; don't mind me, for I frankly confess I shall now eat my luncheon less guiltily than I feared. But tell me, *how* did you refuse him ? "

" I did n't refuse him," said Helen. " I only prevented his asking me."

" How ? "

Then Helen told her all, — everything except her first meeting with Ostrander at the restaurant. A true woman respects the pride of those she loves more even than her own, and while Helen felt that although that incident might somewhat condone her subsequent romantic passion in the duchess's eyes, she could not tell it.

The duchess listened in silence.

" Then you two incompetents have never seen each other since ? " she asked.

" No."

" But you hope to ? "

" I cannot speak for *him*," said Helen.

" And you have never written to him, and don't know whether he is alive or dead ? "

" No."

" Then I have been nursing in my bosom for three years at one and the same time a brave, independent, matter-of-fact young person and the most idiotic, sentimental heroine that ever figured in a romantic opera or a country ballad." Helen did not reply. " Well, my dear," said the duchess after a pause, " I see that you are condemned to pass your days with me in some cheap hotel on the continent." Helen looked up wonderingly. " Yes," she continued, " I suppose I must now make up my mind to sell my place to this gilded South American, who has taken a fancy to it. But I am not going to spoil my day by seeing him *now*. No ; we will excuse ourselves from going to Deep Hill to-day, and we will go back home quietly after luncheon. It will be a mercy to Sir James."

" But," said Helen earnestly, " I can go back to my old life, and earn my own living."

" Not if I can help it," said the duchess grimly. " Your independence has made you

a charming companion to me, I admit; but
I shall see that it does not again spoil your
chances of marrying. Here comes Sir James.
Really, my dear, I don't know which one of
you looks the more relieved."

On their way back through the park Helen
again urged the duchess to give up the idea
of selling Hamley Court, and to consent to
her taking up her old freedom and independence once more. "I shall never, never
forget your loving kindness and protection,"
continued the young girl, tenderly. "You
will let me come to you always when you
want me; but you will let me also shape my
life anew, and work for my living." The
duchess turned her grave, half humorous
face towards her. "That means you have
determined to seek *him*. Well! Perhaps
if you give up your other absurd idea of independence, I may assist you. And now I
really believe, dear, that there is that dreadful South American," pointing to a figure
that was crossing the lawn at Hamley Court,
"hovering round like a vulture. Well, I
can't see him to-day if he calls, but *you* may.
By the way, they say he is not bad-looking,
was a famous general in the South Ameri-

can War, and is rolling in money, and comes
here on a secret mission from his government. But I forget — the rest of our life
is to be devoted to seeking *another*. And
I begin to think I am not a good match-
maker."

Helen was in no mood for an interview
with the stranger, whom, like the duchess,
she was inclined to regard as a portent of fate
and sacrifice. She knew her friend's strait-
ened circumstances, which might make such
a sacrifice necessary to insure a competency
for her old age, and, as Helen feared also, a
provision for herself. She knew the strange
tenderness of this masculine woman, which
had survived a husband's infidelities and a
son's forgetfulness, to be given to her, and
her heart sank at the prospect of separation,
even while her pride demanded that she should
return to her old life again. Then she wondered if the duchess was right ; did she still
cherish the hope of meeting Ostrander again ?
The tears she had kept back all that day as-
serted themselves as she flung open the library
door and ran across the garden into the myrtle
walk. " In hospital ! " The words had been
ringing in her ears through Sir James's com-

placent speech, through the oddly constrained luncheon, through the half-tender, half-masculine reasoning of her companion. He *had* loved her — he had suffered and perhaps thought her false. Suddenly she stopped. At the further end of the walk the ominous stranger whom she wished to avoid was standing looking towards the house.

How provoking! She glanced again; he was leaning against a tree and was obviously as preoccupied as she was herself. He was actually sketching the ivy-covered gable of the library. What presumption! And he was sketching with his left hand. A sudden thrill of superstition came over her. She moved eagerly forward for a better view of him. No! he had two arms!

But his quick eye had already caught sight of her, and before she could retreat she could see that he had thrown away his sketch-book and was hastening eagerly toward her. Amazed and confounded she would have flown, but her limbs suddenly refused their office, and as he at last came near her with the cry of " Helen! " upon his lips, she felt herself staggering, and was caught in his arms.

" Thank God," he said. " Then she *has* let you come to me ! "

She disengaged herself slowly and dazedly from him and stood looking at him with wondering eyes. He was bronzed and worn ; there was the second arm : but still it was *he*. And with the love, which she now knew he had felt, looking from his honest eyes !

" *She* has let me come ! " she repeated vacantly. " Whom do you mean ? "

" The duchess."

" The duchess ? "

" Yes." He stopped suddenly, gazing at her blank face, while his own grew ashy white. " Helen ! For God's sake tell me ! You have not accepted him ? "

" I have accepted no one," she stammered, with a faint color rising to her cheeks. " I do not understand you."

A look of relief came over him. " But," he said amazedly, " has not the duchess told you how I happen to be here ? How, when you disappeared from Paris long ago — with my ambition crushed, and nothing left to me but my old trade of the fighter — I joined a secret expedition to help the Chilian revolutionists ? How I, who might have starved as a painter, gained distinction as a partisan general, and was rewarded with an envoyship in Europe? How I came to Paris to seek you? How I found that even the picture — your picture, Helen — had been sold. How, in tracing it here, I met the duchess at Deep Hill, and learning you were with her, in a moment of impulse told her my whole story. How she told me that though she was your best friend, you had never spoken of me, and how she begged me not to spoil your chance of a good match by revealing myself, and so awakening a past — which she believed you had forgotten. How she implored me at least to let her make a fair test of your affections and your memory, and until then to keep away from you — and to spare you, Helen; and for your sake, I consented. Surely she has told this, *now!*"

"Not a word," said Helen blankly.

"Then you mean to say that if I had not haunted the park to-day, in the hope of seeing you, believing that as you would not recognize me with this artificial arm, I should not break my promise to her, — you would not have known I was even living."

"No!—yes!—stay!" A smile broke over her pale face and left it rosy. "I see it all now. Oh, Philip, don't you understand? She wanted only to try us!"

There was a silence in the lonely wood, broken only by the trills of a frightened bird whose retreat was invaded.

"Not now! Please! Wait! Come with me!"

The next moment she had seized Philip's left hand, and, dragging him with her, was flying down the walk towards the house. But as they neared the garden door it suddenly opened on the duchess, with her glasses to her eyes, smiling.

The General Don Felipe Ostrander did not buy Hamley Court, but he and his wife were always welcome guests there. And Sir James, as became an English gentleman, —amazed though he was at Philip's singular return, and more singular incognito, — afterwards gallantly presented Philip's wife with Philip's first picture.

THE JUDGMENT OF BOLINAS
PLAIN

THE wind was getting up on the Bolinas
Plain. It had started the fine alkaline dust
along the level stage road, so that even that
faint track, the only break in the monotony
of the landscape, seemed fainter than ever.
But the dust cloud was otherwise a relief; it
took the semblance of distant woods where
there was no timber, of moving teams where
there was no life. And as Sue Beasley, standing in the doorway of One Spring House
that afternoon, shading her sandy lashes
with her small red hand, glanced along the
desolate track, even *her* eyes, trained to the
dreary prospect, were once or twice deceived.

" Sue ! "

It was a man's voice from within. Sue
took no notice of it, but remained with her
hand shading her eyes.

" Sue ! Wot yer yawpin' at thar ? "

" Yawpin' " would seem to have been the

local expression for her abstraction, since, without turning her head, she answered slowly and languidly : " Reckoned I see'd som' un on the stage road. But 't ain't nothin' nor nobody."

Both voices had in their accents and delivery something of the sadness and infinite protraction of the plain. But the woman's had a musical possibility in its long-drawn cadence, while the man's was only monotonous and wearying. And as she turned back into the room again, and confronted her companion, there was the like difference in their appearance. Ira Beasley, her husband, had suffered from the combined effects of indolence, carelessness, misadventure, and disease. Two of his fingers had been cut off by a scythe, his thumb and part of his left ear had been blown away by an overcharged gun; his knees were crippled by rheumatism, and one foot was lame from ingrowing nails, — deviations that, however, did not tend to correct the original angularities of his frame. His wife, on the other hand, had a pretty figure, which still retained — they were childless — the rounded freshness of maidenhood. Her features were irregular,

yet not without a certain piquancy of outline ; her hair had the two shades sometimes
seen in imperfect blondes, and her complexion the sallowness of combined exposure
and alkaline assimilation.

She had lived there since, an angular girl
of fifteen, she had been awkwardly helped
by Ira from the tail-board of the emigrant
wagon in which her mother had died two
weeks before, and which was making its first
halt on the Californian plains, before Ira's
door. On the second day of their halt Ira
had tried to kiss her while she was drawing
water, and had received the contents of the
bucket instead, — the girl knowing her own
value. On the third day Ira had some conversation with her father regarding locations
and stock. On the fourth day this conversation was continued in the presence of the
girl ; on the fifth day the three walked to
Parson Davies' house, four miles away, where
Ira and Sue were married. The romance of
a week had taken place within the confines
of her present view from the doorway ; the
episode of her life might have been shut in
in that last sweep of her sandy lashes.

Nevertheless, at that moment some in-

stinct, she knew not what, impelled her when
her husband left the room to put down the
dish she was washing, and, with the towel
lapped over her bare pretty arms, to lean
once more against the doorpost, lazily looking down the plain. A cylindrical cloud of
dust trailing its tattered skirt along the stage
road suddenly assaulted the house, and for
an instant enveloped it. As it whirled away
again something emerged, or rather dropped
from its skirts behind the little cluster of low
bushes which encircled the " One Spring."
It was a man.

" Thar ! I knew it was suthin'," she
began aloud, but the words somehow died
upon her lips. Then she turned and walked
towards the inner door, wherein her husband
had disappeared, — but here stopped again
irresolutely. Then she suddenly walked
through the outer door into the road and
made directly for the spring. The figure of
a man crouching, covered with dust, half
rose from the bushes when she reached them.
She was not frightened, for he seemed utterly
exhausted, and there was a singular mixture
of shame, hesitation, and entreaty in his
broken voice as he gasped out : —

" Look here ! — I say ! hide me somewhere, won't you ? Just for a little. You
see — the fact is — I 'm chased ! They 're
hunting me now, — they 're just behind me.
Anywhere will do till they go by ! Tell you
all about it another time. Quick ! Please
do ! "

In all this there was nothing dramatic nor
even startling to her. Nor did there seem
to be any present danger impending to the
man. He did not look like a horse-thief nor
a criminal. And he had tried to laugh, half-
apologetically, half-bitterly, — the consciousness of a man who had to ask help of a
woman at such a moment.

She gave a quick glance towards the
house. He followed her eyes, and said hurriedly : " Don't tell on me. Don't let any
one see me. I 'm trusting you."

" Come," she said suddenly. " Get on
this side."

He understood her, and slipped to her
side, half-creeping, half-crouching like a dog
behind her skirts, but keeping her figure
between him and the house as she moved
deliberately towards the barn, scarce fifty
yards away. When she reached it she

opened the half-door quickly, said : " In there — at the top — among the hay " — closed it, and was turning away, when there came a faint rapping from within. She opened the door again impatiently ; the man said hastily : " Wanted to tell you — it was a man who insulted a *woman !* I went for him, you see — and " —

But she shut the door sharply. The fugitive had made a blunder. The importation of her own uncertain sex into the explanation did not help him. She kept on towards the house, however, without the least trace of excitement or agitation in her manner, entered the front door again, walked quietly to the door of the inner room, glanced in, saw that her husband was absorbed in splicing a *riata*, and had evidently not missed her, and returned quietly to her dishwashing. With this singular difference : a few moments before she had seemed inattentive and careless of what she was doing, as if from some abstraction ; now, when she was actually abstracted, her movements were mechanically perfect and deliberate. She carefully held up a dish and examined it minutely for cracks, rubbing it cautiously with the towel, but seeing all the while only the man she had left in the barn. A few moments elapsed. Then there came another rush of wind around the house, a drifting cloud of dust before the door, the clatter of hoofs, and a quick shout.

Her husband reached the door, from the inner room, almost as quickly as she did. They both saw in the road two armed mounted men — one of whom Ira recognized as the sheriff's deputy.

"Has anybody been here, just now?" he asked sharply.

"No."

"Seen anybody go by?" he continued.

"No. What's up?"

"One of them circus jumpers stabbed Hal Dudley over the table in Dolores monte shop last night, and got away this morning. We hunted him into the plain and lost him somewhere in this d——d dust."

"Why, Sue reckoned she saw suthin' just now," said Ira, with a flash of recollection. "Did n't ye, Sue?"

"Why the h——ll did n't she say it before? — I beg your pardon, ma'am; did n't see you; you 'll excuse haste."

Both the men's hats were in their hands, embarrassed yet gratified smiles on their faces, as Sue came forward. There was the faintest of color in her sallow cheek, a keen brilliancy in her eyes ; she looked singularly pretty. Even Ira felt a slight antenuptial stirring through his monotonously wedded years.

The young woman walked out, folding the towel around her red hands and forearms — leaving the rounded whiteness of bared elbow and upper arm in charming contrast — and looked gravely past the admiring figures that nearly touched her own. " It was somewhar over thar," she said lazily, pointing up the road in the opposite direction to the barn, " but I ain't sure it *was* any one."

" Then he'd already *passed* the house afore you saw him ? " said the deputy.

" I reckon — if it *was* him," returned Sue.

" He must have got on," said the deputy ; " but then he runs like a deer ; it's his trade."

" Wot trade ? "

" Acrobat."

" Wot's that ? "

The two men were delighted at this divine simplicity. " A man who runs, jumps, climbs — and all that sort, in the circus."

"But is n't he runnin', jumpin', and climbin' away from ye now?" she continued with adorable naïvete.

The deputy smiled, but straightened in the saddle. "We 're bound to come up with him afore he reaches Lowville; and between that and this house it 's a dead level, where a gopher could n't leave his hole without your spottin' him a mile off! Good-by!" The words were addressed to Ira, but the parting glance was directed to the pretty wife as the two men galloped away.

An odd uneasiness at this sudden revelation of his wife's prettiness and its evident effect upon his visitors came over Ira. It resulted in his addressing the empty space before his door with, " Well, ye won't ketch much if ye go on yawpin' and dawdlin' with women-folks like this; " and he was unreasonably delighted at the pretty assent of disdain and scorn which sparkled in his wife's eyes as she added: —

" Not much, I reckon ! "

" That 's the kind of official trash we have

to pay taxes to keep up," said Ira, who
somehow felt that if public policy was not
amenable to private sentiment there was no
value in free government.   Mrs. Beasley,
however, complacently resumed her dishwashing, and Ira returned to his *riata* in
the adjoining room.   For quite an interval
there was no sound but the occasional click
of a dish laid upon its pile, with fingers that,
however, were firm and untremulous.   Presently Sue's low voice was heard.

"Wonder if that deputy caught anything
yet.   I 've a good mind to meander up the
road and see."

But the question brought Ira to the door
with a slight return of his former uneasiness.   He had no idea of subjecting his wife
to another admiring interview.   "I reckon
I 'll go myself," he said dubiously ;   "*you*'d
better stay and look after the house."

Her eyes brightened as she carried a pile
of plates to the dresser ; it was possible she
had foreseen this compromise.   "Yes," she
said cheerfully, "you could go farther than
me."

Ira reflected.   He could also send them
about their business if they thought of re-

turning. He lifted his hat from the floor,
took his rifle down carefully from its pegs,
and slouched out into the road. Sue
watched him until he was well away, then
flew to the back door, stopping only an instant to look at her face in a small mirror
on the wall, — yet without noticing her new
prettiness, — then ran to the barn. Casting
a backward glance at the diminishing figure
of her husband in the distance, she threw
open the door and shut it quickly behind
her. At first the abrupt change from the
dazzling outer plain to the deep shadows of
the barn bewildered her. She saw before
her a bucket half filled with dirty water, and
a quantity of wet straw littering the floor ;
then lifting her eyes to the hay-loft, she detected the figure of the fugitive, unclothed
from the waist upward, emerging from the
loose hay in which he had evidently been
drying himself. Whether it was the excitement of his perilous situation, or whether the
perfect symmetry of his bared bust and arms
— unlike anything she had ever seen before — clothed him with the cold ideality of
a statue, she could not say, but she felt no
shock of modesty ; while the man, accustomed

to the public half-exposure in tights and spangles, was more conscious of detected unreadiness than of shame.

"Gettin' the dust off me," he said, in hurried explanation; "be down in a second." Indeed, in another moment he had resumed his shirt and flannel coat, and swung himself to the floor with a like grace and dexterity, that was to her the revelation of a descending god. She found herself face to face with him, — his features cleansed of dirt and grime, his hair plastered in wet curls on his low forehead. It was a face of cheap adornment, not uncommon in his profession — unintelligent, unrefined, and even unheroic; but she did not know that. Overcoming a sudden timidity, she nevertheless told him briefly and concisely of the arrival and departure of his pursuers.

His low forehead wrinkled. "Thar's no getting away until they come back," he said without looking at her. "Could ye keep me in here to-night?"

"Yes," she returned simply, as if the idea had already occurred to her; "but you must lie low in the loft."

"And could you" — he hesitated, and

went on with a forced smile — " you see, I 've eaten nothing since last night. Could you " —

" I 'll bring you something," she said quickly, nodding her head.

" And if you had " — he went on more hesitatingly, glancing down at his travel-torn and frayed garments — " anything like a coat, or any other clothing? It would disguise me also, you see, and put 'em off the track."

She nodded her head again rapidly : she had thought of that too ; there was a pair of doeskin trousers and a velvet jacket left by a Mexican vaquero who had bought stock from them two years ago. Practical as she was, a sudden conviction that he would look well in the velvet jacket helped her resolve.

" Did they say " — he said, with his forced smile and uneasy glance — " did they — tell you anything about me ? "

" Yes," she said abstractedly, gazing at him.

" You see," he began hurriedly, " I 'll tell you how it was."

" No, don't ! " she said quickly. She meant it. She wanted no facts to stand between her and this single romance of her life. " I must go and get the things," she added, turning away, " before he gets back."

" Who 's *he?* " asked the man.

She was about to reply, " My husband," but without knowing why stopped and said, " Mr. Beasley," and then ran off quickly to the house.

She found the vaquero's clothes, took some provisions, filled a flask of whiskey in the cupboard, and ran back with them, her mouth expanded to a vague smile, and pulsating like a schoolgirl. She even repressed with difficulty the ejaculation " There! " as she handed them to him. He thanked her, but with eyes fixed and fascinated by the provisions. She understood it with a new sense of delicacy, and saying, " I 'll come again when he gets back," ran off and returned to the house, leaving him alone to his repast.

Meantime her husband, lounging lazily along the high road, had precipitated the catastrophe he wished to avoid. For his slouching figure, silhouetted against the horizon on that monotonous level, had been the only one detected by the deputy sheriff and

the constable, his companion, and they had
charged down within fifty yards of him before
they discovered their mistake. They were
not slow in making this an excuse for aban-
doning their quest as far as Lowville: in
fact, after quitting the distraction of Mrs.
Beasley's presence they had, without in the
least suspecting the actual truth, become
doubtful if the fugitive had proceeded so far.
He might at that moment be snugly ensconced behind some low wire-grass ridge,
watching their own clearly defined figures,
and waiting only for the night to evade them.
The Beasley house seemed a proper place of
operation in beating up the field. Ira's cold
reception of the suggestion was duly disposed
of by the deputy. " I have the *right*, ye
know," he said, with a grim pleasantry, " to
summon ye as my posse to aid and assist me
in carrying out the law ; but I ain't the man
to be rough on my friends, and I reckon it
will do jest as well if I ' requisition ' your
house." The dreadful recollection that the
deputy had the power to detail him and the
constable to scour the plain while he remained behind in company with Sue stopped
Ira's further objections. Yet, if he could

only get rid of her while the deputy was in the house, — but then his nearest neighbor was five miles away! There was nothing left for him to do but to return with the men and watch his wife keenly. Strange to say, there was a certain stimulus in this which stirred his monotonous pulses and was not without a vague pleasure. There is a revelation to some natures in newly awakened jealousy that is a reincarnation of love.

As they came into the house a slight circumstance, which an hour ago would have scarcely touched his sluggish sensibilities, now appeared to corroborate his fear. His wife had changed her cuffs and collar, taken off her rough apron, and evidently redressed her hair. This, with the enhanced brightness of her eyes, which he had before noticed, convinced him that it was due to the visit of the deputy. There was no doubt that the official was equally attracted and fascinated by her prettiness, and although her acceptance of his return was certainly not a cordial one, there was a kind of demure restraint and over-consciousness in her manner that might be coquetry. Ira had vaguely observed this quality in other young women, but had never experienced it in his brief courtship. There had been no rivalry, no sexual diplomacy nor insincerity in his capture of the motherless girl who had leaped from the tail-board of her father's wagon almost into his arms, and no man had since come between them. The idea that Sue should care for any other than himself had been simply inconceivable to his placid, matter-of-fact nature. That their sacrament was final he had never doubted. If his two cows, bought with his own money or reared by him, should suddenly have developed an inclination to give milk to a neighbor, he would not have been more astonished. But *they* could have been brought back with a rope, and without a heart throb.

Passion of this kind, which in a less sincere society restricts its expression to innuendo or forced politeness, left the rustic Ira only dumb and lethargic. He moved slowly and abstractedly around the room, accenting his slight lameness more than ever, or dropped helplessly into a chair, where he sat, inanely conscious of the contiguity of his wife and the deputy, and stupidly expectant of — he knew not what. The atmosphere of the little house seemed to him charged with some unwholesome electricity. It kindled his wife's eyes, stimulating the deputy and his follower to coarse playfulness, enthralled his own limbs to the convulsive tightening of his fingers around the rungs of his chair. Yet he managed to cling to his idea of keeping his wife occupied, and of preventing any eyeshot between her and her guests, or the indulgence of dangerously flippant conversation, by ordering her to bring some refreshment. " What's gone o' the whiskey bottle ? " he said, after fumbling in the cupboard.

Mrs. Beasley did not blench. She only gave her head a slight toss. " Ef you men can't get along with the coffee and flapjacks I 'm going to give ye, made with my own hands, ye kin just toddle right along to the first bar, and order your tangle-foot there. Ef it 's a barkeeper you 're looking for, and not a lady, say so ! "

The novel audacity of this speech, and the fact that it suggested that preoccupation he hoped for, relieved Ira for a moment, while it enchanted the guests as a stroke of

coquettish fascination. Mrs. Beasley triumphantly disappeared in the kitchen, slipped
off her cuffs and set to work, and in a few
moments emerged with a tray bearing the
cakes and steaming coffee. As neither she
nor her husband ate anything (possibly owing
to an equal preoccupation) the guests were
obliged to confine their attentions to the
repast before them. The sun, too, was already nearing the horizon, and although its
nearly level beams acted like a powerful
search-light over the stretching plain, twilight would soon put an end to the quest.
Yet they lingered. Ira now foresaw a new
difficulty : the cows were to be brought up
and fodder taken from the barn ; to do this
he would be obliged to leave his wife and
the deputy together. I do not know if Mrs.
Beasley divined his perplexity, but she carelessly offered to perform that evening func-
tion herself. Ira's heart leaped and sank
again as the deputy gallantly proposed to
assist her. But here rustic simplicity seemed
to be equal to the occasion. " Ef I propose
to do Ira's work," said Mrs. Beasley, with
provocative archness, " it 's because I reckon
he 'll do more good helpin' you catch your

man than you 'll do helpin' *me !* So clear out, both of ye ! " A feminine audacity that recalled the deputy to himself, and left him no choice but to accept Ira's aid. I do not know whether Mrs. Beasley felt a pang of conscience as her husband arose gratefully and limped after the deputy ; I only know that she stood looking at them from the door, smiling and triumphant.

Then she slipped out of the back door again, and ran swiftly to the barn, fastening on her clean cuffs and collar as she ran. The fugitive was anxiously awaiting her, with a slight touch of brusqueness in his eagerness.

" Thought you were never coming ! " he said.

She breathlessly explained, and showed him through the half-opened door the figures of the three men slowly spreading and diverging over the plain, like the nearly level sun-rays they were following. The sunlight fell also on her panting bosom, her electrified sandy hair, her red, half-opened mouth, and short and freckled upper lip. The relieved fugitive turned from the three remoter figures to the one beside him, and saw, for the first time, that it was fair. At which he smiled, and her face flushed and was irradiated.

Then they fell to talk, — he grateful, boastful, — as the distant figures grew dim; she quickly assenting, but following his expression rather than his words, with her own girlish face and brightening eyes. But what he said, or how he explained his position, with what speciousness he dwelt upon himself, his wrongs, and his manifold manly virtues, is not necessary for us to know, nor was it, indeed, for her to understand. Enough for her that she felt she had found the one man of all the world, and that she was at that moment protecting him against all the world! He was the unexpected, spontaneous gift to her, the companion her childhood had never known, the lover she had never dreamed of, even the child of her unsatisfied maternal yearnings. If she could not comprehend all his selfish incoherences, she felt it was her own fault; if she could not follow his ignorant assumptions, she knew it was *she* who was deficient; if she could not translate his coarse speech, it was because it was the language of a larger world from which she had been excluded. To this world belonged the beautiful limbs she gazed on, — a very different world from that which had produced the rheumatic deformities and useless mayhem of her husband, or the provincially foppish garments of the deputy. Sitting in the hayloft together, where she had mounted for greater security, they forgot themselves in his monologue of cheap vaporing, broken only by her assenting smiles and her half-checked sighs. The sharp spices of the heated pine-shingles over their heads and the fragrance of the clover-scented hay filled the close air around them. The sun was falling with the wind, but they heeded it not; until the usual fateful premonition struck the woman, and saying "I must go now," she only half-unconsciously precipitated the end. For, as she rose, he caught first her hand and then her waist, and attempted to raise the face that was suddenly bending down as if seeking to hide itself in the hay. It was a brief struggle, ending in a submission as sudden, and their lips met in a kiss, so eager that it might have been impending for days instead of minutes.

" Oh, Sue ! where are ye ? "

It was her husband's voice, out of a darkness that they only then realized. The man threw her aside with a roughness that momentarily shocked her above any sense of surprise or shame: *she* would have confronted her husband in his arms, — glorified and translated, — had he but kept her there. Yet she answered, with a quiet, level voice that astonished her lover, " Here ! I 'm just coming down ! " and walked coolly to the ladder. Looking over, and seeing her husband with the deputy standing in the barnyard, she quickly returned, put her finger to her lips, made a gesture for her companion to conceal himself in the hay again, and was turning away, when, perhaps shamed by her superior calmness, he grasped her hand tightly and whispered, " Come again tonight, dear ; do ! " She hesitated, raised her hand suddenly to her lips, and then quickly disengaging it, slipped down the ladder.

" Ye have n't done much work yet as I kin see," said Ira wearily. " Whitey and Red Tip [the cows] are hangin' over the corral, just waitin'."

" The yellow hen we reckoned was lost is

sittin' in the hayloft, and must n't be disturbed," said Mrs. Beasley, with decision;
" and ye 'll have to take the hay from the
stack to-night. And," with an arch glance
at the deputy, " as I don't see that you two
have done much either, you 're just in time
to help fodder down."

Setting the three men to work with the
same bright audacity, the task was soon completed — particularly as the deputy found no
opportunity for exclusive dalliance with Mrs.
Beasley. She shut the barn door herself,
and led the way to the house, learning inci-
dentally that the deputy had abandoned the
chase, was to occupy a " shake-down " on
the kitchen-floor that night with the constable, and depart at daybreak. The gloom
of her husband's face had settled into a look
of heavy resignation and alternate glances of
watchfulness, which only seemed to inspire
her with renewed vivacity. But the cooking
of supper withdrew her disturbing presence
for a time from the room, and gave him
some relief. When the meal was ready
he sought further surcease from trouble in
copious draughts of whiskey, which she produced from a new bottle, and even pressed

upon the deputy in mischievous contrition
for her previous inhospitality.

" Now I know that it was n't whiskey only
ye came for, I 'll show you that Sue Beasley
is no slouch of a barkeeper either," she
said.

Then, rolling her sleeves above her pretty
arms, she mixed a cocktail in such delightful
imitation of the fashionable barkeeper's dexterity that her guests were convulsed with
admiration. Even Ira was struck with this
revelation of a youthfulness that five years
of household care had checked, but never
yet subdued. He had forgotten that he
had married a child. Only once, when she
glanced at the cheap clock on the mantel,
had he noticed another change, more remarkable still from its very inconsistency
with her burst of youthful spirits. It was
another face that he saw, — older and ma-
tured with an intensity of abstraction that
struck a chill to his heart. It was not *his*
Sue that was standing there, but another
Sue, wrought, as it seemed to his morbid
extravagance, by some one else's hand.

Yet there was another interval of relief
when his wife, declaring she was tired, and

even jocosely confessing to some effect of
the liquor she had pretended to taste, went
early to bed. The deputy, not finding the
gloomy company of the husband to his taste,
presently ensconced himself on the floor, before the kitchen fire, in the blankets that
she had provided. The constable followed
his example. In a few moments the house
was silent and sleeping, save for Ira sitting
alone, with his head sunk on his chest and
his hands gripping the arms of his chair before the dying embers of his hearth.

He was trying, with the alternate quickness and inaction of an inexperienced intellect and an imagination morbidly awakened,
to grasp the situation before him. The
common sense that had hitherto governed
his life told him that the deputy would go
to-morrow, and that there was nothing in
his wife's conduct to show that her coquetry
and aberration would not pass as easily.
But it recurred to him that she had never
shown this coquetry or aberration to *him*
during their own brief courtship, — that she
had never looked or acted like this before.
If this was love, she had never known it;
if it was only " women's ways," as he had

heard men say, and so dangerously attractive, why had she not shown it to him? He remembered that matter-of-fact wedding, the bride without timidity, without blushes, without expectation beyond the transference of her home to his. Would it have been different with another man? — with the deputy, who had called this color and animation to her face? What did it all mean? Were all married people like this? There were the Westons, their neighbors, — was Mrs. Weston like Sue? But he remembered that Mrs. Weston had run away with Mr. Weston from her father's house. It was what they called "a love match." Would Sue have run away with him? Would she now run away with — ?

The candle was guttering as he rose with a fierce start — his first impulse of anger — from the table. He took another gulp of whiskey. It tasted like water; its fire was quenched in the greater heat of his blood. He would go to bed. Here a new and indefinable timidity took possession of him; he remembered the strange look in his wife's face. It seemed suddenly as if the influence of the sleeping stranger in the next room had not only isolated her from him, but would make his presence in her bedroom an intrusion on their hidden secrets. He had to pass the open door of the kitchen. The head of the unconscious deputy was close to Ira's heavy boot. He had only to lift his heel to crush that ruddy, good-looking, complacent face. He hurried past him, up the creaking stairs. His wife lay still on one side of the bed, apparently asleep, her face half-hidden in her loosened, fluffy hair. It was well; for in the vague shyness and restraint that was beginning to take possession of him he felt he could not have spoken to her, or, if he had, it would have been only to voice the horrible, unformulated things that seemed to choke him. He crept softly to the opposite side of the bed, and began to undress. As he pulled off his boots and stockings, his eye fell upon his bare, malformed feet. This caused him to look at his maimed hand, to rise, drag himself across the floor to the mirror, and gaze upon his lacerated ear. She, this prettily formed woman lying there, must have seen it often; she must have known all these years that he was not like other men, — not like the deputy, with his tight riding-boots, his soft hand, and the diamond that sparkled vulgarly on his fat little finger. A cold sweat broke over him. He drew on his stockings again, lifted the outer counterpane, and, half undressed, crept under it, wrapping its corner around his maimed hand, as if to hide it from the light. Yet he felt that he saw things dimly; there was a moisture on his cheeks and eyelids he could not account for; it must be the whiskey "coming out."

His wife lay very still; she scarcely seemed to breathe. What if she should never breathe again, but die as the old Sue he knew, the lanky girl he had married, unchanged and uncontaminated? It would be better than this. Yet at the same moment the picture was before him of her pretty simulation of the barkeeper, of her white bared arms and laughing eyes, all so new, so fresh to him! He tried to listen to the slow ticking of the clock, the occasional stirring of air through the house, and the movement, like a deep sigh, which was the regular, inarticulate speech of the lonely plain beyond, and quite distinct from the evening breeze. He had heard it often, but, like so many things he had learned that day, he never seemed to have caught its meaning before. Then, perhaps, it was his supine position, perhaps some cumulative effect of the whiskey he had taken, but all this presently became confused and whirling. Out of its gyrations he tried to grasp something, to hear voices that called him to " wake," and in the midst of it he fell into a profound sleep.

The clock ticked, the wind sighed, the woman at his side lay motionless for many minutes.

Then the deputy on the kitchen floor rolled over with an appalling snort, struggled, stretched himself, and awoke. A healthy animal, he had shaken off the fumes of liquor with a dry tongue and a thirst for water and fresh air. He raised his knees and rubbed his eyes. The water bucket was missing from the corner. Well, he knew where the spring was, and a turn out of the close and stifling kitchen would do him good. He yawned, put on his boots softly, opened the back door, and stepped out. Everything was dark, but above and around him, to the very level of his feet, all apparently pricked

with bright stars. The bulk of the barn
rose dimly before him on the right, to the
left was the spring. He reached it, drank,
dipped his head and hands in it, and arose
refreshed. The dry, wholesome breath that
blew over this flat disk around him, rimmed
with stars, did the rest. He began to saunter
slowly back, the only reminiscence of his
evening's potations being the figure he recalled of his pretty hostess, with bare arms
and lifted glasses, imitating the barkeeper.
A complacent smile straightened his yellow
mustache. How she kept glancing at him
and watching him, the little witch! Ha!
no wonder! What could she find in the
surly, slinking, stupid brute yonder? (The
gentleman here alluded to was his host.)
But the deputy had not been without a certain provincial success with the fair. He
was true to most men, and fearless to all.
One may not be too hard upon him at this
moment of his life.

For as he was passing the house he stopped
suddenly. Above the dry, dusty, herbal
odors of the plain, above the scent of the
new-mown hay within the barn, there was
distinctly another fragrance, — the smell of

a pipe. But where? Was it his host who
had risen to take the outer air? Then it
suddenly flashed upon him that Beasley did
not smoke, nor the constable either. The
smell seemed to come from the barn. Had
he followed out the train of ideas thus
awakened, all might have been well; but
at this moment his attention was arrested
by a far more exciting incident to him, —
the draped and hooded figure of Mrs. Beasley was just emerging from the house. He
halted instantly in the shadow, and held his
breath as she glided quickly across the in-
tervening space and disappeared in the half-
opened door of the barn. Did she know he
was there? A keen thrill passed over him;
his mouth broadened into a breathless smile.
It was his last! for, as he glided forward
to the door, the starry heavens broke into a
thousand brilliant fragments around him,
the earth gave way beneath his feet, and he
fell forward with half his skull shot away.

Where he fell there he lay without an outcry, with only one movement, — the curved
and grasping fingers of the fighter's hand
towards his guarded hip. Where he fell
there he lay dead, his face downwards, his

good right arm still curved around across
his back. Nothing of him moved but his
blood, - - broadening slowly round him in
vivid color, and then sluggishly thickening
and darkening until it stopped too, and sank
into the earth, a dull brown stain. For an
instant the stillness of death followed the
echoless report, then there was a quick and
feverish rustling within the barn, the hurried
opening of a window in the loft, scurrying
footsteps, another interval of silence, and
then out of the farther darkness the sounds
of horse-hoofs in the muffled dust of the
road. But not a sound or movement in the
sleeping house beyond.

The stars at last paled slowly, the horizon
lines came back, — a thin streak of opal
fire. A solitary bird twittered in the bush
beside the spring. Then the back door of
the house opened, and the constable came
forth, half - awakened and apologetic, and
with the bewildered haste of a belated man.
His eyes were level, looking for his missing
leader as he went on, until at last he stumbled and fell over the now cold and rigid
body. He scrambled to his feet again, cast

a hurried glance around him, — at the half-opened door of the barn, at the floor littered with trampled hay. In one corner lay the ragged blouse and trousers of the fugitive, which the constable instantly recognized. He went back to the house, and reappeared in a few moments with Ira, white, stupefied, and hopelessly bewildered; clear only in his statement that his wife had just fainted at the news of the catastrophe, and was equally helpless in her own room. The constable — a man of narrow ideas but quick action — saw it all. The mystery was plain without further evidence. The deputy had been awakened by the prowling of the fugitive around the house in search of a horse. Sallying out, they had met, and Ira's gun, which stood in the kitchen, and which the deputy had seized, had been wrested from him and used with fatal effect at arm's length, and the now double assassin had escaped on the sheriff's horse, which was missing. Turning the body over to the trembling Ira, he saddled his horse and galloped to Lowville for assistance.

These facts were fully established at the hurried inquest which met that day. There

was no need to go behind the evidence of
the constable, the only companion of the
murdered man and first discoverer of the
body. The fact that he, on the ground
floor, had slept through the struggle and the
report, made the obliviousness of the couple
in the room above a rational sequence. The
dazed Ira was set aside, after half a dozen
contemptuous questions; the chivalry of a
Californian jury excused the attendance of
a frightened and hysterical woman confined
to her room. By noon they had departed
with the body, and the long afternoon shadows settled over the lonely plain and silent
house. At nightfall Ira appeared at the
door, and stood for some moments scanning
the plain; he was seen later by two packers,
who had glanced furtively at the scene of
the late tragedy, sitting outside his doorway,
a mere shadow in the darkness; and a mounted
patrol later in the night saw a light in the
bedroom window where the invalid Mrs.
Beasley was confined. But no one saw her
afterwards. Later, Ira explained that she
had gone to visit a relative until her health
was restored. Having few friends and fewer
neighbors, she was not missed; and even

the constable, the sole surviving guest who had enjoyed her brief eminence of archness and beauty that fatal night, had quite forgotten her in his vengeful quest of the murderer. So that people became accustomed to see this lonely man working in the fields by day, or at nightfall gazing fixedly from his doorway. At the end of three months he was known as the recluse or "hermit" of Bolinas Plain; in the rapid history-making of that epoch it was forgotten that he had ever been anything else.

But Justice, which in those days was apt to nod over the affairs of the average citizen, was keenly awake to offenses against its own officers; and it chanced that the constable, one day walking through the streets of Marysville, recognized the murderer and apprehended him. He was removed to Lowville. Here, probably through some modest doubt of the ability of the County Court, which the constable represented, to deal with purely circumstantial evidence, he was not above dropping a hint to the local Vigilance Committee, who, singularly enough, in spite of his resistance, got possession of the prisoner. It was the rainy season, and business was slack ; the citizens of Lowville were thus enabled to give so notorious a case their fullest consideration, and to assist cheerfully at the ultimate hanging of the prisoner, which seemed to be a foregone conclusion.

But herein they were mistaken. For when the constable had given his evidence, already known to the county, there was a disturbance in the fringe of humanity that lined the walls of the assembly room where the committee was sitting, and the hermit of Bolinas Plain limped painfully into the room. He had evidently walked there : he was soaked with rain and plastered with mud ; he was exhausted and inarticulate. But as he staggered to the witness-bench, and elbowed the constable aside, he arrested the attention of every one. A few laughed, but were promptly silenced by the court. It was a reflection upon its only virtue, — sincerity.

" Do you know the prisoner ? " asked the judge.

Ira Beasley glanced at the pale face of the acrobat, and shook his head.

" Never saw him before," he said faintly.

" Then what are you doing here ? " demanded the judge sternly.

Ira collected himself with evident effort, and rose to his halting feet. First he moistened his dry lips, then he said, slowly and distinctly, " Because *I* killed the deputy of Bolinas."

With the thrill which ran through the crowded room, and the relief that seemed to come upon him with that utterance, he gained strength and even a certain dignity.

" I killed him," he went on, turning his head slowly around the circle of eager auditors with the rigidity of a wax figure, " because he made love to my wife. I killed him because he wanted to run away with her. I killed him because I found him waiting for her at the door of the barn at the dead o' night, when she 'd got outer bed to jine him. He had n't no gun. He had n't no fight. I killed him in his tracks. That man," pointing to the prisoner, " was n't in it at all." He stopped, loosened his collar, and, baring his rugged throat below his disfigured ear, said : " Now take me out and hang me ! "

" What proof have we of this ? Where 's your wife ? Does she corroborate it ? "

A slight tremor ran over him.

"She ran away that night, and never came back again. Perhaps," he added slowly, "because she loved him and could n't bear me ; perhaps, as I 've sometimes allowed to myself, gentlemen, it was because she did n't want to bear evidence agin me."

In the silence that followed the prisoner was heard speaking to one that was near him. Then he rose. All the audacity and confidence that the husband had lacked were in *his* voice. Nay, there was even a certain chivalry in his manner which, for the moment, the rascal really believed.

"It 's true !" he said. "After I stole the horse to get away, I found that woman running wild down the road, cryin' and sobbin'. At first I thought she 'd done the shooting. It was a risky thing for me to do, gentlemen ; but I took her up on the horse and got her away to Lowville. It was that much dead weight agin my chances, but I took it. She was a woman and — I ain't a dog ! "

He was so exalted and sublimated by his fiction that for the first time the jury was impressed in his favor. And when Ira Beasley limped across the room, and, extending his maimed hand to the prisoner, said, "Shake!" there was another dead silence.

It was broken by the voice of the judge addressing the constable.

"What do you know of the deputy's attentions to Mrs. Beasley? Were they enough to justify the husband's jealousy? Did he make love to her?"

The constable hesitated. He was a narrow man, with a crude sense of the principles rather than the methods of justice. He remembered the deputy's admiration; he now remembered, even more strongly, the object of that admiration, simulating with her pretty arms the gestures of the barkeeper, and the delight it gave them. He was loyal to his dead leader, but he looked up and down, and then said, slowly and half-defiantly : "Well, judge, he was a *man.*"

Everybody laughed. That the strongest and most magic of all human passions should always awake levity in any public presentment of or allusion to it was one of the inconsistencies of human nature which even a lynch judge had to admit. He made no attempt to control the tittering of the court, for he felt that the element of tragedy was no longer there. The foreman of the jury arose and whispered to the judge amid another silence. Then the judge spoke : —

"The prisoner and his witness are both discharged. The prisoner to leave the town within twenty-four hours ; the witness to be conducted to his own house at the expense of, and with the thanks of, the Committee."

They say that one afternoon, when a low mist of rain had settled over the sodden Bolinas Plain, a haggard, bedraggled, and worn-out woman stepped down from a common "freighting wagon" before the doorway where Beasley still sat ; that, coming forward, he caught her in his arms and called her "Sue ; " and they say that they lived happily together ever afterwards. But they say — and this requires some corroboration — that much of that happiness was due to Mrs. Beasley's keeping forever in her husband's mind her own heroic sacrifice in disappearing as a witness against him, her own forgiveness of his fruitless crime, and the gratitude he owed to the fugitive.

THE STRANGE EXPERIENCE OF
ALKALI DICK

HE was a "cowboy." A reckless and
dashing rider, yet mindful of his horse's
needs; good-humored by nature, but quick
in quarrel independent of circumstance,
yet shy and sensitive of opinion; abstemi-
ous by education and general habit, yet in-
temperate in amusement; self-centred, yet
possessed of a childish vanity, — taken altogether, a characteristic product of the Western plains, which he never should have left.

But reckless adventure after adventure
had brought him into difficulties, from which
there was only one equally adventurous escape: he joined a company of Indians engaged by Buffalo Bill to simulate before
civilized communities the sports and customs of the uncivilized. In divers Christian
arenas of the nineteenth century he rode as
a northern barbarian of the first might have
disported before the Roman populace, but

harmlessly, of his own free will, and of some
little profit to himself. He threw his lasso
under the curious eyes of languid men and
women of the world, eager for some new
sensation, with admiring plaudits from them
and a half contemptuous egotism of his
own. But outside of the arena he was
lonely, lost, and impatient for excitement.

An ingenious attempt to " paint the town
red " did not commend itself as a spectacle
to the householders who lived in the vicinity
of Earl's Court, London, and Alkali Dick
was haled before a respectable magistrate
by a serious policeman, and fined as if he
had been only a drunken coster. A later
attempt at Paris to " incarnadine " the
neighborhood of the Champs de Mars, and
" round up " a number of boulevardiers,
met with a more disastrous result, — the
gleam of steel from mounted gendarmes,
and a mandate to his employers.

So it came that one night, after the conclusion of the performance, Alkali Dick
rode out of the corral gate of the Hippo-
drome with his last week's salary in his
pocket and an imprecation on his lips. He
had shaken the sawdust of the sham arena

from his high, tight-fitting boots ; he would shake off the white dust of France, and the effeminate soil of all Europe also, and embark at once for his own country and the Far West!

A more practical and experienced man would have sold his horse at the nearest market and taken train to Havre, but Alkali Dick felt himself incomplete on *terra firma* without his mustang, — it would be hard enough to part from it on embarking, — and he had determined to ride to the seaport.

The spectacle of a lithe horseman, clad in a Rembrandt sombrero, velvet jacket, turnover collar, almost Van Dyke in its proportions, white trousers and high boots, with long curling hair falling over his shoulders, and a pointed beard and mustache, was a picturesque one, but still not a novelty to the late-supping Parisians who looked up under the midnight gas as he passed, and only recognized one of those men whom Paris had agreed to designate as " Booflo-bils," going home.

At three o'clock he pulled up at a wayside cabaret, preferring it to the publicity of a larger hotel, and lay there till morning.

The slight consternation of the cabaret-keeper and his wife over this long-haired phantom, with glittering, deep-set eyes, was soothed by a royally-flung gold coin, and a few words of French slang picked up in the arena, which, with the name of Havre, comprised Dick's whole knowledge of the language. But he was touched with their ready and intelligent comprehension of his needs, and their genial if not so comprehensive loquacity. Luckily for his quick temper, he did not know that they had taken him for a traveling quack-doctor going to the Fair of Yvetot, and that madame had been on the point of asking him for a magic balsam to prevent migraine.

He was up betimes and away, giving a wide berth to the larger towns; taking by-ways and cut-offs, yet always with the Western pathfinder's instinct, even among these alien, poplar-haunted plains, low-banked willow-fringed rivers, and cloverless meadows. The white sun shining everywhere, — on dazzling arbors, summer - houses, and trellises ; on light green vines and delicate pea-rows; on the white trousers, jackets, and shoes of smart shopkeepers or holiday mak-

ers; on the white headdresses of nurses and
the white-winged caps of the Sisters of St.
Vincent, — all this grew monotonous to this
native of still more monotonous wastes. The
long, black shadows of short, blue-skirted,
sabotted women and short, blue-bloused, sabotted men slowly working in the fields, with
slow oxen, or still slower heavy Norman
horses; the same horses gayly bedecked,
dragging slowly not only heavy wagons, but
their own apparently more monstrous weight
over the white road, fretted his nervous
Western energy, and made him impatient to
get on.

At the close of the second day he found
some relief on entering a trackless wood, —
not the usual formal avenue of equidistant
trees, leading to nowhere, and stopping upon
the open field, — but apparently a genuine
forest as wild as one of his own " oak bot-
toms." Gnarled roots and twisted branches
flung themselves across his path; his mustang's hoofs sank in deep pits of moss and
last year's withered leaves; trailing vines
caught his heavy-stirruped feet, or brushed
his broad sombrero; the vista before him
seemed only to endlessly repeat the same

sylvan glade ; he was in fancy once more
in the primeval Western forest, and encompassed by its vast, dim silences. He did not
know that he had in fact only penetrated
an ancient park which in former days re-
sounded to the winding fanfare of the chase,
and was still, on stated occasions, swept over
by accurately green-coated Parisians and
green - plumed Dianes, who had come down
by train ! To him it meant only unfettered
and unlimited freedom.

He rose in his stirrups, and sent a characteristic yell ringing down the dim aisles
before him. But, alas ! at the same moment, his mustang, accustomed to the firmer
grip of the prairie, in lashing out, stepped
upon a slimy root, and fell heavily, rolling
over his clinging and still unlodged rider.
For a few moments both lay still. Then
Dick extricated himself with an oath, rose gid-
dily, dragged up his horse, — who, after the
fashion of his race, was meekly succumbing
to his reclining position, — and then became
aware that the unfortunate beast was badly
sprained in the shoulder, and temporarily
lame. The sudden recollection that he was
some miles from the road, and that the sun

was sinking, concentrated his scattered faculties. The prospect of sleeping out in that summer woodland was nothing to the pioneer-bred Dick; he could make his horse and himself comfortable anywhere — but he was delaying his arrival at Havre. He must regain the high road, — or some wayside inn. He glanced around him; the westering sun was a guide for his general direction; the road must follow it north or south; he would find a " clearing " somewhere. But here Dick was mistaken; there seemed no interruption of, no encroachment upon this sylvan tract, as in his western woods. There was no track or trail to be found; he missed even the ordinary woodland signs that denoted the path of animals to water. For the park, from the time a Northern Duke had first alienated it from the virgin forest, had been rigidly preserved.

Suddenly, rising apparently from the ground before him, he saw the high roof-ridges and *tourelles* of a long, irregular, gloomy building. A few steps further showed him that it lay in a cup-like depression of the forest, and that it was still a long descent from where he had wandered to where

it stood in the gathering darkness. His mustang was moving with great difficulty; he
uncoiled his lariat from the saddle-horn,
and, selecting the most open space, tied one
end to the trunk of a large tree, — the forty
feet of horsehair rope giving the animal a
sufficient degree of grazing freedom.

Then he strode more quickly down the
forest side towards the building, which now
revealed its austere proportions, though Dick
could see that they were mitigated by a
strange, formal flower-garden, with quaint
statues and fountains. There were grim
black allées of clipped trees, a curiously
wrought iron gate, and twisted iron espa-
liers. On one side the edifice was supported
by a great stone terrace, which seemed to
him as broad as a Parisian boulevard. Yet
everywhere it appeared sleeping in the de-
sertion and silence of the summer twilight.
The evening breeze swayed the lace curtains
at the tall windows, but nothing else moved.
To the unsophisticated Western man it
looked like a scene on the stage.

His progress was, however, presently
checked by the first sight of preservation he
had met in the forest, — a thick hedge, which

interfered between him and a sloping lawn beyond. It was up to his waist, yet he began to break his way through it, when suddenly he was arrested by the sound of voices. Before him, on the lawn, a man and woman, evidently servants, were slowly advancing, peering into the shadows of the wood which he had just left. He could not understand what they were saying, but he was about to speak and indicate by signs his desire to find the road when the woman, turning towards her companion, caught sight of his face and shoulders above the hedge. To his surprise and consternation, he saw the color drop out of her fresh cheeks, her round eyes fix in their sockets, and with a despairing shriek she turned and fled towards the house. The man turned at his companion's cry, gave the same horrified glance at Dick's face, uttered a hoarse " Sacré ! " crossed himself violently, and fled also.

Amazed, indignant, and for the first time in his life humiliated, Dick gazed speechlessly after them. The man, of course, was a sneaking coward; but the woman was rather pretty. It had not been Dick's experience to have women run *from* him ! Should he

follow them, knock the silly fellow's head
against a tree, and demand an explanation ?
Alas, he knew not the language! They had
already reached the house and disappeared
in one of the offices. Well! let them go —
for a mean " low down " pair of country bump-
kins! — *he* wanted no favors from them!

He turned back angrily into the forest
to seek his unlucky beast. The gurgle of
water fell on his ear ; hard by was a spring,
where at least he could water the mustang.
He stooped to examine it ; there was yet
light enough in the sunset sky to throw back
from that little mirror the reflection of his
thin, oval face, his long, curling hair, and
his pointed beard and mustache. Yes! this
was his face, — the face that many women
in Paris had agreed was romantic and picturesque. Had those wretched greenhorns
never seen a real man before ? Were they
idiots, or insane ? A sudden recollection of
the silence and seclusion of the building suggested certainly an asylum, — but where were
the keepers ?

It was getting darker in the wood ; he
made haste to recover his horse, to drag it
to the spring, and there bathe its shoulder

in the water mixed with whiskey taken from his flask. His saddle-bag contained enough bread and meat for his own supper; he would camp for the night where he was, and with the first light of dawn make his way back through the wood whence he came. As the light slowly faded from the wood he rolled himself in his saddle-blanket and lay down.

But not to sleep. His strange position, the accident to his horse, an unusual irritation over the incident of the frightened servants, — trivial as it might have been to any other man, — and, above all, an increasing childish curiosity, kept him awake and restless. Presently he could see also that it was growing lighter beyond the edge of the wood, and that the rays of a young crescent moon, while it plunged the forest into darkness and impassable shadow, evidently was illuminating the hollow below. He threw aside his blanket, and made his way to the hedge again. He was right; he could see the quaint, formal lines of the old garden more distinctly, — the broad terrace, the queer, dark bulk of the house, with lights now gleaming from a few of its open windows.

Before one of these windows opening on

the terrace was a small, white, draped table
with fruits, cups, and glasses, and two or
three chairs. As he gazed curiously at these
new signs of life and occupation, he became
aware of a regular and monotonous tap upon
the stone flags of the terrace. Suddenly he
saw three figures slowly turn the corner of
the terrace at the further end of the building, and walk towards the table. The cen-
tral figure was that of an elderly woman, yet
tall and stately of carriage, walking with a
stick, whose regular tap he had heard, supported on the one side by an elderly curé
in black *soutaine*, and on the other by a tall
and slender girl in white.

They walked leisurely to the other end of
the terrace, as if performing a regular exercise, and returned, stopping before the
open French window ; where, after remaining in conversation a few moments, the
elderly lady and her ecclesiastical companion
entered. The young girl sauntered slowly
to the steps of the terrace, and leaning against
a huge vase as she looked over the garden,
seemed lost in contemplation. Her face was
turned towards the wood, but in quite another direction from where he stood.

There was something so gentle, refined, and graceful in her figure, yet dominated by a girlish youthfulness of movement and gesture, that Alkali Dick was singularly interested. He had probably never seen an ingénue before; he had certainly never come in contact with a girl of that caste and seclusion in his brief Parisian experience. He was sorely tempted to leave his hedge and try to obtain a nearer view of her. There was a fringe of lilac bushes running from the garden up the slope; if he could gain their shadows, he could descend into the garden. What he should do after his arrival he had not thought; but he had one idea — he knew not why — that if he ventured to speak to her he would not be met with the abrupt rustic terror he had experienced at the hands of the servants. *She* was not of that kind! He crept through the hedge, reached the lilacs, and began the descent softly and securely in the shadow. But at the same moment she arose, called in a youthful voice towards the open window, and began to descend the steps. A half-expostulating reply came from the window, but the young girl answered it with the

laughing, capricious confidence of a spoiled
child, and continued her way into the garden.
Here she paused a moment and hung over
a rose - tree, from which she gathered a
flower, afterwards thrust into her belt. Dick
paused, too, half-crouching, half-leaning over
a lichen-stained, cracked stone pedestal from
which the statue had long been overthrown
and forgotten.

To his surprise, however, the young girl,
following the path to the lilacs, began leisurely to ascend the hill, swaying from side
to side with a youthful movement, and swing-
ing the long stalk of a lily at her side. In
another moment he would be discovered!
Dick was frightened; his confidence of the
moment before had all gone; he would fly,
— and yet, an exquisite and fearful joy kept
him motionless. She was approaching him,
full and clear in the moonlight. He could
see the grace of her delicate figure in the
simple white frock drawn at the waist with
broad satin ribbon, and its love-knots of pale
blue ribbons on her shoulders; he could see
the coils of her brown hair, the pale, olive
tint of her oval cheek, the delicate, swelling
nostril of her straight, clear-cut nose; he

could even smell the lily she carried in her
little hand. Then, suddenly, she lifted her
long lashes, and her large gray eyes met his.

Alas! the same look of vacant horror
came into her eyes, and fixed and dilated
their clear pupils. But she uttered no outcry, — there was something in her blood that
checked it; something that even gave a
dignity to her recoiling figure, and made
Dick flush with admiration. She put her
hand to her side, as if the shock of the ex-
ertion of her ascent had set her heart to
beating, but she did not faint. Then her
fixed look gave way to one of infinite sadness, pity, and pathetic appeal. Her lips
were parted; they seemed to be moving, apparently in prayer. At last her voice came,
wonderingly, timidly, tenderly: " Mon Dieu!
c'est donc vous? Ici? C'est vous que Ma-
rie a crue voir! Que venez-vous faire ici,
Armand de Fontonelles? Répondez!"

Alas, not a word was comprehensible to
Dick; nor could he think of a word to say in
reply. He made an uncouth, half-irritated,
half-despairing gesture towards the wood he
had quitted, as if to indicate his helpless
horse, but he knew it was meaningless to the

frightened yet exalted girl before him. Her little hand crept to her breast and clutched a rosary within the folds of her dress, as her soft voice again arose, low but appealingly :

" Vous souffrez ! Ah, mon Dieu ! Peut-on vous secourir ? Moi-même — mes prières pourraient elles intercéder pour vous? Je supplierai le ciel de prendre en pitié l'âme de mon ancêtre. Monsieur le curé est là, — je lui parlerai. Lui et ma mère vous viendront en aide."

She clasped her hands appealingly before him.

Dick stood bewildered, hopeless, mystified ; he had not understood a word ; he could not say a word. For an instant he had a wild idea of seizing her hand and leading her to his helpless horse, and then came what he believed was his salvation, — a sudden flash of recollection that he had seen the word he wanted, the one word that would explain all, in a placarded notice at the Cirque of a bracelet that had been *lost*, — yes, the single word " *perdu.*" He made a step towards her, and in a voice almost as faint as her own, stammered, " *Perdu !* "

With a little cry, that was more like a sigh

than an outcry, the girl's arms fell to her side; she took a step backwards, reeled, and fainted away.

Dick caught her as she fell. What had he said! — but, more than all, what should he do now? He could not leave her alone and helpless, — yet how could he justify another disconcerting intrusion? He touched her hands; they were cold and lifeless; her eyes were half closed; her face as pale and drooping as her lily. Well, he must brave the worst now, and carry her to the house, even at the risk of meeting the others and terrifying them as he had her. He caught her up, — he scarcely felt her weight against his breast and shoulder, — and ran hurriedly down the slope to the terrace, which was still deserted. If he had time to place her on some bench beside the window within their reach, he might still fly undiscovered! But as he panted up the steps of the terrace with his burden, he saw that the French window was still open, but the light seemed to have been extinguished. It would be safer for her if he could place her *inside* the house, — if he but dared to enter. He was desperate, — and he dared!

He found himself alone, in a long salon
of rich but faded white and gold hangings,
lit at the further end by two tall candles on
either side of the high marble mantel, whose
rays, however, scarcely reached the window
where he had entered. He laid his burden
on a high-backed sofa. In so doing, the rose
fell from her belt. He picked it up, put it
in his breast, and turned to go. But he was
arrested by a voice from the terrace : —

" Renèe ! "

It was the voice of the elderly lady, who,
with the curé at her side, had just appeared
from the rear of the house, and from the
further end of the terrace was looking towards the garden in search of the young
girl. His escape in that way was cut off.
To add to his dismay, the young girl, perhaps roused by her mother's voice, was beginning to show signs of recovering consciousness. Dick looked quickly around him.
There was an open door, opposite the window, leading to a hall which, no doubt,
offered some exit on the other side of the
house. It was his only remaining chance !
He darted through it, closed it behind him,
and found himself at the end of a long

hall or picture-gallery, strangely illuminated through high windows, reaching nearly to the roof, by the moon, which on that side of the building threw nearly level bars of light and shadows across the floor and the quaint portraits on the wall.

But to his delight he could see at the other end a narrow, lance-shaped open postern door showing the moonlit pavement without — evidently the door through which the mother and the curé had just passed out. He ran rapidly towards it. As he did so he heard the hurried ringing of bells and voices in the room he had quitted — the young girl had evidently been discovered — and this would give him time. He had nearly reached the door, when he stopped suddenly — his blood chilled with awe! It was his turn to be terrified — he was standing, apparently, before *himself!*

His first recovering thought was that it was a mirror — so accurately was every line and detail of his face and figure reflected. But a second scrutiny showed some discrepancies of costume, and he saw it was a panelled portrait on the wall. It was of a man of his own age, height, beard, complexion, and fea-

tures, with long curls like his own, falling
over a lace Van Dyke collar, which, however,
again simulated the appearance of his own
hunting-shirt. The broad-brimmed hat in
the picture, whose drooping plume was lost
in shadow, was scarcely different from Dick's
sombrero. But the likeness of the face to
Dick was marvelous — convincing! As he
gazed at it, the wicked black eyes seemed to
flash and kindle at his own, — its lip curled
with Dick's own sardonic humor!

He was recalled to himself by a step in
the gallery. It was the curé who had entered
hastily, evidently in search of one of the
servants. Partly because it was a man and
not a woman, partly from a feeling of bravado — and partly from a strange sense,
excited by the picture, that he had some
claim to be there, he turned and faced the
pale priest with a slight dash of impatient
devilry that would have done credit to the
portrait. But he was sorry for it the next
moment!

The priest, looking up suddenly, discovered what seemed to him to be the portrait
standing before its own frame and glaring
at him. Throwing up his hands with an

averted head and an "*Exorcis*—*!*" he
wheeled and scuffled away. Dick seized the
opportunity, darted through the narrow door
on to the rear terrace, and ran, under cover
of the shadow of the house, to the steps into
the garden. Luckily for him, this new and
unexpected diversion occupied the inmates
too much with what was going on in the
house to give them time to search outside.
Dick reached the lilac hedge, tore up the
hill, and in a few moments threw himself,
panting, on his blanket. In the single look
he had cast behind, he had seen that the
half-dark salon was now brilliantly lighted
— where no doubt the whole terrified household was now assembled. He had no fear
of being followed ; since his confrontation
with his own likeness in the mysterious portrait, he understood everything. The apparently supernatural character of his visitation
was made plain ; his ruffled vanity was
soothed — his vindication was complete. He
laughed to himself and rolled about, until in
his suppressed merriment the rose fell from
his bosom, and — he stopped! Its freshness and fragrance recalled the innocent
young girl he had frightened. He remem-

bered her gentle, pleading voice, and his
cheek flushed. Well, he had done the best
he could in bringing her back to the house —
at the risk of being taken for a burglar —
and she was safe now ! If that stupid French
parson did n't know the difference between a
living man and a dead and painted one, it
was n't his fault. But he fell asleep with
the rose in his fingers.

He was awake at the first streak of dawn.
He again bathed his horse's shoulder, saddled, but did not mount him, as the beast,
although better, was still stiff, and Dick
wished to spare him for the journey to still
distant Havre, although he had determined
to lie over that night at the first wayside
inn. Luckily for him, the disturbance at
the château had not extended to the forest,
for Dick had to lead his horse slowly and
could not have escaped; but no suspicion
of external intrusion seemed to have been
awakened, and the woodland was, evidently,
seldom invaded.

By dint of laying his course by the sun
and the exercise of a little woodcraft, in the
course of two hours he heard the creaking
of a hay-cart, and knew that he was near a

traveled road. But to his discomfiture he
presently came to a high wall, which had
evidently guarded this portion of the woods
from the public. Time, however, had made
frequent breaches in the stones ; these had
been roughly filled in with a rude *abatis* of
logs and treetops pointing towards the road.
But as these were mainly designed to prevent intrusion into the park rather than
egress from it, Dick had no difficulty in
rolling them aside and emerging at last with
his limping steed upon the white high-road.
The creaking cart had passed ; it was yet
early for traffic, and Dick presently came
upon a wine-shop, a bakery, a blacksmith's
shop, laundry, and a somewhat pretentious
café and hotel in a broader space which
marked the junction of another road.

Directly before it, however, to his consternation, were the massive, but timeworn,
iron gates of a park, which Dick did not
doubt was the one in which he had spent
the previous night. But it was impossible
to go further in his present plight, and he
boldly approached the restaurant. As he
was preparing to make his usual explana-
tory signs, to his great delight he was ad-

dressed in a quaint, broken English, mixed
with forgotten American slang, by the white-
trousered, black-alpaca coated proprietor.
More than that — he was a Social Democrat
and an enthusiastic lover of America — had
he not been to "Bos-town" and New York,
and penetrated as far west as "Booflo,"
and had much pleasure in that beautiful and
free country? Yes! it was a "go-a-'ed"
country — you "bet-your-lif'." One had
reason to say so: there was your electricity
— your street cars — your "steambots" —
ah! such steambots — and your "r-rail-
r-roads." Ah! observe! compare your r-rail-
r-roads and the buffet of the Pullman with
the line from Paris, for example — and
where is one? Nowhere! Actually, positively, without doubt, nowhere!

Later, at an appetizing breakfast — at
which, to Dick's great satisfaction, the good
man had permitted and congratulated himself to sit at table with a free-born American
— he was even more loquacious. For what
then, he would ask, was this incompetence,
this imbecility, of France? He would tell.
It was the vile corruption of Paris, the grasping of capital and companies, the fatal in-

fluence of the still clinging noblesse, and
the insidious Jesuitical power of the priests.
As for example, Monsieur " the Booflo-bil "
had doubtless noticed the great gates of the
park before the café ?   It was the preserve,
— the hunting-park of one of the old grand
seigneurs, still kept up by his descendants,
the Comtes de Fontonelles — hundreds of
acres that had never been tilled, and kept
as wild waste wilderness, — kept for a day's
pleasure in a year !   And, look you ! the
peasants starving around its walls in their
small garden patches and pinched farms !
And the present Comte de Fontonelles cas-
cading gold on his mistresses in Paris ; and
the Comtesse, his mother, and her daughter
living there to feed and fatten and pension
a brood of plotting, black-cowled priests. Ah,
bah ! where was your Republican France,
then ?   But a time would come.   The " Booflo-bil " had, without doubt, noticed, as he
came along the road, the breaches in the
wall of the park ?

Dick, with a slight dry reserve, " reckoned
that he had."

" They were made by the scythes and
pitchforks of the peasants in the Revolution

of '93, when the count was *emigré*, as one
says with reason ' skedadelle,' to England.
Let them look the next time that they burn
not the château, — ' bet your lif' ! ' "

" The château," said Dick, with affected
carelessness. " Wot 's the blamed thing
like ? "

It was an old affair, — with armor and a
picture-gallery, — and bricabrac. He had
never seen it. Not even as a boy, — it was
kept very secluded then. As a man — you
understand — he could not ask the favor.
The Comtes de Fontonelles and himself were
not friends. The family did not like a café
near their sacred gates, — where had stood
only the huts of their retainers. The American would observe that he had not called it
"*Café de Château*," nor "*Café de Fontonelles*," — the gold of California would not
induce him. Why did he remain there ?
Naturally, to goad them ! It was a prin-
ciple, one understood. To *goad* them and
hold them in 'check ! One kept a café, —
why not ? One had one's principles, — one's
conviction, — that was another thing ! That
was the kind of " 'air-pin " — was it not ? —
that *he*, Gustav Ribaud, was like !

Yet for all his truculent socialism, he was quick, obliging, and charmingly attentive to Dick and his needs. As to Dick's horse, he should have the best veterinary surgeon — there was an incomparable one in the person of the blacksmith — see to him, and if it were an affair of days, and Dick must go, he himself would be glad to purchase the beast, his saddle, and accoutrements. It was an affair of business, — an advertisement for the café! He would ride the horse himself before the gates of the park. It would please his customers. Ha! he had learned a trick or two in free America.

Dick's first act had been to shave off his characteristic beard and mustache, and even to submit his long curls to the village barber's shears, while a straw hat, which he bought to take the place of his slouched sombrero, completed his transformation. His host saw in the change only the natural preparation of a voyager, but Dick had really made the sacrifice, not from fear of detection, for he had recovered his old swaggering audacity, but from a quick distaste he had taken to his resemblance to the portrait. He was too genuine a Westerner,

and too vain a man, to feel flattered at his
resemblance to an aristocratic bully, as he
believed the ancestral De Fontonelles to be.
Even his momentary sensation as he faced
the curé in the picture-gallery was more
from a vague sense that liberties had been
taken with his, Dick's, personality, than
that he had borrowed anything from the
portrait.

But he was not so clear about the young
girl. Her tender, appealing voice, although
he knew it had been addressed only to a vision, still thrilled his fancy. The pluck that
had made her withstand her fear so long —
until he had uttered that dreadful word —
still excited his admiration. His curiosity
to know what mistake he had made — for
he knew it must have been some frightful
blunder — was all the more keen, as he had
no chance to rectify it. What a brute she
must have thought him — or *did* she really
think him a brute even then ? — for her look
was one more of despair and pity ! Yet she
would remember him only by that last word,
and never know that he had risked insult
and ejection from her friends to carry her to
her place of safety. He could not bear to go

across the seas carrying the pale, unsatisfied
face of that gentle girl ever before his eyes!
A sense of delicacy — new to Dick, but always the accompaniment of deep feeling —
kept him from even hinting his story to his
host, though he knew — perhaps *because* he
knew — that it would gratify his enmity to
the family. A sudden thought struck Dick.
He knew her house, and her name. He
would write her a note. Somebody would
be sure to translate it for her.

He borrowed pen, ink, and paper, and in
the clean solitude of his fresh chintz bedroom, indited the following letter: —

Dear Miss Fontonelles, — Please excuse me for having skeert you. I had n't
any call to do it; I never reckoned to do it
— it was all jest my derned luck; I only
reckoned to tell you I was lost — in them
blamed woods — don't you remember? —
" lost " — *perdoo!* — and then you up and
fainted! I would n't have come into your
garden, only, you see, I 'd just skeered by
accident two of your helps, reg'lar softies,
and I wanted to explain. I reckon they
allowed I was that man that that picture

in the hall was painted after. I reckon
they took *me* for him — see? But he ain't
my style, nohow, and I never saw the picture at all until after I'd toted you, when
you fainted, up to your house, or I'd have
made my kalkilations and acted according.
I'd have laid low in the woods, and got away
without skeerin' you. You see what I mean?
It was mighty mean of me, I suppose, to
have tetched you at all, without saying, "Excuse me, miss," and toted you out of the
garden and up the steps into your own par-
lor without asking your leave. But the
whole thing tumbled so suddent. And it
didn't seem the square thing for me to lite
out and leave you lying there on the grass.
That's why! I'm sorry I skeert that old
preacher, but he came upon me in the picture hall so suddent, that it was a mighty
close call, I tell you, to get off without a
shindy. Please forgive me, Miss Fontonelles.
When you get this, I shall be going back
home to America, but you might write to
me at Denver City, saying you're all right.
I liked your style; I liked your grit in
standing up to me in the garden until you
had your say, when you thought I was the

Lord knows what — though I never understood a word you got off — not knowing French. But it's all the same now. Say! I've got your rose!

Yours very respectfully,
RICHARD FOUNTAINS.

Dick folded the epistle and put it in his pocket. He would post it himself on the morning before he left. When he came downstairs he found his indefatigable host awaiting him, with the report of the veterinary blacksmith. There was nothing seriously wrong with the mustang, but it would be unfit to travel for several days. The landlord repeated his former offer. Dick, whose money was pretty well exhausted, was fain to accept, reflecting that *she* had never seen the mustang and would not recognize it. But he drew the line at the sombrero, to which his host had taken a great fancy. He had worn it before *her!*

Later in the evening Dick was sitting on the low veranda of the café, overlooking the white road. A round white table was beside him, his feet were on the railing, but his eyes were resting beyond on the high,

mouldy iron gates of the mysterious park.
What he was thinking of did not matter,
but he was a little impatient at the sudden
appearance of his host — whom he had
evaded during the afternoon — at his side.
The man's manner was full of bursting loquacity and mysterious levity.

Truly, it was a good hour when Dick had
arrived at Fontonelles, — "just in time."
He could see now what a world of imbeciles
was France. What stupid ignorance ruled,
what low cunning and low tact could achieve,
— in effect, what jugglers and mountebanks,
hypocritical priests and licentious and lying
noblesse went to make up existing society.
Ah, there had been a fine excitement, a
regular coup d'théâtre at Fontonelles, — the
château yonder ; here at the village, where
the news was brought by frightened grooms
and silly women ! He had been in the thick
of it all the afternoon ! He had examined
it, — interrogated them like a juge d'instruc-
tion, — winnowed it, sifted it. And what
was it all ? An attempt by these wretched
priests and noblesse to revive in the nineteenth century — the age of electricity and
Pullman cars — a miserable mediæval legend

of an apparition, a miracle! Yes, one is asked to believe that at the chateau yonder was seen last night three times the apparition of Armand de Fontonelles!

Dick started. "Armand de Fontonelles!" He remembered that she had repeated that name.

"Who's he?" he demanded abruptly.

"The first Comte de Fontonelles! When monsieur knows that the first comte has been dead three hundred years, he will see the imbecility of the affair!"

"Wot did he come back for?" growled Dick.

"Ah! it was a legend. Consider its artfulness! The Comte Armand had been a hard liver, a dissipated scoundrel, a reckless beast, but a mighty hunter of the stag. It was said that on one of these occasions he had been warned by the apparition of St. Hubert; but he had laughed, — for, observe, *he* always jeered at the priests too; hence this story! — and had declared that the flaming cross seen between the horns of the sacred stag was only the torch of a poacher, and he would shoot it! Good! the body of the comte, dead, but without a wound,

was found in the wood the next day, with
his discharged arquebus in his hand. The
Archbishop of Rouen refused his body the
rites of the Church until a number of masses
were said every year and — paid for ! One
understands ! one sees their ' little game ; '
the count now appears, — he is in purga-
tory ! More masses, — more money ! There
you are. Bah ! One understands, too, that
the affair takes place, not in a café like this,
— not in a public place, — but at a château
of the noblesse, and is seen by " — the proprietor checked the characters on his fingers
— *two* retainers ; one young demoiselle of
the noblesse, daughter of the châtelaine herself ; and, my faith, it goes without saying,
by a fat priest, the curé ! In effect, two
interested ones ! And the priest, — his lie
is magnificent ! Superb ! *For he saw the
comte in the picture-gallery, — in effect,
stepping into his frame !* "

"Oh, come off the roof, said Dick impatiently ; " they must have seen *something*,
you know. The young lady would n't lie ! " "

Monsieur Ribaud leaned over, with a mysterious, cynical smile, and lowering his voice
said : —

" You have reason to say so. You have
hit it, my friend. There *was* a something!
And if we regard the young lady, you shall
hear. The story of Mademoiselle de Fontonelles is that she has walked by herself
alone in the garden, — you observe, *alone*
— in the moonlight, near the edge of the
wood. You comprehend? The mother and
the curé are in the house, — for the time
effaced ! Here at the edge of the wood —
though why she continues, a young demoiselle, to the edge of the wood does not make
itself clear — she beholds her ancestor, as
on a pedestal, young, pale, but very handsome and *exalté*, — pardon ! "

" Nothing," said Dick hurriedly ; " go
on ! "

" She beseeches him why! He says he
is lost! She faints away, on the instant,
there — regard me! — *on the edge of the
wood*, she says. But her mother and Monsieur le Curé find her pale, agitated, distressed, *on the sofa in the salon*. One is
asked to believe that she is transported
through the air — like an angel — by the
spirit of Armand de Fontonelles. Incred-
ible ! "

" Well, wot do *you* think ? " said Dick
sharply.

The café proprietor looked around him
carefully, and then lowered his voice signifi-
cantly : —

" A lover ! "

" A what ? " said Dick, with a gasp.

" A lover ! " repeated Ribaud. " You
comprehend ! Mademoiselle has no *dot*, —
the property is nothing, — the brother has
everything. A Mademoiselle de Fontonelles
cannot marry out of her class, and the noblesse are all poor. Mademoiselle is young,
— pretty, they say, of her kind. It is an
intolerable life at the old château ; mademoiselle consoles herself ! "

Monsieur Ribaud never knew how near
he was to the white road below the railing
at that particular moment. Luckily, Dick
controlled himself, and wisely, as Monsieur
Ribaud's next sentence showed him.

" A romance, — an innocent, foolish liai-
son, if you like, — but, all the same, if
known of a Mademoiselle de Fontonelles, a
compromising, a fatal entanglement. There
you are. Look ! for this, then, all this
story of cock and bulls and spirits ! Made-

moiselle has been discovered with her lover by some one. This pretty story shall stop their mouths ! "

" But wot," said Dick brusquely, " wot if the girl was really skeert at something she 'd seen, and fainted dead away, as she said she did, — and — and " — he hesitated — " some stranger came along and picked her up ? "

Monsieur Ribaud looked at him pityingly.

" A Mademoiselle de Fontonelle is picked up by her servants, by her family, but not by the young man in the woods, alone. It is even more compromising ! "

" Do you mean to say," said Dick furiously, " that the ragpickers and sneaks that wade around in the slumgallion of this country would dare to spatter that young gal ? "

" I mean to say, yes, — assuredly, positively yes ! " said Ribaud, rubbing his hands with a certain satisfaction at Dick's fury. " For you comprehend not the position of la jeune fille in all France ! Ah ! in America the young lady she go everywhere alone ; I have seen her — pretty, charming, fascinating — alone with the young man. But

here, no, never! Regard me, my friend.
The French mother, she say to her daughter's fiancé, 'Look! there is my daughter.
She has never been alone with a young man
for five minutes, — not even with you. Take
her for your wife!' It is monstrous! it is
impossible! it is so!'"

There was a silence of a few minutes, and
Dick looked blankly at the iron gates of the
park of Fontonelles. Then he said : " Give
me a cigar."

Monsieur Ribaud instantly produced his
cigar case. Dick took a cigar, but waved
aside the proffered match, and entering the
café, took from his pocket the letter to
Mademoiselle de Fontonelles, twisted it in a
spiral, lighted it at a candle, lit his cigar with
it, and returning to the veranda held it in
his hand until the last ashes dropped on the
floor. Then he said, gravely, to Ribaud : —

" You 've treated me like a white man,
Frenchy, and I ain't goin' back on yer —
though your ways ain't my ways — nohow ;
but I reckon in this yer matter at the shotto
you 're a little too previous! For though I
don't as a gin'ral thing take stock in ghosts,
I believe every word that them folk said up

thar. And," he added, leaning his hand somewhat heavily on Ribaud's shoulder, " if you 're the man I take you for, you 'll believe it too ! And if that chap, Armand de Fontonelles, had n't hev picked up that gal at that moment, he would hev deserved to roast in hell another three hundred years ! That 's why I believe her story. So you 'll let these yer Fontonelles keep their ghosts for all they 're worth ; and when you next feel inclined to talk about that girl's *lover*, you 'll think of me, and shut your head ! You hear me, Frenchy, I 'm shoutin' ! And don't you forget it ! "

Nevertheless, early the next morning, Monsieur Ribaud accompanied his guest to the railway station, and parted from him with great effusion. On his way back an old-fashioned carriage with a postilion passed him. At a sign from its occupant, the postilion pulled up, and Monsieur Ribaud, bowing to the dust, approached the window, and the pale, stern face of a dignified, white-haired woman of sixty that looked from it.

" Has he gone ? " said the lady.

" Assuredly, madame ; I was with him at the station."

" And you think no one saw him ? "

" No one, madame, but myself."

" And — what kind of a man was he ? "

Monsieur Ribaud lifted his shoulders, threw out his hands despairingly, yet with a world of significance, and said: —

" An American."

" Ah ! "

The carriage drove on and entered the gates of the château. And Monsieur Ribaud, café proprietor and Social Democrat, straightened himself in the dust and shook his fist after it.

A NIGHT ON THE DIVIDE

With the lulling of the wind towards evening it came on to snow — heavily, in straight, quickly succeeding flakes, dropping like white lances from the sky. This was followed by the usual Sierran phenomenon. The deep gorge, which, as the sun went down, had lapsed into darkness, presently began to reappear; at first the vanished trail came back as a vividly whitening streak before them; then the larches and pines that ascended from it like buttresses against the hillsides glimmered in ghostly distinctness, until at last the two slopes curved out of the darkness as if hewn in marble. For the sudden storm, which extended scarcely two miles, had left no trace upon the steep granite face of the high cliffs above; the snow, slipping silently from them, left them still hidden in the obscurity of night. In the vanished landscape the gorge alone stood out, set in a chaos of cloud and storm

through which the moonbeams struggled in-
effectually.

It was this unexpected sight which burst
upon the occupants of a large covered "station wagon" who had chanced upon the
lower end of the gorge. Coming from a
still lower altitude, they had known nothing
of the storm, which had momentarily ceased,
but had left a record of its intensity in
nearly two feet of snow. For some moments
the horses floundered and struggled on, in
what the travelers believed to be some old
forgotten drift or avalanche, until the extent
and freshness of the fall became apparent.
To add to their difficulties, the storm recom-
menced, and not comprehending its real
character and limit, they did not dare to attempt to return the way they came. To go
on, however, was impossible. In this quan-
dary they looked about them in vain for
some other exit from the gorge. The sides
of that gigantic white furrow terminated
in darkness. Hemmed in from the world
in all directions, it might have been their
tomb.

But although *they* could see nothing beyond
their prison walls, they themselves were per-

fectly visible from the heights above them. And Jack Tenbrook, quartz miner, who was sinking a tunnel in the rocky ledge of shelf above the gorge, stepping out from his cabin at ten o'clock to take a look at the weather before turning in, could observe quite distinctly the outline of the black wagon, the floundering horses, and the crouching figures by their side, scarcely larger than pygmies on the white surface of the snow, six hundred feet below him. Jack had courage and strength, and the good humor that accompanies them, but he contented himself for a few moments with lazily observing the travelers' discomfiture. He had taken in the situation with a glance; he would have helped a brother miner or mountaineer, although he knew that it could only have been drink or bravado that brought *him* into the gorge in a snowstorm, but it was very evident that these were " greenhorns," or eastern tourists, and it served their stupidity and arrogance right! He remembered also how he, having once helped an Eastern visitor catch the mustang that had " bucked " him, had been called " my man," and presented with five dollars; he recalled how he had once

spread the humble resources of his cabin
before some straying members of the San
Francisco party who were "opening" the
new railroad, and heard the audible wonder
of a lady that a civilized being could live
so "coarsely"! With these recollections in
his mind, he managed to survey the distant
struggling horses with a fine sense of humor,
not unmixed with self-righteousness. There
was no real danger in the situation; it meant
at the worst a delay and a camping in the
snow till morning, when he would go down
to their assistance. They had a spacious
traveling equipage, and were, no doubt, well
supplied with furs, robes, and provisions for
a several hours' journey; his own pork bar-
rel was quite empty, and his blankets worn.
He half smiled, extended his long arms in a
decided yawn, and turned back into his cabin
to go to bed. Then he cast a final glance
around the interior. Everything was all
right; his loaded rifle stood against the wall;
he had just raked ashes over the embers of
his fire to keep it intact till morning. Only
one thing slightly troubled him; a grizzly
bear, two-thirds grown, but only half tamed,
which had been given to him by a young

lady named "Miggles," when that charming
and historic girl had decided to accompany
her paralytic lover to the San Francisco hospital, was missing that evening. It had
been its regular habit to come to the door
every night for some sweet biscuit or sugar
before going to its lair in the underbrush
behind the cabin. Everybody knew it along
the length and breadth of Hemlock Ridge,
as well as the fact of its being a legacy from
the fair exile. No rifle had ever yet been
raised against its lazy bulk or the stupid,
small-eyed head and ruff of circling hairs
made more erect by its well-worn leather
collar. Consoling himself with the thought
that the storm had probably delayed its return, Jack took off his coat and threw it on
his bunk. But from thinking of the storm
his thoughts naturally returned again to the
impeded travelers below him, and he half
mechanically stepped out in his shirt-sleeves
for a final look at them.

But here something occurred that changed
his resolution entirely. He had previously
noticed only the three foreshortened, crawl-
ing figures around the now stationary wagon
bulk. They were now apparently making

arrangements to camp for the night. But
another figure had been added to the group,
and as it stood perched upon a wagon seat
laid on the snow Jack could see that its
outline was not bifurcated like the others.
But even that general suggestion was not
needed! the little head, the symmetrical
curves visible even at that distance, were
quite enough to indicate that it was a woman! The easy smile faded from Jack's
face, and was succeeded by a look of concern
and then of resignation. He had no choice
now; he *must* go! There was a woman
there, and that settled it. Yet he had arrived at this conclusion from no sense of
gallantry, nor, indeed, of chivalrous trans-
port, but as a matter of simple duty to the
sex. He was giving up his sleep, was going
down six hundred feet of steep trail to offer
his services during the rest of the night as
much as a matter of course as an Eastern
man would have offered his seat in an omni-
bus to a woman, and with as little expectation of return for his courtesy.

Having resumed his coat, with a bottle of
whiskey thrust into its pocket, he put on a
pair of india-rubber boots reaching to his

thighs, and, catching the blanket from his bunk, started with an axe and shovel on his shoulder on his downward journey. When the distance was half completed he shouted to the travelers below; the cry was joyously answered by the three men; he saw the fourth figure, now unmistakably that of a slender youthful woman, in a cloak, helped back into the wagon, as if deliverance was now sure and immediate. But Jack on arriving speedily dissipated that illusive hope; they could only get through the gorge by taking off the wheels of the wagon, placing the axle on rude sledge-runners of split saplings, which, with their assistance, he would fashion in a couple of hours at his cabin and bring down to the gorge. The only other alternative would be for them to come to his cabin and remain there while he went for assistance to the nearest station, but that would take several hours and necessitate a double journey for the sledge if he was lucky enough to find one. The party quickly acquiesced in Jack's first suggestion.

"Very well," said Jack, "then there's no time to be lost; unhitch your horses and we'll dig a hole in that bank for them to

stand in out of the snow." This was speedily
done. " Now," continued Jack, " you'll just
follow me up to my cabin ; it's a pretty
tough climb, but I'll want your help to
bring down the runners."

Here the man who seemed to be the head
of the party — of middle age and a superior,
professional type — for the first time hesitated. " I forgot to say that there is a lady
with us, — my daughter," he began, glancing
towards the wagon.

" I reckoned as much," interrupted Jack
simply, " and I allowed to carry her up myself the roughest part of the way. She kin
make herself warm and comf'ble in the cabin
until we've got the runners ready."

" You hear what our friend says, Amy?"
suggested the gentleman, appealingly, to the
closed leather curtains of the wagon.

There was a pause. The curtain was suddenly drawn aside, and a charming little
head and shoulders, furred to the throat and
topped with a bewitching velvet cap, were
thrust out. In the obscurity little could be
seen of the girl's features, but there was a
certain willfulness and impatience in her attitude. Being in the shadow, she had the

advantage of the others, particularly of Jack, as his figure was fully revealed in the moonlight against the snowbank. Her eyes rested for a moment on his high boots, his heavy mustache, so long as to mingle with the unkempt locks which fell over his broad shoulders, on his huge red hands streaked with black grease from the wagon wheels, and some blood, stanched with snow, drawn from bruises in cutting out brambles in the brush; on — more awful than all — a monstrous, shiny " specimen " gold ring encircling one of his fingers, — on the whiskey bottle that shamelessly bulged from his side pocket, and then — slowly dropped her dissatisfied eyelids.

" Why can't I stay *here?* " she said languidly. " It 's quite nice and comfortable."

" Because we can't leave you alone, and we must go with this gentleman to help him."

Miss Amy let the tail of her eye again creep shudderingly over this impossible Jack. " I thought the — the gentleman was going to help *us*," she said dryly.

" Nonsense, Amy, you don't understand," said her father impatiently. " This gentleman is kind enough to offer to make some sledge-runners for us at his cabin, and we must help him."

"But I can stay here while you go. I'm not afraid."

"Yes, but you're *alone* here, and something might happen."

"Nothing could happen," interrupted Jack, quickly and cheerfully. He had flushed at first, but he was now considering that the carrying of a lady as expensively attired and apparently as delicate and particular as this one might be somewhat difficult. "There's nothin' that would hurt ye here," he continued, addressing the velvet cap and furred throat in the darkness, "and if there was it could n't get at ye, bein', so to speak, in the same sort o' fix as you. So you're all right," he added positively.

Inconsistently enough, the young lady did not accept this as gratefully as might have been imagined, but Jack did not see the slight flash of her eye as, ignoring him, she replied markedly to her father, "I'd much rather stop here, papa."

"And," continued Jack, turning also to her father, "you can keep the wagon and

the whole gorge in sight from the trail all
the way up. So you can see that everything's all right. Why, I saw *you* from
the first." He stopped awkwardly, and
added, " Come along ; the sooner we 're off
the quicker the job's over."

" Pray don't delay the gentleman and —
the job," said Miss Amy sweetly.

Reassured by Jack's last suggestion, her
father followed him with the driver and the
second man of the party, a youngish and
somewhat undistinctive individual, but to
whose gallant anxieties Miss Amy responded
effusively. Nevertheless, the young lady had
especially noted Jack's confession that he
had seen them when they first entered the
gorge. " And I suppose," she added to herself mentally, " that he sat there with his
boozing companions, laughing and jeering at
our struggles."

But when the sound of her companions'
voices died away, and their figures were
swallowed up in the darkness behind the
snow, she forgot all this, and much else that
was mundane and frivolous, in the impres-
sive and majestic solitude which seemed to
descend upon her from the obscurity above.

At first it was accompanied with a slight thrill of vague fear, but this passed presently into that profound peace which the mountains alone can give their lonely or perturbed children. It seemed to her that Nature was never the same, on the great plains where men and cities always loomed into such ridiculous proportions, as when the Great Mother raised herself to comfort them with smiling hillsides, or encompassed them and drew them closer in the loving arms of her mountains. The long white *cañada* stretched before her in a purity that did not seem of the earth; the vague bulk of the mountains rose on either side of her in a mystery that was not of this life. Yet it was not oppressive; neither was its restfulness and quiet suggestive of obliviousness and slumber; on the contrary, the highly rarefied air seemed to give additional keenness to her senses; her hearing had become singularly acute; her eyesight pierced the uttermost extremity of the gorge, lit by the full moon that occasionally shone through slowly drifting clouds. Her nerves thrilled with a delicious sense of freedom and a strange desire to run or climb. It seemed

to her, in her exalted fancy, that these soli-
tudes should be peopled only by a kingly
race, and not by such gross and material
churls as this mountaineer who helped them.
And, I grieve to say, — writing of an ideal-
ist that *was*, and a heroine that *is* to be, —
she was getting outrageously hungry.

There were a few biscuits in her travel-
ing-bag, and she remembered that she had
been presented with a small jar of California honey at San José. This she took out
and opened on the seat before her, and
spreading the honey on the biscuits, ate them
with a keen schoolgirl relish and a pleasant
suggestion of a sylvan picnic in spite of the
cold. It was all very strange ; quite an experience for her to speak of afterwards.
People would hardly believe that she had
spent an hour or two, all alone, in a deserted wagon in a mountain snow pass. It
was an adventure such as one reads of in
the magazines. Only something was lack-
ing which the magazines always supplied, —
something heroic, something done by somebody. If that awful-looking mountaineer —
that man with the long hair and mustache,
and that horrible gold ring, — why such a

ring? — was only different! But he was probably gorging beefsteak or venison with her father and Mr. Waterhouse, — men were always such selfish creatures! — and had quite forgotten all about her. It would have been only decent for them to have brought her down something hot; biscuits and honey were certainly cloying, and somehow did n't agree with the temperature. She was really half starved! And much they cared! It would just serve them right if something *did* happen to her, — or *seem* to happen to her, — if only to frighten them. And the pretty face that was turned up in the moonlight wore a charming but decided pout.

Good gracious, what was that? The horses were either struggling or fighting in their snow shelters. Then one with a frightened neigh broke from its halter and dashed into the road, only to be plunged snorting and helpless into the drifts. Then the other followed. How silly! Something had frightened them. Perhaps only a rabbit or a mole; horses were such absurdly nervous creatures! However, it is just as well; somebody would see them or hear them, —

that neigh was quite human and awful, —
and they would hurry down to see what was
the matter. *She* could n't be expected to
get out and look after the horses in the snow.
Anyhow, she *would n't!* She was a good
deal safer where she was ; it might have been
rats or mice about that frightened them !
Goodness !

She was still watching with curious wonder the continued fright of the animals, when
suddenly she felt the wagon half bumped,
half lifted from behind. It was such a lazy,
deliberate movement that for a moment she
thought it came from the party, who had
returned noiselessly with the runners. She
scrambled over to the back seat, unbuttoned
the leather curtain, lifted it, but nothing
was to be seen. Consequently, with feminine
quickness, she said, " I see you perfectly,
Mr. Waterhouse — don't be silly ! " But
at this moment there was another shock to
the wagon, and from beneath it arose what
at first seemed to her to be an uplifting of
the drift itself, but, as the snow was shaken
away from its heavy bulk, proved to be the
enormous head and shoulders of a bear !

Yet even then she was not *wholly* fright-

ened, for the snout that confronted her had
a feeble inoffensiveness ; the small eyes were
bright with an eager, almost childish curiosity rather than a savage ardor, and the
whole attitude of the creature lifted upon its
hind legs was circus-like and ludicrous rather
than aggressive. She was enabled to say
with some dignity, " Go away ! Shoo ! " and
to wave her luncheon basket at it with exemplary firmness. But here the creature
laid one paw on the back seat as if to steady
itself, with the singular effect of collapsing
the whole side of the wagon, and then opened
its mouth as if in some sort of inarticulate
reply. But the revelation of its red tongue,
its glistening teeth, and, above all, the hot,
suggestive fume of its breath, brought the
first scream from the lips of Miss Amy. It
was real and convincing ; the horses joined
in it; the three screamed together ! The bear
hesitated for an instant, then, catching sight
of the honey-pot on the front seat, which the
shrinking-back of the young girl had disclosed,
he slowly reached forward his other paw and
attempted to grasp it. This exceedingly
simple movement, however, at once doubled
up the front seat, sent the honey-pot a dozen

feet into the air, and dropped Miss Amy
upon her knees in the bed of the wagon.
The combined mental and physical shock
was too much for her; she instantly and
sincerely fainted; the last thing in her ears
amidst this wreck of matter being the
" wheep " of a bullet and the sharp crack of
a rifle.

.   .   .   .

She recovered her consciousness in the
flickering light of a fire of bark, that played
upon the rafters of a roof thatched with
bark and upon a floor of strewn and shred-
ded bark. She even suspected she was lying
upon a mattress of bark underneath the
heavy bearskin she could feel and touch.
She had a delicious sense of warmth, and,
mingled with this strange spicing of woodland freedom, even a sense of home protection. And surely enough, looking around,
she saw her father at her side.

He briefly explained the situation. They
had been at first attracted by the cry of the
frightened horses and their plunging, which
they could see distinctly, although they saw
nothing else. " But, Mr. Tenbrook " —

" Mr. Who ? " said Amy, staring at the
rafters.

" The owner of this cabin — the man who helped us — caught up his gun, and, calling us to follow, ran like lightning down the trail. At first we followed blindly, and unknowingly, for we could only see the struggling horses, who, however, seemed to be *alone*, and the wagon from which you did not seem to have stirred. Then, for the first time, my dear child, we suddenly saw your danger. Imagine how we felt as that hideous brute rose up in the road and began attacking the wagon. We called on Tenbrook to fire, but for some inconceivable reason he did not, although he still kept running at the top of his speed. Then we heard you shriek — "

" I did n't shriek, papa; it was the horses."

" My child, I knew your voice."

" Well, it was only a *very little* scream — because I had tumbled." The color was coming back rapidly to her pink cheeks.

" And, then, at your scream, Tenbrook fired! — it was a wonderful shot for the distance, so everybody says — and killed the bear, though Tenbrook says it ought n't to. I believe he wanted to capture the creature

alive. They 've queer notions, those hunt-
ers. And then, as you were unconscious, he
brought you up here."

" *Who* brought me ? "

" Tenbrook; he 's as strong as a horse.
Slung you up on his shoulders like a feather
pillow."

" Oh ! "

" And then, as the wagon required some
repairing from the brute's attack, we concluded to take it leisurely, and let you rest
here for a while."

" And where is — where are *they* ? "

" At work on the wagon. I determined
to stay with you, though you are perfectly
safe here."

" I suppose I ought — to thank — this
man, papa ? "

" Most certainly, though of course, *I* have
already done so. But he was rather curt
in reply. These half-savage men have such
singular ideas. He said the beast would
never have attacked you except for the
honey-pot which it scented. That 's absurd."

" Then it 's all my fault ? "

" Nonsense ! How could *you* know ? "

"And I've made all this trouble. And frightened the horses. And spoilt the wagon. And made the man run down and bring me up here when he did n't want to!"

"My dear child! Don't be idiotic! Amy! Well, really!"

For the idiotic one was really wiping two large tears from her lovely blue eyes. She subsided into an ominous silence, broken by a single sniffle. "Try to go to sleep, dear; you 've had quite a shock to your nerves," added her father soothingly. She continued silent, but not sleeping.

"I smell coffee."

"Yes, dear."

"You 've been having coffee, papa?"

"We *did* have some, I think," said the wretched man apologetically, though why he could not determine.

"Before I came up? while the bear was trying to eat me?"

"No, after."

"I 've a horrid taste in my mouth. It 's the honey. I 'll never eat honey again. Never!"

"Perhaps it 's the whiskey."

"What?"

" The whiskey. You were quite faint and chilled, you know. We gave you some."

" Out of — that — black — bottle ? "

" Yes."

Another silence.

" I 'd like some coffee. I don't think he 'd begrudge me that, if he did save my life."

" I dare say there 's some left." Her father at once bestirred himself and presently brought her some coffee in a tin cup. It was part of Miss Amy's rapid convalescence, or equally of her debilitated condition, that she made no comment on the vessel. She lay for some moments looking curiously around the cabin ; she had no doubt it had a worse look in the daylight, but somehow the firelight brought out a wondrous luxury of color in the bark floor and thatching. Besides, it was not " smelly," as she feared it would be ; on the contrary the spicy aroma of the woods was always dominant. She remembered that it was this that always made a greasy, oily picnic tolerable. She raised herself on her elbow, seeing which her father continued confidently, " Perhaps, dear, if you sat up for a few moments you might be strong enough

presently to walk down with me to the
wagon. It would save time."

Amy instantly lay down again. "I don't
know what you can be thinking of, papa.
After this shock really I don't feel as if I
could *stand* alone, much less *walk*. But, of
course," with pathetic resignation, "if you
and Mr. Waterhouse supported me, perhaps
I might crawl a few steps at a time."

"Nonsense, Amy. Of course, this man
Tenbrook will carry you down as he brought
you up. Only I thought, — but there are
steps, they're coming now. No! — only *he*."

The sound of crackling in the underbrush
was followed by a momentary darkening of
the open door of the cabin. It was the tall
figure of the mountaineer. But he did not
even make the pretense of entering; standing at the door he delivered his news to the
interior generally. It was to the effect that
everything was ready, and the two other men
were even then harnessing the horses. Then
he drew back into the darkness.

"Papa," said Amy, in a sudden frightened
voice, "I've lost my bracelet."

"Haven't you dropped it somewhere there
in the bunk?" asked her father.

" No. It's on the floor of the wagon. I remember now it fell off when I tumbled! And it will be trodden upon and crushed! Couldn't you run down, ahead of me, and warn them, papa, dear? Mr. Tenbrook will have to go *so* slowly with me." She tumbled out of the bunk with singular alacrity, shook herself and her skirts into instantaneous gracefulness, and fitted the velvet cap on her straying hair. Then she said hurriedly, " Run quick, papa dear, and as you go, call him in and say I am quite ready."

Thus adjured, the obedient parent disappeared in the darkness. With him also disappeared Miss Amy's singular alacrity. Sitting down carefully again on the edge of the bunk, she leaned against the post with a certain indefinable languor that was as touching as it was graceful. I need not tell any feminine readers that there was no dissimulation in all this, — no coquetry, no ostentation, — and that the young girl was perfectly sincere! But the masculine reader might like to know that the simple fact was that, since she had regained consciousness, she had been filled with remorse for her capricious and ungenerous rejection of Tenbrook's

proffered service. More than that, she felt
she had periled her life in that moment of
folly, and that this man — this hero — had
saved her. For hero he was, even if he did
not fulfill her ideal, — it was only *she* that
was not a heroine. Perhaps if he had been
more like what she wished she would have
felt this less keenly; love leaves little room
for the exercise of moral ethics. So Miss
Amy Forester, being a good girl at bottom,
and not exactly loving this man, felt towards
him a frank and tender consideration which
a more romantic passion would have shrunk
from showing. Consequently, when Tenbrook entered a moment later, he found
Amy paler and more thoughtful, but, as he
fancied, much prettier than before, looking
up at him with eyes of the sincerest solicitude.

Nevertheless, he remained standing near
the door, as if indicating a possible intrusion, his face wearing a look of lowering
abstraction. It struck her that this might
be the effect of his long hair and general
uncouthness, and this only spurred her to a
fuller recognition of his other qualities.

"I am afraid," she began, with a charming embarrassment, "that instead of resting satisfied with your kindness in carrying me up here, I will have to burden you again with my dreadful weakness, and ask you to carry me down also. But all this seems so little after what you have just done and for which I can never, *never* hope to thank you!" She clasped her two little hands together, holding her gloves between, and brought them down upon her lap in a gesture as prettily helpless as it was unaffected.

"I have done scarcely anything," he said, glancing away towards the fire, "and — your father has thanked me."

"You have saved my life!"

"No! no!" he said quickly. "Not that! You were in no danger, except from my rifle, had I missed."

"I see," she said eagerly, with a little posthumous thrill at having been after all a kind of heroine, "and it was a wonderful shot, for you were so careful not to touch me."

"Please don't say any more," he said, with a slight movement of half awkwardness, half impatience. "It was a rough job, but it's over now."

He stopped and chafed his red hands abstractedly together. She could see that he had evidently just washed them — and the glaring ring was more in evidence than ever. But the thought gave her an inspiration.

" You 'll at least let me shake hands with you ! " she said, extending both her own with childish frankness.

" Hold on, Miss Forester," he said, with sudden desperation. " It ain't the square thing ! Look here ! I can't play this thing on you ! — I can't let you play it on me any longer ! You were n't in any danger, — you *never* were ! That bear was only a half-wild thing I helped to ra'r myself ! It 's taken sugar from my hand night after night at the door of this cabin as it might have taken it from yours here if it was alive now. It slept night after night in the brush, not fifty yards away. The morning 's never come yet — till now," he said hastily, to cover an odd break in his voice, " when it did n't brush along the whole side of this cabin to kinder wake me up and say ' So long,' afore it browsed away into the cañon. Thar ain't a man along the whole Divide who

did n't know it ; thar ain't a man along the
whole Divide that would have drawn a bead
or pulled a trigger on it till now.   It never
had an enemy but the bees ; it never even
knew why horses and cattle were frightened
of it.   It was n't much of a pet, you 'd say,
Miss Forester ; it was n't much to meet a
lady's eye ; but we of the woods must take
our friends where we find 'em and of our
own kind.   It ain't no fault of yours, Miss,
that you did n't know it ; it ain't no fault
of yours what happened ; but when it comes
to your *thanking* me for it, why — it 's —
it 's rather rough, you see — and gets me."
He stopped short as desperately and as abruptly as he had begun, and stared blankly
at the fire.

A wave of pity and shame swept over the
young girl and left its high tide on her cheek.
But even then it was closely followed by the
feminine instinct of defence and defiance.
The *real* hero — the *gentleman* — she rea-
soned bitterly, would have spared her all this
knowledge.

"But why," she said, with knitted brows,
"why, if you knew it was so precious and
so harmless — why did you fire upon it ? "

"Because," he said almost fiercely, turning upon her, " because you *screamed*, and *then I knew it had frightened you!* " He stopped instantly as she momentarily recoiled from him, but the very brusqueness of his action had dislodged a tear from his dark eyes that fell warm on the back of her hand, and seemed to blot out the indignity. " Listen, Miss," he went on hurriedly, as if to cover up his momentary unmanliness. " I knew the bear was missing to-night, and when I heard the horses scurrying about I reckoned what was up. I knew no harm could come to you, for the horses were unharnessed and away from the wagon. I pelted down that trail ahead of them all like grim death, calkilatin' to get there before the bear ; they would n't have understood me ; I was too high up to call to the creature when he did come out, and I kinder hoped you would n't see him. Even when he turned towards the wagon, I knew it was n't *you* he was after, but suthin' else, and I kinder hoped, Miss, that you, being different and quicker-minded than the rest, would see it too. All the while them folks were yellin' behind me to fire — as if I did n't

know my work. I was half-way down — and
then you screamed ! And then I forgot everything, — everything but standing clear of
hitting you, — and I fired. I was that savage
that I wanted to believe that he 'd gone mad,
and would have touched you, till I got down
there and found the honey-pot lying along-
side of him. But there, — it 's all over now !
I would n't have let on a word to you only I
could n't bear to take *your thanks* for it,
and I could n't bear to have you thinking
me a brute for dodgin' them." He stopped,
walked to the fire, leaned against the chimney under the shallow pretext of kicking the
dull embers into a blaze, which, however,
had only the effect of revealing his two glistening eyes as he turned back again and
came towards her. " Well," he said, with
an ineffectual laugh, " it 's all over now, it 's
all in the day's work, I reckon, — and now,
Miss, if you 're ready, and will just fix yourself your own way so as to ride easy, I 'll
carry you down."   And slightly bending his
strong figure, he dropped on one knee beside
her with extended arms.

Now it is one thing to be carried up a hill
in temperate, unconscious blood and practi-

cal business fashion by a tall, powerful man
with steadfast, glowering eyes, but quite another thing to be carried down again by the
same man, who has been crying, and when
you are conscious that you are going to cry
too, and your tears may be apt to mingle.
So Miss Amy Forester said: "Oh, wait,
please! Sit down a moment. Oh, Mr. Tenbrook, I am so very, very sorry," and, clap-
ping her hand to her eyes, burst into tears.

"Oh, please, please don't, Miss Forester,"
said Jack, sitting down on the end of the
bunk with frightened eyes, "please don't do
that! It ain't worth it. I'm only a brute
to have said anything."

"No, no! You are *so* noble, *so* forgiv-
ing!" sobbed Miss Forester, "and *I* have
made you go and kill the only thing you
cared for, that was all your own."

"No, Miss, — not all my own, either, —
and that makes it so rough. For it was only
left in trust with me by a friend. It was
her only companion."

"*Her* only companion?" echoed Miss
Forester, sharply lifting her bowed head.

"Except," said Jack hurriedly, miscom-
prehending the emphasis with masculine fatu-

ity, — " except the dying man for whom she lived and sacrificed her whole life. She gave me this ring, to always remind me of my trust. I suppose," he added ruefully, looking down upon it, " it's no use now. I'd better take it off."

Then Amy eyed the monstrous object with angelic simplicity. " I certainly should," she said with infinite sweetness; " it would only remind you of your loss. But," she added, with a sudden, swift, imploring look of her blue eyes, " if you could part with it to me, it would be such a reminder and token of — of your forgiveness."

Jack instantly handed it to her. " And now," he said, " let me carry you down."

" I think," she said hesitatingly, " that — I had better try to walk," and she rose to her feet.

" Then I shall know that you have not forgiven me," said Jack sadly.

" But I have no right to trouble " —

Alas! she had no time to finish her polite objection, for the next moment she felt herself lifted in the air, smelled the bark thatch within an inch of her nose, saw the firelight vanish behind her, and subsiding into his

curved arms as in a hammock, the two passed
forth into the night together.

"I can't find your bracelet anywhere,
Amy," said her father, when they reached
the wagon.

"It was on the floor in the hut," said Amy
reproachfully. "But, of course, you never
thought of that!"

.   .   .   .

My pen halts with some diffidence between
two conclusions to this veracious chronicle.
As they agree in result, though not in theory
or intention, I may venture to give them
both. To one coming from the lips of the
charming heroine herself I naturally yield the
precedence. "Oh, the bear story! I don't
really remember whether that was before I
was engaged to John or after. But I had
known him for some time; father introduced him at the Governor's ball at Sacramento. Let me see! — I think it was in
the winter of '56. Yes! it was very amus-
ing; I always used to charge John with
having trained that bear to attack our carriage so that he might come in as a hero!
Oh, of course, there are a hundred absurd
stories about him, — they used to say that

he lived all alone in a cabin like a savage, and all that sort of thing, and was a friend of a dubious woman in the locality, whom the common people made a heroine of, — Miggles, or Wiggles, or some such preposterous name. But look at John there; can you conceive it?" The listener, glancing at a very handsome, clean-shaven fellow, faultlessly attired, could not conceive such an absurdity. So I therefore simply give the opinion of Joshua Bixley, Superintendent of the Long Divide Tunnel Company, for what it is worth: "I never took much stock in that bear story, and its captivating old Forester's daughter. Old Forester knew a thing or two, and when he was out here consolidating tunnels, he found out that Jack Tenbrook was about headed for the big lead, and brought him out and introduced him to Amy. You see, Jack, clear grit as he was, was mighty rough style, and about as simple as they make 'em, and they had to get up something to account for that girl's taking a shine to him. But they seem to be happy enough — and what are you going to do about it?"

And I transfer this philosophic query to the reader.

THE YOUNGEST PROSPECTOR IN CALAVERAS

HE was scarcely eight when it was believed that he could have reasonably laid
claim to the above title. But he never did.
He was a small boy, intensely freckled to
the roots of his tawny hair, with even a suspicion of it in his almond-shaped but somewhat full eyes, which were the greenish hue
of a ripe gooseberry. All this was very unlike his parents, from whom he diverged in
resemblance in that fashion so often seen in
the Southwest of America, as if the youth
of the boundless West had struck a new
note of independence and originality, over-
riding all conservative and established rules
of heredity. Something of this was also
shown in a singular and remarkable reticence and firmness of purpose, quite unlike
his family or schoolfellows. His mother was
the wife of a teamster, who had apparently
once "dumped" his family, consisting of a

boy and two girls, on the roadside at Burnt
Spring, with the canvas roof of his wagon to
cover them, while he proceeded to deliver
other freight, not so exclusively his own, at
other stations along the road, returning to
them on distant and separate occasions with
slight additions to their stock, habitation,
and furniture. In this way the canvas roof
was finally shingled and the hut enlarged,
and, under the quickening of a smiling California sky and the forcing of a teeming
California soil, the chance-sown seed took
root and became known as Medliker's Ranch,
or " Medliker's," with its bursting garden
patch and its three sheds or " lean-to's."

The girls helped their mother in a childish,
imitative way ; the boy, John Bunyan, after
a more desultory and original fashion —
when he was not " going to " or ostensibly
" coming from " school, for he was seldom
actually there. Something of this fear was
in the mind of Mrs. Medliker one morning
as she looked up from the kettle she was
scrubbing, with premonition of " more wor-
riting," to behold the Reverend Mr. Staples,
the local minister, hale John Bunyan Medliker into the shanty with one hand. Let-

ting Johnny go, he placed his back against
the door and wiped his face with a red
handkerchief. Johnny dropped into a chair,
furtively glancing at the arm by which Mr.
Staples had dragged him, and feeling it
with the other hand to see if it was really
longer.

"I've been requested by the schoolmaster," said the Rev. Mr. Staples, putting
his handkerchief back into his broad felt
hat with a gasping smile, "to bring our
young friend before you for a matter of
counsel and discipline. I have done so,
Sister Medliker, with some difficulty," — he
looked down at John Bunyan, who again
felt his arm and was satisfied that it *was*
longer — "but we must do our dooty, even
with difficulty to ourselves, and, perhaps, to
others. Our young friend, John Bunyan,
stands on a giddy height — on slippery
places, and," continued Mr. Staples, with a
lofty disregard to consecutive metaphor, "his
feet are taking fast hold of destruction."
Here the child drew a breath of relief, possibly at the prospect of being on firm ground
of any kind at last; but Sister Medliker,
to whom the Staples style of exordium had

only a Sabbath significance, turned to her offspring abruptly : —

"And what's these yer doin's now, John? and me a slavin' to send ye to school?"

Thus appealed to, Johnny looked for a reply at his feet, at his arm, and at the kettle. Then he said : "*I* ain't done nothin', but *he*" — indicating Staples — "hez been nigh onter pullin' off my arm."

"It's now almost a week ago," continued Mr. Staples, waving aside the interruption with a smile of painful Christian tolerance, "or perhaps ten days — I won't be too sure — that the schoolmaster discovered that Johnny had in his possession two or three flakes of fine river gold — each of the value of half a dollar, or perhaps sixty-two and one half cents. On being questioned where he got them he refused to say; although subsequently he alleged that he had 'found' them. It being a single instance, he was given the benefit of the doubt, and nothing more was said about it. But a few days after he was found trying to pass off, at Mr. Smith's store, two other flakes of a different size, and a small nugget of the value of four or five dollars. At this point I was called

in ; he repeated to me, I grieve to say, the
same untruthfulness, and when I suggested
to him the obvious fact that he had taken it
from one of the miner's sluice boxes and
committed the grievous sin of theft, he wick-
edly denied it — so that we are prevented
from carrying out the Christian command of
restoring it even *one* fold, instead of four or
five fold as the Mosaic Law might have required. We were, alas! unable to ascertain
anything from the miners themselves, though
I grieve to say they one and all agreed that
their ' take ' that week was not at all what
they had expected. I even went so far as to
admit the possibility of his own statement,
and besought him at least to show me where
he had found it. He at first refused with
great stubbornness of temper, but later consented to accompany me privately this afternoon to the spot." Mr. Staples paused, and
sinking his voice gloomily, and with his
eyes fixed upon Johnny, continued slowly :
" When I state that, after several times trying to evade me on the way, he finally led
me to the top of Bald Hill, where there is
not a scrap of soil, and not the slightest
indication, and still persisted that he found

it *there*, you will understand, Sister Medliker, the incorrigibility of his conduct, and
how he has added the sin of 'false witness'
to his breaking the Eighth Commandment.
But I leave him to your Christian discipline!
Let us hope that if, through his stiff-necked
obduracy, he has haply escaped the vengeance of man's law, he will not escape the
rod of the domestic tabernacle."

"Ye kin leave him to me," said Mrs.
Medliker, in her anxiety to get rid of the
parson, assuming a confidence she was far
from feeling.

"So be it, Sister Medliker," said Staples,
drawing a long, satisfactory breath; "and
let us trust that when you have rastled with
his flesh and spirit, you will bring us joyful
tidings to Wednesday's Mother's Meeting."

He clapped his soft hat on his head, cast
another glance at the wicked Johnny, opened
the door with his hand behind him, and
backed himself into the road.

"Now, Johnny," said Mrs. Medliker, setting her lips together as the door closed,
"look me right in the face, and say where
you stole that gold."

But Johnny evidently did not think that

his mother's face at that moment offered any moral support, for he did not look at her; but, after gazing at the kettle, said slowly, " I did n't steal no gold."

" Then," said Mrs. Medliker triumphantly, " if ye did n't steal it, you 'd say right off *how* ye got it."

Children are often better logicians than their elders. To John Bunyan the stealing of gold and the mere refusal to say where he got it were two distinct and separate things; that the negation of the second proposition meant the affirmation of the first he could not accept. But then children are also imitative, and fearful of the older intellect. It struck Johnny that his mother might be right, and that to her it really meant the same thing. So, after a moment's silence he replied more confidently, " I suppose I stoled it."

But he was utterly unprepared for the darkening change in his mother's face, and her furious accents. " You stole it? — you *stole* it, you limb ! And you sit there and brazenly tell me ! Who did you steal it from ? Tell me quick, afore I wring it out of you !"

Completely astounded and bewildered at this new turn of affairs, Johnny again fell back upon the dreadful truth, and gasped, " I don't know."

" You don't know, you devil! Did you take it from Frazer's ? "

" No."

" From the Simmons Brothers ? "

" No."

" From the Blazing Star Company ? "

" No."

" From a store ? "

" No."

" Then, in created goodness ! — *where* did you get it ? "

Johnny raised his brown-gooseberry eyes for a single instant to his mother's and said, " I found it."

Mrs. Medliker gasped again and stared hopelessly at the ceiling. Yet she was conscious of a certain relief. After all, it was *possible* that he had found it — liar as he undoubtedly was.

" Then why don't you say where, you awful child ? "

" Don't want to ! "

Johnny would have liked to add that he

saw no reason why he should tell. Other
people who found gold were not obliged to
tell. There was Jim Brody, who had struck
a lead and kept the locality secret. Nobody
forced him to tell. Nobody called him a
thief; nobody had dragged him about by
the arm until he showed it. Why was it
wrong that a little boy should find gold? It
was n't agin the Commandments. Mr. Staples had never got up and said, "Thou shalt
not find gold!" His mother had never
made him pray not to find it! The schoolmaster had never read him awful stories of
boys who found gold and never said anything about it, and so came to a horrid end.
All this crowded his small boy's mind, and,
crowding, choked his small boy's utterance.

"You jest wait till your father comes
home," said Mrs. Medliker, "and he 'll see
whether you 'want to' or not. And now
get yourself off to bed and stay there."

Johnny knew that his father — whose
teams had increased to five wagons, and
whose route extended forty miles further —
was not due for a week, and that the catastrophe was yet remote. His present punishment he had expected. He went into the

adjoining bedroom, which he occupied with his sister, and began to undress. He lingered for some time over one stocking, and finally cautiously removed from it a small piece of flake gold which he had kept concealed all day under his big toe, to the great discomfort of that member. But this was only a small, ordinary self-martyrdom of boyhood. He scratched a boyish hieroglyphic on the metal, and when his mother's back was turned scraped a small hole in the adobe wall, inserted the gold in it, and covered it up with a plaster made of the moistened débris. It was safe — so was his secret — for it need not, perhaps, be stated here that Johnny *had* told the truth and *had* honestly found the gold! But where? — yes, that was his own secret! And now, Johnny, with the instinct of all young animals, dismissed the whole subject from his mind, and, reclining comfortably upon his arm, fell into an interesting study of the habits of the red ant as exemplified in a crack of the adobe wall, and with the aid of a burnt match succeeded in diverting for the rest of the afternoon the attention of a whole laborious colony.

The next morning, however, brought trouble to him in the curiosity of his sisters, heightened by their belief that he could at any moment be taken off to prison — which was their understanding of their mother's story. I grieve to say that to them this invested him with a certain romantic heroism, from the gratification of which the hero himself was not exempt. Nevertheless, he successfully evaded their questioning, and on broader impersonal grounds. As girls, it was none of their business ! He was n't a-going to tell them *his* secrets ! And what did they know about gold, anyway ? They could n't tell it from brass ! The attitude of his mother was, however, still perplexing. She was no longer actively indignant, but treated him with a mysterious reserve that was the more appalling. The fact was that she no longer believed in his theft, — indeed, she had never seriously accepted it, — but his strange reticence and secretiveness piqued her curiosity, and even made her a little afraid of him. The capacity for keeping a secret she believed was manlike, and reminded her — for no reason in the world — of Jim Medliker, her husband, whom she feared.

Well, she would let them fight it out between them. More than that, she was finally
obliged to sink her reserve in employing him
in the necessary " chores " for the house,
and he was sent on an errand to the country
store at the cross-roads. But he first ex-
tracted his gold-flake from the wall, and put
it in his pocket.

On arriving at the store, it was plain even
to his boyish perceptions that the minister
had circulated his miserable story. Two or
three of the customers spoke to each other
in a whisper, and looked at him. More than
that, when he began his homeward journey
he saw that two of the loungers were evidently following him. Half in timidity and
half in boyish mischief he once or twice
strayed from the direct road, and snatched
a fearful joy in observing their equal diver-
gence. As he passed Mr. Staples's house
he saw that reverend gentleman sneak out of
his back gate, and, without seeing the two
others, join in the inquisitorial procession.
But the events of the past day had had their
quickening effect upon Johnny's intellect.
A brilliantly wicked thought struck him.
As he was passing a perfectly bare spot on

the road he managed, without being noticed,
to cast his glittering flake of gold on the
sterile ground at the other side of the road,
where the minister's path would lie. Then,
at a point where the road turned, he concealed himself in the brush. The Reverend
Mr. Staples hurried forward as he lost sight
of the boy in the sweep of the road, but
halted suddenly. Johnny's heart leaped.
The minister looked around him, stooped,
picked up the piece of gold, thrust it hurriedly in his waistcoat pocket, and continued
his way. When he reached the turn of the
road, before passing it, he availed himself
of his solitude to pause and again examine
the treasure, and again return it to his
pocket. But, to Johnny's surprise, he here
turned back, walked quickly to the spot
where he had found it, carefully examined
the locality, kicking the loose soil and stones
around with his feet until he had apparently
satisfied himself that there was no more, and
no gold-bearing indications in the soil. At
this moment, however, the two other in-
quisitors came in sight, and Mr. Staples
turned quickly and hurried on. Before he
had passed the brush where Johnny was

concealed, the two men overtook him and exchanged greetings. They both spoke of "Johnny" and his crime; of having followed him with a view of finding out where he went to procure his gold, and of his having again evaded them. Mr. Staples agreed with their purpose, but, to Johnny's intense astonishment, *said nothing about his own find!* When they had passed on, the boy slipped from his place of concealment and followed them at a distance until his own house came in view. Here the two men diverged, but the minister continued on towards the other "store" and post-office on the main road.

He would have told his mother what he had seen, and his surprise that the minister had not spoken of finding the gold to the other men, but he was checked, first by his mother's attitude towards him, which was clearly the same as the minister's, and, second, by the knowledge that she would have condemned his dropping the gold in the minister's path, — though he knew not *why*, — or asked his reason for it, which he was equally sure he could not formulate, though he also knew not why. But that evening, as he was returning from the spring with water, he heard the minister's voice in the kitchen. It had been a day of surprises and revelations to Johnny, but the climax seemed to be reached as he entered the room; and he now stood transfixed and open-mouthed as he heard Mr. Staples say: —

"It 's all very well, Sister Medliker, to comfort your heart with vain hopes and delusions. A mother's leanin's is the soul's deceivin's, — and yer leanin' on a broken reed. If the boy truly found that gold he 'd have come to ye and said: 'Behold, mother, I have found gold in the highways and byways; rejoice and be exceedin' glad!' and hev poured it inter yer lap. Yes," continued Mr. Staples aggressively to the boy, as he saw him stagger back with his pail in hand, "yes, sir, *that* would have been the course of a Christian child!"

For a moment Johnny felt the blood boiling in his ears, and a thousand words seemed crowding in his throat. "Then" — he gasped and choked. "Then" — he began again, and stopped with the suffocation of indignation.

But Mr. Staples saw in his agitation only

an awakened conscience, and, nudging Mrs.
Medliker, leaned eagerly forward for a reply.
" Then," he repeated, with suave encour-
agement, " go on, Johnny! Speak it out!"

" Then," said Johnny, in a high, shrill
falsetto that startled them, " then wot for
did *you* pick up that piece o' gold in the
road this arternoon, and say nothin' of it to
the men who followed ye? Ye did; I seed
yer! And ye did n't say nothin' of it to
anybody; and ye ain't sayin' nothin' of it
now ter maw! and ye 've got it in yer vest!
And it 's mine, and I dropped it! Gimme
it."

Astonishment, confusion, and rage swelled
and empurpled Staples' face. It was *his*
turn to gasp for breath. Yet in the same
moment he made an angry dash at the boy.
But Mrs. Medliker interfered. This was an
entirely new feature in the case. Great is
the power of gold. A single glance at the
minister's confusion had convinced her that
Johnny's accusation was true, and it was
Johnny's *money* — constructively *hers* —
that the minister was concealing. His mere
possession of that gold had more effect in
straightening out her loose logic than any
sense of hypocrisy.

" You leave the boy be, Brother Staples," said Mrs. Medliker sharply. " I reckon wot's his is hisn, spite of whar he got it."

Mr. Staples saw his mistake, and smiled painfully as he fumbled in his waistcoat pocket. " I believe I *did* pick up something," he said, " that may or may not have been gold, but I have dropped it again or thrown it away ; and really it is of little concern in our moral lesson. For we have only *his* word that it was really his ! How do we *know* it ? "

" Cos it has my marks on it," said Johnny quickly ; " it had a criss-cross I scratched on it. I kin tell it good enuf."

Mr. Staples turned suddenly pale and rose. " Of course," he said to Mrs. Medliker with painful dignity, " if you set so much value upon a mere worldly trifle, I will endeavor to find it. It may be in my other pocket." He backed out of the door in his usual fashion, but instantly went over to the post-office, where, as he afterwards alleged, he had changed the ore for coin in a moment of inadvertence. But Johnny's hieroglyphics were found on it, and in some mysterious way the story got about. It had

two effects that Johnny did not dream of.
It had forced his mother into an attitude of
complicity with him; it had raised up for
him a single friend. Jake Stielitzer, quartz
miner, had declared that Burnt Spring was
" playing it low down " on Johnny! That
if they really believed that the boy took gold
from their sluice boxes, it was their duty to
watch their *claims* and not the boy. That
it was only their excuse for " snooping "
after him, and they only wanted to find his
" strike," which was as much his as their
claims were their own! All this with great
proficiency of epithet, but also a still more
recognized proficiency with the revolver,
which made the former respected.

" That 's the real nigger in the fence,
Johnny," said Jake, twirling his huge mustache, " and they only want to know where
your lead is, — and don't yer tell 'em! Let
'em bile over with waitin' first, and that 'll
put the fire out. Does yer pop know?"

" No," said Johnny.

" Nor yer mar?"

" No."

Jake whistled. " Then it 's only *you*,
yourself?

Johnny nodded violently, and his brown eyes glistened.

" It 's a heap of information to be packed away in a chap of your size, Johnny. Makes you feel kinder crowded inside, eh? *Must* keep it to yourself, eh ? "

" Have to," said Johnny with a gasp that was a little like a sigh.

It caused Jake to look at him attentively. " See here, Johnny," he said, " now ef ye wanted to tell somebody about it, — somebody as was a friend of yours, — *me*, f'r instance ? "

Johnny slowly withdrew the freckled, warty little hand that had been resting confidingly in Jake's and gently sidled away from him. Jake burst into a loud laugh.

" All right, Johnny boy," he said with a hearty slap upon the boy's back, " keep yer head shut ef yer wanter ! Only ef anybody else comes bummin' round ye, like this, jest turn him over *to me*, and I 'll lift him outer his boots ! "

Jake kept his word, and his distance thereafter. Indeed, it was after this first and last conversation with him that the influence of his powerful protection was so strong that

all active criticisms of Johnny ceased, and
only a respectful surveillance of his movements lingered in the settlement. I do
not know that this was altogether distasteful
to the child; it would have been strange,
indeed, if he had not felt at times exalted
by this mysterious influence that he seemed
to have acquired over his fellow creatures.
If he were merely hunting blackberries in
the brush, he was always sure, sooner or
later, to find a ready hand offered to help
and accompany him; if he trapped a squirrel
or tracked down a wild bees' hoard, he generally found a smiling face watching him.
Prospectors sometimes stopped him with:
" Well, Johnny, as a chipper and far-minded
boy, now *whar* would *you* advise us to dig ? "
I grieve to say that Johnny was not above
giving his advice, — and that it was invari-
ably of not the smallest use to the recipient.

And so the days passed. Mr. Medliker's
absence was protracted, and the hour of retribution and punishment still seemed far away.
The blackberries ripened and dried upon the
hillside, and the squirrels had gathered their
hoards; the bees no longer came and went
through the thicket, but Johnny was still in

daily mysterious possession of his grains of
gold! And then one day — after the fate
of all heroic humanity — his secret was im-
perilled by the blandishments and machina-
tions of the all-powerful sex.

Florry Fraser was a little playmate of
Johnny's. Why, with his doubts of his
elder sister's intelligence and integrity, he
should have selected a child two years
younger, and of singular simplicity, was,
like his other secret, his own. What *she*
saw in him to attract her was equally
strange; possibly it may have been his
brown-gooseberry eyes or his warts; but
she was quite content to trot after him, like
a young squaw, carrying his "bow-arrow,"
or his "trap," supremely satisfied to share
his woodland knowledge or his scanter confidences. For nobody who knew Johnny suspected that she was privy to his great secret.
Howbeit, wherever his ragged straw hat,
thatched with his tawny hair, was detected
in the brush, the little nankeen sunbonnet
of Florry was sure to be discerned not far
behind. For two weeks they had not seen
each other. A fell disease, nurtured in ignorance, dirt, and carelessness, was striking

right and left through the valleys of the
foothills, and Florry, whose sister had just
recovered from an attack, had been seques-
tered with her. But one morning, as Johnny
was bringing his wood from the stack behind
the house, he saw, to his intense delight, a
picket of the road fence slipped aside by a
small red hand, and a moment after Florry
squeezed herself through the narrow opening.
Her round cheeks were slightly flushed, and
there was a scrap of red flannel around her
plump throat that heightened the whiteness
of her skin.

"My!" said Johnny, with half-real, half-
affected admiration, "how splendiferous!"

"Sore froat," said Florry, in a whisper,
trying to insert her two chubby fingers between the bandage and her chin. "I mussent go outer the garden patch! I mussent
play in the woods, for I'll be seed! I
mussent stay long, for they'll ketch me outer
bed!"

"Outer bed?" repeated Johnny, with intense admiration, as he perceived for the
first time that Florry was in a flannel night-
gown, with bare legs and feet.

"Ess."

Whereupon these two delightful imps chuckled and wagged their heads with a sincere enjoyment that this mere world could not give! Johnny slipped off his shoes and stockings and hurriedly put them on the infant Florry, securing them from falling off with a thick cord. This added to their enjoyment.

" We can play cubby house in the stone heap," whispered Florry.

" Hol' on till I tote in this wood," said Johnny. " You hide till I come back."

Johnny swiftly delivered his load with an alacrity he had never shown before. Then they played " cubby house " — not fifty feet from the cabin, with a hushed but guilty satisfaction. But presently it palled. Their domain was too circumscribed for variety. " Robinson Crusoe up the tree " was impossible, as being visible from the house windows. Johnny was at his wits' end. Florry was fretful and fastidious. Then a great thought struck him and left him cold. " If I show you a show, you won't tell ? " he said suddenly.

" No."

" Wish yer-ma-die ? "

" Ess."

" Got any penny ? "

" No."

" Got any slate pencil ? "

" No."

" Ain't got any pins nor nuthin' ? You kin go in for a pin."

But Florry had none of childhood's fluctuating currency with her, having, so to speak, no pockets.

" Well," said Johnny, brightening up, " ye kin go in for luv."

The child clipped him with her small arms and smiled, and, Johnny leading the way, they crept on all fours through the thick ferns until they paused before a deep fissure in the soil half overgrown with bramble. In its depths they could hear the monotonous trickle of water. It was really the source of the spring that afterwards reappeared fifty yards nearer the road, and trickled into an unfailing pool known as the Burnt Spring, from the brown color of the surrounding bracken. It was the water supply of the ranch, and the reason for •Mr. Medliker's original selection of that site. Johnny lingered for an instant, looked carefully around,

and then lowered himself into the fissure.
A moment later he reached up his arms to
Florry, lowered her also, and both disappeared from view. Yet from time to time
their voices came faintly from below — with
the gurgle of water — as of festive gnomes
at play.

At the end of ten minutes they reappeared, a little muddy, a little bedraggled,
but flushed and happy. There were two
pink spots on Florry's cheeks, and she
clasped something tightly in her little red
fist.

"There," said Johnny, when they were
seated in the straw again, "now mind you
don't tell."

But here suddenly Florry's lips began to
quiver, and she gave vent to a small howl of
anguish.

"You ain't bit by a trant'ler nor nuthin'?"
said Johnny anxiously. "Hush up!"

"N—o—o! But"—

"But what?" said Johnny.

"Mar said I *must* tell! Mar said I was
to fin' out where you get the truly gold!
Mar said I was to get you to take me,"
howled Florry, in an agony of remorse.

Johnny gasped. "You Injin !" he began.

"But I won't — Johnny !" said Florry, clutching his leg frantically. "I won't and I sha'n't ! I ain't no Injin !"

Then, between her sobs, she told him how her mother and Mr. Staples had said that she was to ask Johnny the next time they met to take her where they found the "truly gold," and she was to remember where it was and to tell them. And they were going to give her a new dolly and a hunk of gingerbread. "But I won't — and I sha'n't !" she said passionately. She was quite pale again.

Johnny was convinced, but thoughtful. "Tell 'em," he said hoarsely, "tell 'em a big whopper ! They won't know no better. They 'll never guess where." And he briefly recounted the wild-goose chase he had given the minister.

"And get the dolly and the cake," said Florry, her eyes shining through her tears.

"In course," said Johnny. "They 'll get the dolly back, but you kin have eated the cake first." They looked at each other, and their eyes danced together over this heaven-sent inspiration. Then Johnny took off her shoes and stockings, rubbed her cold feet with his dirty handkerchief, and said: "Now you trot over to your mar!"

He helped her through the loose picket of the fence and was turning away when her faint voice again called him.

"Johnny!"

He turned back; she was standing on the other side of the fence holding out her arms to him. He went to her with shining eyes, lifted her up, and from her hot but loving little lips took a fatal kiss.

For only an hour later Mrs. Fraser found Florry in her bed, tossing with a high fever and a light head. She was talking of "Johnny" and "gold," and had a flake of the metal in her tiny fist. When Mr. Staples was sent for, and with the mother and father, hung anxiously above her bed, to their eager questioning they could only find out that Florry had been to a high mountain, ever so far away, and on the top of it there was gold lying around, and a shining figure was giving it away to the people.

"And who were the people, Florry dear," said Mr. Staples persuasively; "anybody ye know here?"

"They woz angels," said Florry, with a frightened glance over her shoulder.

I grieve to say that Mr. Staples did not look as pleased at the celestial vision as he might have, and poor Mrs. Fraser probably saw that in her child's face which drove other things from her mind. Yet Mr. Staples persisted : —

"And who led you to this beautiful mountain?   Was it Johnny?"

"No."

"Who then?"

Florry opened her eyes on the speaker. "I fink it was Dod," she said, and closed them again.

But here Dr. Duchesne hurried in, and after a single glance at the child hustled Mr. Staples from the room.   For there were grave complications that puzzled him. Florry seemed easier and quieter under his kindly voice and touch, but did not speak again, — and so, slowly sinking, passed away that night in a dreamless sleep.   This was followed by a mad panic at Burnt Spring the next day, and Mrs. Medliker fled with her two girls to Sacramento, leaving Johnny, ostensibly strong and active, to keep house

until his father's return. But Mr. Medliker's return was again delayed, and in the
epidemic, which had now taken a fast hold
of the settlement, Johnny's secret — and indeed the boy himself — was quite forgotten.
It was only on Mr. Medliker's arrival it was
known that he had been lying dangerously
ill, alone, in the abandoned house. In his
strange reticence and firmness of purpose
he had kept his sufferings to himself, — as
he had his other secret, — and they were revealed only in the wasted, hollow figure that
feebly opened the door to his father.

On which intelligence Mr. Staples was, as
usual, promptly on the spot with his story of
Johnny's secret to the father, and his usual
eager questioning to the fast-sinking boy.
" And now, Johnny," he said, leaning over
the bed, " tell us *all*. There is One from
whom no secrets are hid. Remember, too,
that dear Florry, who is now with the angels,
has already confessed."

Perhaps it was because Johnny, even at
that moment, hated the man ; perhaps it
was because at that moment he loved and
believed in Florry, or perhaps it was only
that because at that moment he was nearer

the greater Truth than his questioner, but he said, in a husky voice, " You lie ! "

Staples drew back with a flushed face, but lips that writhed in a pained and still persistent eagerness. " But, Johnny, at least tell us where — wh — wow — wow."

I am obliged to admit that these undignified accents came from Mr. Staples' own lips, and were due to the sudden pressure of Mr. Medliker's arm around his throat. The teamster was irascible and prompt through much mule-driving, and his arm was, from the same reason, strong and sinewy. Mr. Staples felt himself garroted and dragged from the room, and only came to under the stars outside, with the hoarse voice of Mr. Medliker in his ears : —

" You 're a minister of the gospel, I know, but ef ye say another word to my Johnny, I 'll knock the gospel stuffin' out of ye. Ye hear me ! *I 've driven mules afore !* "

He then strode back into the room. " Ye need n't answer, Johnny, he 's gone."

But so, too, had Johnny, for he never answered the question in this world, nor, please God, was he required to in the next. He lay still and dead. The community was

scandalized the next day when Mr. Medliker
sent for a minister from Sacramento to offi-
ciate at his child's funeral, in place of Mr.
Staples, and then the subject was dropped.

.   .   .   .

But the influence of Johnny's hidden
treasure still remained as a superstition in
the locality.   Prospecting parties were con-
tinually made up to discover the unknown
claim, but always from evidence and data
altogether apocryphal.   It was even alleged
that a miner had one night seen the little
figures of Johnny and Florry walking over
the hilltop, hand in hand, but that they had
vanished among the stars at the very moment he thought he had discovered their
secret.   And then it was forgotten; the
prosperous Mr. Medliker, now the proprietor
of a stage-coach route, moved away to Sacramento; Medliker's Ranch became a station
for changing horses, and, as the new railway
in time superseded even that, sank into a
blacksmith's shop on the outskirts - of the
new town of Burnt Spring.   And then one
day, six years after, news fell as a bolt from
the blue !

It was thus recorded in the county paper :

" A piece of rare good fortune, involving, it is said, the development of a lead of extraordinary value, has lately fallen to the lot of Mr. John Silsbee, the popular blacksmith, on the site of the old Medliker Ranch. In clearing out the failing water-course known as Burnt Spring, Mr. Silsbee came upon a rich ledge or pocket at the actual source of the spring, — a fissure in the ground a few rods from the road. The present yield has been estimated to be from eight to ten thousand dollars. But the event is considered as one of the most remarkable instances of the vagaries of 'prospecting' ever known, as this valuable 'pot-hole' existed undisturbed *for eight years* not *fifty yards* from the old cabin that was in former times the residence of J. Medliker, Esq., and the station of the Pioneer Stage Company, and was utterly unknown and unsuspected by the previous inhabitants! Verily truth is stranger than fiction ! "

A TALE OF THREE TRUANTS

THE schoolmaster at Hemlock Hill was
troubled that morning. Three of his boys
were missing. This was not only a notable
deficit in a roll-call of twenty, but the absentees were his three most original and distinctive scholars. He had received no pre-
liminary warning or excuse. Nor could he
attribute their absence to any common local
detention or difficulty of travel. They lived
widely apart and in different directions.
Neither were they generally known as
" chums," or comrades, who might have
entered into an unhallowed combination to
" play hookey."

He looked at the vacant places before
him with a concern which his other scholars
little shared, having, after their first lively
curiosity, not unmixed with some envy of
the derelicts, apparently forgotten them.
He missed the cropped head and inquisitive
glances of Jackson Tribbs on the third

bench, the red hair and brown eyes of
Providence Smith in the corner, and there
was a blank space in the first bench where
Julian Fleming, a lanky giant of seventeen,
had sat. Still, it would not do to show his
concern openly, and, as became a man who
was at least three years the senior of the
eldest, Julian Fleming, he reflected that they
were " only boys," and that their friends
were probably ignorant of the good he was
doing them, and so dismissed the subject.
Nevertheless, it struck him as wonderful how
the little world beneath him got on without
them. Hanky Rogers, bully, who had been
kept in wholesome check by Julian Fleming, was lively and exuberant, and his conduct was quietly accepted by the whole
school; Johnny Stebbins, Tribbs's bosom
friend, consorted openly with Tribbs's particular enemy ; some of the girls were singularly gay and conceited. It was evident
that some superior masculine oppression had
been removed.

He was particularly struck by this last
fact, when, the next morning, no news coming of the absentees, he was impelled to
question his flock somewhat precisely con-

cerning them. There was the usual shy
silence which follows a general inquiry from
the teacher's desk; the children looked at
one another, giggled nervously, and said nothing.

"Can you give me any idea as to what
might have kept them away?" said the
master.

Hanky Rogers looked quickly around, began, "Playin' hook—" in a loud voice, but
stopped suddenly without finishing the word,
and became inaudible. The master saw fit
to ignore him.

"Bee-huntin'," said Annie Roker viva-
ciously.

"Who is?" asked the master.

"Provy Smith, of course. Allers bee-
huntin'. Gets lots o' honey. Got two full
combs in his desk last week. He's awful
on bees and honey. Ain't he, Jinny?"
This in a high voice to her sister.

The younger Miss Roker, thus appealed
to, was heard to murmur that of all the
sneakin' bee-hunters she had ever seed,
Provy Smith was the worst. "And squirrels
— for nuts," she added.

The master became attentive, — a clue

seemed probable here. "Would Tribbs and Fleming be likely to go with him?" he asked.

A significant silence followed. The master felt that the children recognized a doubt of this, knowing the boys were not "chums;" possibly they also recognized something incriminating to them, and with characteristic freemasonry looked at one another and were dumb.

He asked no further questions, but, when school was dismissed, mounted his horse and started for the dwelling of the nearest culprit, Jackson Tribbs, four miles distant. He had often admired the endurance of the boy, who had accomplished the distance, including the usual meanderings of a country youth, twice a day, on foot, in all weathers, with no diminution of spirits or energy. He was still more surprised when he found it a mountain road, and that the house lay well up on the ascent of the pass. Autumn was visible only in a few flaming sumacs set among the climbing pines, and here, in a little clearing to the right, appeared the dwelling he was seeking.

"Tribbses," or "Tribbs's Run," was de-

voted to the work of cutting down the pines
midway on a long regularly sloping moun-
tain-side, which allowed the trunks, after
they were trimmed and cut into suitable
lengths, to be slid down through rude runs,
or artificial channels, into the valley below,
where they were collected by teams and conveyed to the nearest mills. The business
was simple in the extreme, and was carried
on by Tribbs senior, two men with saws and
axes, and the natural laws of gravitation.
The house was a long log cabin; several
sheds roofed with bark or canvas seemed
consistent with the still lingering summer
and the heated odors of the pines, but were
strangely incongruous to those white patches
on the table-land and the white tongue
stretching from the ridge to the valley. But
the master was familiar with those Sierran
contrasts, and as he had never ascended the
trail before, it might be only the usual prospect of the dwellers there. At this moment
Mr. Tribbs appeared from the cabin, with his
axe on his shoulder. Nodding carelessly to
the master, he was moving away, when the
latter stopped him.

" Is Jackson here ? " he asked.

"No," said the father, half impatiently, still moving on. "Hain't seen him since yesterday."

"Nor has he been at school," said the master, "either yesterday or to-day."

Mr. Tribbs looked puzzled and grieved. "Now I reckoned you had kep' him in for some devilment of his'n, or lessons."

"Not *all night!*" said the master, somewhat indignant at this presumption of his arbitrary functions.

"Humph!" said Mr. Tribbs. "Mariar!" Mrs. Tribbs made her appearance in the doorway. "The schoolmaster allows that Jackson ain't bin to school at all." Then, turning to the master, he added, "Thar! you settle it between ye," and quietly walked away.

Mrs. Tribbs looked by no means satisfied with or interested in the proposed tête-à-tête. "Hev ye looked in the bresh" (*i. e.*, brush or underwood) "for him?" she said querulously.

"No," said the master, "I came here first. There are two other boys missing, — Providence Smith and Julian Fleming. Did either of them " —

But Mrs. Tribbs had interrupted him with a gesture of impatient relief. "Oh, that's all, is it? Playin' hookey together, in course. 'Scuse me, I must go back to my bakin'." She turned away, but stopped suddenly, touched, as the master fondly believed, by some tardy maternal solicitude. But she only said: "When he *does* come back, you just give him a whalin', will ye?" and vanished into her kitchen.

The master rode away, half ashamed of his foolish concern for the derelicts. But he determined to try Smith's father, who owned a small rancho lower down on a spur of the same ridge. But the spur was really nearer Hemlock Hill, and could have been reached more directly by a road from there. He, however, kept along the ridge, and after half an hour's ride was convinced that Jackson Tribbs could have communicated with Provy Smith without coming nearer Hemlock Hill, and this revived his former belief that they were together. He found the paternal Smith engaged in hoeing potatoes in a stony field. The look of languid curiosity with which he had regarded the approach of the master changed to one of equally languid

aggression as he learned the object of his
visit.

" Wot are ye comin' to *me* for? I ain't
runnin' your school," he said slowly and
aggressively. " I started Providence all
right for it mornin' afore last, since when I
never set eyes on him. That lets *me* out.
My business, young feller, is lookin' arter
the ranch. Yours, I reckon, is lookin' arter
your scholars."

" I thought it my business to tell you
your son was absent from school," said the
master coldly, turning away. " If you are
satisfied, I have nothing more to say." Nevertheless, for the moment he was so startled
by this remarkable theory of his own re-
sponsibility in the case that he quite accepted the father's callousness, — or rather
it seemed to him that his unfortunate charges
more than ever needed his protection. There
was still the chance of his hearing some news
from Julian Fleming's father; he lived at
some distance, in the valley on the opposite
side of Hemlock Hill; and thither the master made his way. Luckily he had not gone
far before he met Mr. Fleming, who was a
teamster, en route. Like the fathers of the

other truants, he was also engaged in his vocation. But, unlike the others, Fleming senior was jovial and talkative. He pulled up his long team promptly, received the master's news with amused interest, and an invitation to spirituous refreshment from a demijohn in his wagon.

" Me and the ole woman kind o' speki-lated that Jule might hev been over with Aunt Marthy; but don't you worry, Mr. Schoolmaster. They 're limbs, every one o' them, but they 'll fetch up somewhere, all square! Just you put two fingers o' that corn juice inside ye, and let 'em slide. Ye did n't hear what the 'lekshun news was when ye was at Smith's, did ye ? "

The master had not inquired. He con-fessed he had been worried about the boys. He had even thought that Julian might have met with an accident.

Mr. Fleming wiped his mouth, with a humorous affectation of concern. " Met with an *accident ?* Yes, I reckon not *one* accident, but *two* of 'em. These yer acci-dents Jule 's met with had two legs, and were mighty lively accidents, you bet, and took him off with 'em; or mebbe they had four

legs, and he's huntin' 'em yet. Accidents!
Now I never thought o' that! Well, when
you come across him and *them accidents*,
you just whale 'em, all three! And ye
won't take another drink? Well, so long,
then! Gee up!" He rolled away, with a
laugh, in the heavy dust kicked up by his
plunging mules, and the master made his
way back to the schoolhouse. His quest
for that day was ended.

But the next morning he was both astounded and relieved, at the assembling of
school, to find the three truants back in
their places. His urgent questioning of
them brought only the one and same response from each: " Got lost on the ridge."
He further gathered that they had slept out
for two nights, and were together all the
time, but nothing further, and no details
were given. The master was puzzled. They
evidently expected punishment ; that was no
doubt also the wish of their parents ; but
if their story was true, it was a serious question if he ought to inflict it. There was
no means of testing their statement ; there
was equally none by which he could con-
trovert it. It was evident that the whole

school accepted it without doubt; whether
they were in possession of details gained
from the truants themselves which they had
withheld from him, or whether from some
larger complicity with the culprits, he could
not say. He told them gravely that he
should withhold equally their punishment
and their pardon until he could satisfy himself of their veracity, and that there had
been no premeditation in their act. They
seemed relieved, but here, again, he could
not tell whether it sprang from confidence
in their own integrity or merely from youthful hopefulness that delayed retribution never
arrived!

It was a month before their secret was
fully disclosed. It was slowly evolved from
corroborating circumstances, but always with
a shy reluctance from the boys themselves,
and a surprise that any one should think it
of importance. It was gathered partly from
details picked up at recess or on the play-
ground, from the voluntary testimony of
teamsters and packers, from a record in the
county newspaper, but always shaping itself
into a consecutive and harmonious narra-
tive.

It was a story so replete with marvelous escape and adventure that the master hesitated to accept it in its entirety until after it had long become a familiar history, and was even forgotten by the actors themselves. And even now he transcribes it more from the circumstances that surrounded it than from a hope that the story will be believed.

WHAT HAPPENED

Master Provy Smith had started out that eventful morning with the intention of fighting Master Jackson Tribbs for the " Kingship " of Table Ridge — a trifling territory of ten leagues square — Tribbs having infringed on his boundaries and claimed absolute sovereignty over the whole mountain range. Julian Fleming was present as referee and bottle-holder. The battle ground selected was the highest part of the ridge. The hour was six o'clock, which would allow them time to reach school before its opening, with all traces of their conflict removed. The air was crisp and cold, — a trifle colder than usual, — and there was a singular thickening of the sun's rays on the ridge, which made the distant peaks indistinct and

ghostlike. However, the two combatants
stripped "to the buff," and Fleming patronizingly took position at the "corner," leaning upon a rifle, which, by reason of his
superior years, and the wilderness he was
obliged to traverse in going to school, his
father had lent him to carry. It was that
day a providential weapon.

Suddenly, Fleming uttered the word,
"Sho!" The two combatants paused in
their first "squaring off" to see, to their
surprise, that their referee had faced round,
with his gun in his hand, and was staring in
another direction.

"B'ar!" shouted the three voices together.
A huge bear, followed by its cubs, was seen
stumbling awkwardly away to the right,
making for the timber below. In an instant
the boys had hurried into their jackets again,
and the glory of fight was forgotten in the
fever of the chase. Why should they pound
each other when there was something to
really *kill?* They started in instant pur-
suit, Julian leading.

But the wind was now keen and bitter in
their faces, and that peculiar thickening of
the air which they had noticed had become

first a dark blue and then a whitening pall, in which the bear was lost. They still kept on. Suddenly Julian felt himself struck between the eyes by what seemed a snowball, and his companions were as quickly spattered by gouts of monstrous clinging snowflakes. Others as quickly followed — it was not snowing, it was snowballing. They at first laughed, affecting to retaliate with these whirling, flying masses shaken like clinging feathers from a pillow; but in a few seconds they were covered from head to foot by snow, their limbs impeded or pinioned against them by its weight, their breath gone. They stopped blindly, breathlessly. Then, with a common instinct, they turned back. But the next moment they heard Julian cry, "Look out!" Coming towards them out of the storm was the bear, who had evidently turned back by the same instinct. An ungovernable instinct seized the younger boys, and they fled. But Julian stopped with leveled rifle. The bear stopped too, with sullen, staring eyes. But the eyes that glanced along the rifle were young, true, and steady. Julian fired. The hot smoke was swept back by the gale into his face, but the bear turned and disappeared in the storm again. Julian ran on to where his companions had halted, at the report, a little ashamed of their cowardice. "Keep on that way!" he shouted hoarsely. "No use tryin' to go where the b'ar could n't. Keep on!"

"Keep on — whar? There ain't no trail — no nuthin'!" said Jackson querulously, to hold down a rising fear. It was true. The trail had long since disappeared; even their footprints of a moment before were filled up by the piling snow; they were isolated in this stony upland, high in air, without a rock or tree to guide them across its vast white level. They were bitterly cold and benumbed. The stimulus of the storm and chase had passed, but Julian kept driving them before him, himself driven along by the furious blast, yet trying to keep some vague course along the waste. So an hour passed. Then the wind seemed to have changed, or else they had traveled in a circle — they knew not which, but the snow was in their faces now. But, worst of all, the snow had changed too; it no longer fell in huge blue flakes, but in millions of stinging gray granules. Julian's face grew hard and his eyes bright. He knew it was no longer a snow - squall, but a lasting storm. He stopped ; the boys tumbled against him. He looked at them with a strange smile.

" Hev you two made up ? " he said.

" No—o ! "

" Make up, then."

" What ? "

" Shake hands."

They clasped each other's red, benumbed fingers and laughed, albeit a little frightened at Julian. " Go on ! " he said, curtly.

They went on dazedly, stupidly, for another hour.

Suddenly Provy Smith's keen eyes sparkled. He pointed to a singular irregular mound of snow before them, plainly seen above the dreary level. Julian ran to it with a cry, and began wildly digging. " I knew I hit him," he cried, as he brushed the snow from a huge and hairy leg. It was the bear — dead, but not yet cold. He had succumbed with his huge back to the blast, the snow piling a bulwark behind him, where it had slowly roofed him in. The half-frozen lads threw themselves fearlessly

against his furry coat and crept between his
legs, nestling themselves beneath his still
warm body with screams of joy. The snow
they had thrown back increased the bulwark,
and drifting over it, in a few moments inclosed
them in a thin shell of snow. Thoroughly
exhausted, after a few grunts of satisfaction,
a deep sleep fell upon them, from which they
were awakened only by the pangs of hunger.
Alas! their dinners — the school dinners —
had been left on the inglorious battlefield.
Nevertheless, they talked of eating the bear
if it came to the worst. They would have
tried it even then, but they were far above
the belt of timber; they had matches — what
boy has not? — but no *wood*. Still, they
were reassured, and even delighted, with
this prospect, and so fell asleep again, stew-
ing with the dead bear in the half-impervi-
ous snow, and woke up in the morning rav-
enous, yet to see the sun shining in their
faces through the melted snow, and for Jackson Tribbs to quickly discover, four miles
away as the crow flies, the cabin of his father
among the flaming sumacs.

They started up in the glare of the sun,
which at first almost blinded them. They

then discovered that they were in a depression of the table-land that sloped before them to a deep gully in the mountain-
side, which again dropped into the cañon
below. The trail they had lost, they now
remembered, must be near this edge. But
it was still hidden, and in seeking it there
was danger of some fatal misstep in the
treacherous snow. Nevertheless, they sallied out bravely, although they would fain
have stopped to skin the bear, but Julian's
mandate was peremptory. They spread themselves along the ridge, at times scraping the
loose snow away in their search for the lost
trail.

Suddenly they all slipped and fell, but
rose again quickly, laughing. Then they
slipped and fell again, but this time with
the startling consciousness that it was not
they who had slipped, but *the snow!* As
they regained their feet they could plainly
see now that a large crack on the white field,
some twenty feet in width, extended between
them and the carcass of the bear, showing
the glistening rock below. Again they were
thrown down with a sharp shock. Jackson
Tribbs, who had been showing a strange ex-

citement, suddenly gave a cry of warning. "Lie flat, fellers! but keep a-crawlin' and jumpin'. We 're goin' down a slide!" And the next moment they were sliding and tossing, apparently with the whole snow-field, down towards the gullied precipice.

What happened after this, and how long it lasted, they never knew. For, hurried along with increasing momentum, but always mechanically clutching at the snow, and bounding from it as they swept on, they sometimes lost breath, and even consciousness. At times they were half suffocated in rolling masses of drift, and again free and skimming over its arrested surface, but always falling, as it seemed to them, almost perpendicularly. In one of these shocks they seemed to be going through a thicket of underbrush; but Provy Smith knew that they were the tops of pine-trees. At last there was one shock longer and lasting, followed by a deepening thunder below them. The avalanche had struck a ledge in the mountain side, and precipitated its lower part into the valley.

Then everything was still, until Provy heard Julian's voice calling. He answered, but there was no response from Tribbs. Had he gone over into the valley? They set up a despairing shout! A voice — a smothered one — that might be his, came apparently from the snow beneath them. They shouted again; the voice, vague and hollow, responded, but it was now surely his.

"Where are you?" screamed Provy.

"Down the chimbley."

There was a black square of adobe sticking out of the snow near them. They ran to it. There was a hole. They peered down, but could see nothing at first but a faint glimmer.

"Come down, fellows! It ain't far!" said Tribbs's voice.

"Wot yer got there?" asked Julian cautiously.

"Suthin' to eat."

That was enough. In another instant Julian and Provy went down the chimney. What was a matter of fifteen feet after a thousand? Tribbs had already lit a candle, by which they could see that they were in the cabin of some tunnel-man at work on the ridge. He had probably been in the tunnel when the avalanche fell, and escaped, though his cabin was buried. The three discoverers helped themselves to his larder. They laughed and ate as at a picnic, played cards, pretended it was a robber's cave, and finally, wrapping themselves in the miner's blankets, slept soundly, knowing where they were, and confident also that they could find the trail early the next morning. They did so, and without going to their homes came directly to school — having been absent about fifty hours. They were in high spirits, except for the thought of approaching punishment, never dreaming to evade it by anything miraculous in their adventures.

Such was briefly their story. Its truth was corroborated by the discovery of the bear's carcass, by the testimony of the tunnel-man, who found his larder mysteriously ransacked in his buried cabin, and, above all, by the long white tongue that for many months hung from the ledge into the valley. Nobody thought the lanky Julian a hero, — least of all himself. Nobody suspected that Jackson Tribbs's treatment of a " slide " had been gathered from experiments in his father's " runs " — and he was glad they did not.   The master's pardon obtained, the three truants cared little for the opinion of Hemlock Hill. They knew *themselves*   that was enough.